# TIGER'S EYE

# TIGER'S EYE

KATE SPULER

First published in Australia in 2019.
ISBN: 978-0-6469-9166-5

Cover Design by Joel Tippie
Typeset by Joel Tippie

Printed and bound in Australia by Griffin Press.
First printed in the USA, January 2020 by Bang Printing.

# TIGER'S EYE

# 1

# CARLA

I'VE SEEN MY LAST TOMORROW. I fight back bitter tears as the stench of despair embraces me like a familiar winter cloak. I let my spent legs crumble and welcome the assault of gravel against my cheek.

*Destroy me,* I dare my captors. *Just as you destroyed the others.* I watch my freed cart careen off the track and slam into the jagged wall. The shockwaves ripple through the stale air.

I don't fear punishment. I just want this to end.

A firm hand grasps mine and squeezes gently, long enough for me to identify its owner. Theo.

"Carla," Theo says quietly, but with an edge of urgency.

The sound of his voice stirs my spirit. I try to focus on it, but the blackened walls begin to sweep in circles around me. I manage a tortured breath, and his face appears out of the haze, pleading with me to calm down so we can make it in time. To save ourselves. To see our families again.

My family! Now I am imagining the face of a young boy. My brother. Rory. Rory! My breath quickens as I remember. I have to see him again. I have to get up.

"Carla, please," Theo says. His voice is desperate now. "Can you hear me?"

My head spins as I try to focus my thoughts.

"We don't have much time, Carla. You must get up." Theo tugs at my wrist, and his green eyes bore into mine.

I am reminded of all of the times he's spoken about his family and realize there is no choice. If not for my family, I must do it for his.

Theo's voice is stern, "Stand up now, Carla."

The tense muscles in my thighs bulge as I shakily force myself upright.

"Good," he praises. He seizes my cart and levers it back onto the track, grunting with exertion. "Now hold on."

I grasp the grimy handles of the mining cart.

"That's it. Now push, Carla."

I heave against the cart, but the wheels resist movement.

Ore is strewn across the track from the excavation of the tiger's eye. I raise a hand to wipe a drip of sweat off my face, no doubt smearing fiery streaks of gem dust across my cheeks. I mentally curse the golden gemstone.

I grip the handles firmly and strain my exhausted muscles, urging the stubborn cart to move. It emits a begrudging creak as it slowly gains momentum. I lean harder, and soon I break into a run once more. The cart makes two clicks as it crosses each beam of the tracks. Click, *click*. Click, *click*. The monotonous noise begins to form words in my mind. Ro-*ry*, Ro-*ry*, Ro-*ry*.

Theo matches my pace on the adjacent track, his cart adding to the symphony.

I can't give up. There is no other way.

Theo shouts, "We can do this, Carla."

My feet pound into the ground with determination, matching the rhythm of the clicking. Just ahead of me, the tunnel opens out into a wider cavern, marking the start of the main tunnel. The exit gate of the mines lies just beyond.

I glance wearily at the empty tracks around us. The other prisoners are already inside, safe. Why couldn't I have stuck to the status quo like everyone else? Why couldn't I have resisted my reckless curiosity? How could I be so thoughtless?

Theo's voice booms, "Carla! We can make it."

He doesn't seem to know how hopeless it is. We still have to make it through the tunnel before we reach the gate, which is already closing. We won't make it. My feet echo my futility and begin to slacken. I can't go on. What's the point? We're already dead.

I glance up. We are in the main tunnel now. The worst part. I don't dare stop. Darkness consumes us, and my heart lurches with fear. My body tenses in anticipation.

I don't have to wait long. Squeals and shrieks pierce my eardrums. They swoop close to us, hundreds of them smashing into our carts. I can feel their furry, vulgar bodies on my face and arms. Tearing at my skin and tangling my hair. Teeth rip into my face. Bats. This is their territory. We are imposters, and they will make us pay. My screams add to the gruesome concerto.

*Just keep going,* I implore myself. My stomach squirms at the crunching sound as the tiny flapping bodies are crushed by my cart. There is an eternity of shrill screeching before we finally approach the light. The end of the tunnel. I gasp with relief as we reach the open cavern and leave the terrifying beasts to their loathsome lair.

The vast metal gate is just in view, but it's shutting. The other miners in our squad shout frantically at us. I squint, and see that they've shoved a wooden beam in the opening—a makeshift lever. It won't last long. *Stay open*, I command. I glare at the gate, hoping I can somehow control it with my mind. I know I can't go any faster. Blackness invades the edges of my vision.

My mind flashes back to the lifeless-looking bodies of children with tubes sticking out of them. Like hospital drips, but somehow seeming more sinister. Why did I go in? I know we're not allowed in any of those rooms. If only the door hadn't been left ajar, tempting me. Making sure we wouldn't be back in time. Guilt washes over me and my throat seizes, making it even harder to catch a breath.

Theo reaches out and pulls my cart along with his, but my legs are screaming and I stumble. He lets go. The gate is seconds from closing, and Theo bellows at me to push harder, run faster. My lungs burn, engulfed in fire. He reaches the gate before I do. He pushes his cart through but refuses to cross until I reach him.

Finally my cart slams into the closing gate. There's not enough room to force it through. Theo yells at me. I drop the cart and clamber over it, frantic hands pulling me through the tiny gap. Theo practically squashes me as he, too, scrambles to safety. His desperate breath fans my hair.

*Slam!* The gate wins the battle, and the entire

Compound rattles. I whimper softly, and the miners gather around, hugging us.

But my mind is focused on just one thing. My cart is outside the gate. He will execute me. Us. The entire squad. I begin to shiver, and soon my entire body is trembling. Theo holds me.

"It's all right, you're safe now," he whispers.

But all I can do is shake my head at how wrong he is, because I know I've failed. For everyone. There is nothing I can do now, and I welcome the emptiness as I sink deeper into my mind, and out of the world as I know it.

# 2

# AXTON

I snap my fingers, and a deep blue screen appears. I point at the search box and say her name. The image of a teen with bright eyes and a resolute expression appears; her location is etched beside it.

Intense determination swells from within.

I am coming. I will find her.

# 3

# CARLA

THE FIRST THING THAT COMES TO MIND WHEN I WAKE IS FOOD. The familiar ache in my stomach is a reminder that I missed dinner. Pointless saliva floods my mouth as my thoughts drift to Mom's cooking back home in California. What I wouldn't give for a plate of lasagna, or spicy pork ribs, or . . .

"Morning, sunshine," Theo interrupts my reverie of recipes.

His soothing tone immediately puts me in a good mood. That is, until I remember that I'm probably going to die today. Even worse, Theo will be punished too. We all will. The normal rustle and chatter of the unit around me belies the darkness threatening us all.

I stare at the concrete ceiling for a few minutes, trying not to think about the fact that I've sentenced my entire squad to death. Which means, of course, that's all I think about.

"All right, Carla," Theo says. "Enough moping. Time to rise and shine."

I grimace, the weight of the day ahead settling on me. I gaze around the room for a moment, wondering if I've had my last night in this inhumane prison.

"I don't want to," I mumble, squeezing my eyes tight once again.

I bury my face in the pillow, but instantly regret it when the scratchy hessian bag grates against my face. I take a moment to debate whether the intense discomfort of my bed outweighs its benefit in postponing my fate.

"Get up," Verity roars, and I bolt upright. Now I'm definitely awake. I prefer Theo's method of waking me, to be honest.

As I blink my gritty eyes, I can't help but think about what I've done. There is an overabundance of rules here at the Compound, and if someone slips up, the entire unit is punished. We've heard stories of other units who made such mistakes—none survived unscathed. Last week, a boy in the next row was removed from an Assembly for speaking to someone in another unit. For trying to make a friend. We never saw him again, and rumor had it that the guard knifed him in the stomach.

However, there's one rule they drill into us the most—that each of us must *always* return with a full cart of tiger's eye. Of course that would be the rule that I've carelessly managed to break.

At least my hunger has almost been erased. I've got bigger things to worry about. Like death. Still, I feel like I should have the right to a final meal of my choice. Even prisoners on death row get that, don't they? Maybe a farewell feast at McDonald's: Big Mac, fries, and a hot apple pie to finish, thanks.

My stomach activates in response.

Make that a triple Big Mac. Frozen Coke on the side.

"Had a good night's sleep, Carla?" asks Damon, one of the members of our squad. He doesn't wait for a response. "I hope so, because you probably won't get another."

I death stare him.

He smirks. "Nah, we'll be okay, Carla. No point worrying about it."

I walk away from him, holding back a moan as my back twinges; a kind of cold pain has crept into my spine the last few nights, waking me often and making my cart seem even heavier.

I help the squad tidy our area and try not to think about my family. The thought of Rory upsets me the most. He's my brother, yet I'll never see him grow up or finish high school or get married. And he'll have to live the rest of his life without me. But I'm grateful that at least he's still got our parents. Please let them be okay.

My last memory of our family is from the Friday morning before summer break. My final day of normality. I was still eating breakfast when Mom and Dad hugged me and rushed out the door to take Rory to school. He hated the bus.

I remember brushing the knots from Milly's coat and running her through her tricks, before heading to the bus stop. The sunshine was glorious, and dragonflies zigzagged gleefully between slicks of water on the road. I was looking forward to hanging out at Pebble Beach with my friends on the holidays. I could already imagine inhaling burgers and salty fries slathered with ketchup at the little stand across the road.

As I meandered across the park on my regular shortcut to the bus stop, brutal hands pushed me to the ground. I felt a jab in the small of my back. Then nothing. Next thing I knew, instead of planning for college, I was waking up in a concrete prison. Freshman class at the Compound, majoring in mining and misery.

Nobody seems to know why they brought us here; only that we're trapped deep underground. And why me? My friends would have scoffed at the thought of anyone choosing me to mine gemstones for twelve hours a day. It's obvious they need us for labor, and I'm hardly the muscle-bound athlete.

The heavy stomping of the guard's platformed boots interrupts my thoughts, just as Verity mutters in a low voice, "He's coming." Her pretty eyes glare at me, full of blame, and Theo responds with a scowl in her direction. His support only makes me feel worse.

*Clip, clop,* echo the boots against the cold concrete. I quickly get in line behind Theo. Verity takes her position at the front as the group leader. When we aren't under the command of the guard, she's our boss. A prisoner like us, except she is blamed for our mistakes. Which is why she's especially bitter towards me today. Everyone is, to some extent. Can I blame them?

Theo should be the most upset with me, because only he knows what I did in the mines. He refused to go into the room with me, but he had my back and acted as lookout. Only he knows that I couldn't fight my inquisitive nature. That I've seen things that can't be unseen. Now I'm late with my cart and we will all face the consequences.

"It's not your fault," Theo whispers to me.

I almost laugh. "Don't patronize me," is all I can get out.

"Really, Carla, it could have been any of us."

But it wasn't. It was me.

*Clip, clop.* A constant beating rhythm. I certainly get the feeling that those boots are used as a tool to intimidate us. One of many. The foreboding sound deters any thought of defiance. As do the impromptu awakenings with buckets of ice water. Though maybe the latter is simply for their own entertainment. Either way, there's little chatter among the unit about breaking out.

But we like to wonder, Theo and I. Deep into the night, we whisper plans of escape—knocking the guards out with a metal pipe and searching for an escape route, traversing deep into the mines and never coming back (not our best idea), or hiding in a cart until they unknowingly wheel us out with the tiger's eye.

It's all speculation, though. Mostly to keep our minds busy and to help us resist the urge to punch the guards when they come too close.

I wonder if they'll be taking us to Assembly now, rather than waiting for Thursday. It would be the perfect venue to kick off punishment proceedings. During Assembly, the Commander—the *almighty* leader, as the guards call him—chastises us for our inadequate efforts, reinforces the goal of overflowing carts, and threatens us with punishment. The same spiel every week.

Theo and I utilize this hour. Most of the guards are in a team briefing in another part of the building, and there are only two guards on duty. The pair spend the whole time in a corner muttering to each other under their breaths, and sometimes we get the chance to sneak out the door and scout around.

Even though the guards constantly remind us that we are too deep underground to escape, it doesn't stop Theo and I from quietly exploring the various passageways. Still, it's not like we can flee through a fissure in the wall. Here, a crevice only means rats, and there are plenty of those. The hideous type, with evil faces, that like to chew on your hair once you've fallen asleep.

Rats or bats; make your choice. We get both.

We stand frozen as the boots arrive at the entrance to our unit. Through the glass door, we see the guard press the touchpad with his thumb, and the door slides open.

"Silence," he shouts. His icy eyes are mere pinpricks in his unsmiling face.

*I'll speak when I like*, I think to myself. Then I take back the thought. I don't want to die any sooner than necessary.

He adjusts the strap of his high-tech gun to make sure we notice it, and hitches up his signature silver belt. Hence our highly creative nickname for him—Silver Belt.

There's an extra energy about him today. These sick skunks enjoy bestowing punishment. Especially for a big crime. I shudder. I've heard there are things worse than death.

Today, he's cradling a black box in his fleshy hands. And wearing an anticipatory smirk on his face. The show is about to begin.

"Follow me." The guard's cruel voice bounces menacingly off the unyielding walls. Theo and I exchange glances and fall into line.

Our unit plods after him. I tie my hair into a loose ponytail with a piece of string I found ages ago. It's a weak attempt to guard myself against the immense heat of the Compound. Freezing at night, sweltering by day. *Probably not for much longer,* I remind myself. *Soon I'll pay for the tiger's eye cart sitting outside the gate.* I'll be as dead and irrelevant as the bats I've rolled the cart over.

Mostly, it's guilt that consumes me.

*I'm sorry, Theo,* I think. Whatever hope he once had of escaping has been obliterated. Now it's too late.

The guard leads us through a door that Theo and I

had found, but not fully explored. We were never game to traverse too far into the passages below. One time, Theo ventured further than ever, and something scared him. He fled and wouldn't tell me what it was, despite my pleas.

We make our way down some stairs like a disjointed caterpillar. The treading of our feet on steel becomes a cadence; a poorly rehearsed orchestra. The light slowly fades, and soon we are descending in almost complete darkness.

Theo trips, and grunts indicate others are slipping too. But the guard slows for no one. He has a headlamp, but the stairs are so twisted that only the few people directly behind him benefit from the illumination.

My heart is racing, and I'm panting heavily. Are we speeding up? I wish I had some water. I wish I was home in bed. I wish that wishes came true.

Suddenly I hear a difference in the tempo. We have reached the bottom. But I suspect this is not the end.

Only the beginning of the end.

I am drenched in sweat and try to distance my mind from my physical presence, in preparation for punishment.

But we don't stop. It gets darker. I reach around, hoping to find Theo's arm. Someone behind me grabs mine, and they hold on tight. It's the only thing keeping me upright.

We continue down a long tunnel for several minutes before speeding up again. Thankfully, there's a dim light now. I can just see Theo's feet ahead of me when I squint.

Eventually, we stop at a closed door. Silver Belt jams his thumb onto the pad and it lights up. We enter in single file. Inside, I glimpse glowing red circles on the ground. Two rows of seven—one for every member of our unit.

Now I see what might have frightened Theo. Various instruments adorn every inch of the wall; a hundred unidentifiable tools of the torture trade.

"Find your number," Silver Belt orders.

I spot cameras in the corners of the room. Maybe they'll re-watch our deaths later to prolong their pleasure. I decide then and there that I will refuse to give in to the pain. Refuse to give them that satisfaction. I will die on my own terms. My final victory.

I glance at the embossing on my wrist. I am number 323, allocated at the first night's initiation. My arms were forced under a laser that seared the skin with a number and left red welts that blackened and fell off over the following days.

I straighten my shoulders and locate my red circle. Four guards appear, glaring at us from the front of the room. Silver Belt stands with them on a slightly raised platform. A disquieting grin lurks on his mean face. He is still fondling the box with his meaty fingers. What could possibly be inside?

On second thoughts, I hope I never find out.

Silver Belt clears his throat. He stands directly in front of me, and I wonder if it's on purpose. I'm like the reverse of teacher's pet in here. I want to turn my head to locate Theo, but I can't with Silver Belt standing there. Theo can't be far away. *Please don't hurt Theo,* I think. *It's my fault.* Why should anyone else be punished for what I did?

I hope Theo can't see me from where he's standing. I don't want him to have to watch me suffer. Tears well up. I won't let them spill.

Silver Belt holds the box out so another guard can pry open the latch. I catch the glint of metal inside. *Needles.* Fourteen perfectly lined up needles arranged on red velvet in two neat rows. Such pretty packaging should cradle exquisite perfumes or lipstick. Not the cause of my death.

I search instinctively for some way to stop this. Should we try to overpower the guards, or shut off the power, or . . .

"Bow your heads," the guard bellows. The vibrations of his voice carry around the room and echo multiple times. I think I see the corners of his mouth curl upwards.

I tilt my head. *I did this.* Straighten my back. *I did this.* Close my eyes. *I did this.* If only I had said goodbye to my family. I'm not ready to die. *Please.* I don't want to die! I need to see them again. Another tear slides down my cheek, and I pray that none of the guards see it. Twice the punishment for the weak. I've seen it happen.

"Right arm out."

I thrust my hand in front of me. My arm quivers, so I clench the muscles. I want to open my eyes so I know when my turn will come, but I can't face it. I am committed to the darkness.

All I can see are vague shadows through my eyelids. Footsteps echo in the dimness. Every time it sounds as if he's coming closer to me, I tense and expect a jab, but the steps pound in another direction. A cruel waiting game.

Without warning, I feel a disturbance in the air in front of me and squeeze my eyes tighter. I hold my breath. Something cold plunges into the flesh of my forearm. I don't flinch. I distance myself from the pain. I can feel the cool liquid pulsing through my veins.

"Now comes the fun part." I hear the smile, and know his cruel lips are spread wide. "Ladies and gentlemen, the fine poison you have generously accepted is sophisticated. We have set a timer on the activation of the chemical substance within each syringe, so the extraordinary pain will begin at a different time for each of you."

He smirks, "That way, you can enjoy each other's performances." I hear his pride in the cruel scheme.

"Your time starts now."

Finally, I understand this malicious game. The ones in immediate pain are lucky. The rest have the unwelcome bonus of increasing trepidation. Knowing that at any second the pain could consume your body, but never knowing which second that will be.

He continues, "Death occurs five hours after the pain commences."

Five hours. I could be dead in five hours.

"One of you has just over five hours left to live. The rest, a little longer."

I open my eyes for a split second and catch him as he runs his tongue across his thick lips. I see the flash of a metal tongue piercing.

Then the screaming begins.

It doesn't take long to work out who it is. Verity. So that's how the evil worm rewards her for her leadership. She was the strongest of us all. And now, at this very moment, she has been relegated to the weakest.

Yet perhaps the luckiest.

# 4

# AXTON

I GRIP THE LEATHER STRAP AND WRAP IT AROUND MY
WAIST, FASTENING THE BUCKLES IN FRONT. I ready myself
for the jump.

"Approaching drop zone now," the captain announces
through the speakers. The doors of the pod open and I
lean out, welcoming the vicious blast of wind on my face.

I scan the ground far below. In the dawn twilight,
I can just make out the Compound, spreading like an
uncontained virus in all directions. Beyond it, green.
Dense, thick jungle that's blown out in the last couple of
decades. The effects of global warming, they say—more
carbon dioxide equals more green. Too much green.

I brace for exit.

"Someone's keen," a voice calls out. He's right about that. We've practiced jumps like this in training hundreds of times, and I don't understand why some soldiers are still hesitant to toss themselves over. Granted, this time is different. The real deal.

"Ready to initiate jump," the captain drawls. He almost sounds bored. No risk in the cockpit, I guess.

My friend, Greg, gives me the thumbs up. I glance at the other soldiers, some of whom I've rarely spoken to. They either ignore me or give me a limp smile. Everyone's nervous.

I take a deep breath and eject from the pod. The last thing I register is Greg's solemn face, and I dimly wonder whether I'll ever see him again.

# 5

# CARLA

I ESTIMATE THAT I'VE BEEN STANDING FOR OVER AN HOUR, BUT THERE'S REALLY NO WAY OF KNOWING. It seems as though we are falling through an unmarked void towards our deaths. Verity's screams still fill the room, but their endless monotony has rendered them mute.

Another scream joins hers, but I can't place it.

In between screams, Damon whispers some variant of, "This is your fault, Carla. I hate you."

My stomach jumps each time, and I scream a silent apology back. I push the guilt even deeper. As long as Theo still accepts me, I will be okay. I guess we're already technically dead, but the human soul has a hardwired desire for survival. So we breathe on.

After another eternity, I am empty. Not sad. Not scared. All I feel is a slight dread for the beginning of the pain. Maybe I am already dead; I can't tell.

Sound fades. If I think hard enough about my old life, perhaps I can forget the present. I allow my mind to drift to the bay not far from home. There is a beautiful little beach. Serene and calm. We made our way there every weekend, Rory and I. Built sand castles and swam in the ocean. Mom always worried about dangerous sea creatures, but we were carefree. On a good day, the whole family came down, even Dad; but that was mainly when we were much younger. Dad always said how lucky we were that not many people lived near us. Often, we were the only ones as far as the eye could see.

Sometimes, Rory and I would go to the rocks at the end of the inlet while Mom and Dad stayed on the beach underneath the umbrella. We would find small crabs and fish in the rockpools. I remember daring Rory to touch a crab. It was only tiny, but so were his fingers.

He wasn't old enough then to know it wasn't a good idea. He shrieked as the crab's pincer clamped onto his pointer finger, and I laughed. Rory burst into tears and ran across the rocks towards Mom and Dad with that little crab swinging from the tip of his finger. I was rolling around in fits of laughter on the sand for a solid five minutes.

Later, I felt bad when I saw the little laceration on his fingertip, so I fetched a Band-Aid and bought him an ice-cream. He shared it with me. The world was good again.

And in this moment, it truly hit me that I will never be there for him ever again. His hardships will be his alone.

How did my world turn into this? It's so unfair. I start to get fired up. Why did they choose me? Or Theo? Or any of us? I wonder if my family still goes to the beach sometimes, and if the memory of Rory and the crab still comes back to them too. What if they can't bear to go there because I'm not there anymore? Did they ever find out what happened to me?

Now a knife, twisting in my gut like a frantic snake. Twirling round and round. It's happening, and there's nothing I can do to stop it. I want to protest, but I am immobile. My skin seems to tighten around me, squeezing flesh into the bone. Hundreds of needles hurtle inside my neck like angry porcupines.

A third voice adds to the cacophony of the screams. It is mine. The white inside my brain is all I can register. White darkness. Dark white. How can white be dark? I can never come back.

Goodbye, Theo.

              *     *     *

I vaguely feel the rough floor on my face. Or is that the air? Forty days and forty nights of cold ocean breeze. Twinkling stars of hot lava. Burning. I didn't think death would be like this. Oh, I must have made it to some kind of netherworld. Which means I am alone. There's no way Theo would end up down here.

"All right," the voice cuts through the confusion, and suddenly the pain is gone. "It is done. Get out of here before we change our minds."

What?

"Go on, move it!"

Wait, what is going on? Is the devil releasing me? Can he do that? I thought eternity was . . . well . . . eternity. Maybe this is his waiting room. I'd better make a move. There's a slight problem. Standing up seems beyond my capability. I struggle, but none of my joints are listening. Maybe in this netherworld we fly? I wiggle my shoulders but no wings pop out. This is crazy. Maybe I should open my eyes.

That's better. Wait, this is exactly like the place I just left.

Strong arms grab me and lift me up. I turn to see Theo's warm eyes. What is he doing here? He seems so real.

"You're not dead," he whispers.

"But—"

"Shh, just hold on to me."

Stunned, I put one arm around his shoulders and he carries me out of the room as if I'm nothing.

He leans me against the wall and stares at me. He brushes the hair off my face. I am drowning in his soft eyes.

"You're fine," he murmurs.

I smile wanly and he helps hold me up. But I don't think I am fine. I certainly don't feel fine. In fact, I think I would best be classified as distinctly, absolutely, not fine. I'm supposed to be dead.

"I think they couldn't afford to lose all of us," he says, once we reach outside. "So they just decided to scare us instead."

My mind can't keep up.

"Carla?" Theo touches my hand. "Are you okay?" I look down. "I mean, okay in the vaguest definition of the word?"

I nod, and the waterworks explode.

"Oh, Carla," Theo sighs as he lifts me into his arms again and begins the long, winding flight of stairs back to our room. He is panting heavily after a few minutes.

"Sorry," Theo wheezes. "Need a break."

"I can walk." I'm feeling better now.

He slumps with relief and sets me down. We keep going, Theo half-supporting me with his arm.

We reach the top of the stairs and continue along the winding passageways. Fortunately, the lights are on now, but I have no idea where we are in the Compound. Theo does, though. He gazes straight ahead with his chin up. I wish I were that confident.

We finally reach something I recognize—the Monitor Rooms. This is where they send us every three days for surveillance. Whatever that means. But at least it's a break from the physical hardships of the mines.

And those who are deemed 'ready' after surveillance are allowed to leave the Compound. The leavers are so excited and grateful to go; some tell me they think they are being returned home. I'm not sure I'd trust the future of a leaver. There always seems to be something odd about them.

But we have no say in any of it. We are the powerless pawns of this operation. All rights were stripped the moment we were seized. Along with watches, phones, identification and personal belongings. We are told nothing and the only reason we can keep track of the passing days is that a siren sounds when it's time to sleep or wake up. Theo keeps a secret tally count in the floor to keep track of the days. He says I showed up about three weeks after he was captured.

We hurry past the Monitor Rooms, and finally reach Unit 14. The guard presses the scanner beside the door, and we are back to relative safety.

We slump on the ground. Half dead, but at least we are still half alive. Though I'm not entirely certain that living is a positive at this point.

"Must be about dinner time," mutters Felix, one of the younger boys in our unit. Strange. Normally it's Verity who tells us to get ready for dinner. I search the room. Where is she? I frantically scan each of the familiar faces in the room again. It's not that I especially liked her. But I sure don't like to think that people can just disappear, either. She's not here. I turn to Theo.

"Verity?" I say, panicked.

He shrugs.

"She's not here. You didn't see her?"

I can't believe it.

"No, I didn't . . . "

Everyone else either shakes their head or ignores me. I sit on my makeshift bedding. They can't kill our leader! She did the most out of all of us. She is the person here who least deserves to die. I may have resented the things she made us do, but she was amazing. Only sixteen, yet she seemed many years my elder. They nominated her as our leader for a reason. Who's going to keep us in line now? It can't be one of us—we're a bunch of clowns without her. Only thirteen left.

*Ding.* The bell rings, a familiar sound that means we'll be a little less starving in a few minutes. What can I say about the food at this fine establishment? Wouldn't rate much on TripAdvisor. True, it's consistent—a rock-hard roll covered in a fine film of greenish mold, accompanied by a textureless stew with all the flavor of unsalted mud. It really is that bad. Theo says it's the crushed-up bones of rats, but I hope that's his idea of a joke.

The small trapdoor in the side wall opens, revealing trays filled with familiar sludge. I'm glad to see it today. No one moves. It was always Verity who counted the rolls. Sometimes, they'd give us extras—or not enough—so she'd divide them equally.

"Well," Felix says softly, "I guess I'll do it."

He stands, his small mohawk flopping slightly to the left. It's still blue at the tips where the boys colored it with a highlighter pen that we found. It was a risk, but nothing was said. And it helps keep the tiny spark of hope and rebellion alive.

Felix picks up each roll, counting out loud, before placing it into a bowl of stew and passing it out.

"12, 13 . . . " He stops. His face turns grim. " . . 14," he whispers.

We all know what this is. It is not an act of kindness that results in the fortuitous receipt of one extra roll today, nor is it a mistake. It is a stab into hope, designed to shrivel any lurking sliver of optimism. I feel most sorry for Felix. His handsome face just aged a decade. Although they never said anything, he and Verity had a strong bond that ran deeper than just camaraderie. We all noticed the subtle glances and intentional brushes of skin as they stood close.

No one says a word as Felix gazes at the fourteenth piece of bread in his hand for a moment, before ripping it silently into thirteen small pieces and dropping them into the remaining bowls of stew. He gestures, and we eat. We finish our bowls while they are still lukewarm. The remaining one gets passed around the group for each to take a sip. I choke on mine, remembering Theo's comments about the source of the food.

He nudges me as the others are preparing for bed. He puts his hand out and places something into mine. It's his piece of roll. Not the small extra piece, but his entire roll.

"Why?" I whisper.

"Because you nearly died today, and I didn't."

I shake my head, but gratefully tear off some of the bread. I shove the rest back into his pocket, feeling the closest to being full that I have in a long time. I squeeze his hand. We are the last ones to return our bowls and crawl into our beds, next to each other. Just in time for the lights-out siren.

It means no talking, but Theo leans toward me.

"I'm sorry it was you, not me," he says. "I wish I was the one who had to go through that."

I shake my head. "Obviously, genius, you didn't have a choice."

"I know, but—"

"You think you could've handled it better?"

He sits up. "Wow, Carla. You know I'm not—"

I am amused at his discomfort. "I'm kidding," I say, smirking. "I know you're a manly man."

He punches me lightly on the arm.

"And that's what I get after a near-death experience?" I ask.

"No," Theo says. He stabs his fingers into my side, tickling me, and I have to hold back a squeal. "*This* is what you get."

Just like that, in this moment, I am content. This unfamiliar sensation is firing up my senses, and I need to use everything I've got not to laugh out loud and bring the guards running with their guns. I haven't laughed in so long.

"Stop it," I whisper desperately, a giggle escaping. He finally stops. I find it hard to breathe without releasing the build-up of laughter. I sense the glares of the others in the darkness, but for once, I don't care.

I cling to this feeling as long as I can.

*　　*　　*

I have strange dreams that night. They begin with happiness and Theo and I. We are playing a game of Scrabble against Mom, Dad and Rory, and we are winning.

But soon the dream transforms. Now we are lining up single file; not only our unit, but everyone. Even my family. Hundreds of guards surround us on either side. I cannot see what we are lining up for, but I don't hear any screams. The line in front of me is shrinking, and soon there's only one person before me. A massive canyon beckons. The boy in front, I realize, is Felix, except his mohawk has been roughly shaved off.

He takes a step, but something seems very wrong with him. Felix appears to have no emotion at all. His face is passive, as if he's watching an unstimulating movie for the hundredth time. Then he falls off the edge and into the depths below. He doesn't scream, or hesitate. Is there water? Is it shallow?

33

It is my turn. I know I must jump. One leap, and it will all be over. I tense my muscles, but I can't do it. The guards point their guns and yell. I try again to jump. My feet do not move. I glance down to see that I am literally buried in the ground up to my calves. There's nothing I can do.

I'm going to be shot. I desperately don't want to be.

I don't want to die.

I'm not ready.

The guards start barking orders. Lining up their guns for the final shot. They are moving to one side to make sure the momentum of the bullets will push me off the edge.

"This is your final warning. Move forward, or we will shoot," the voice blares. Can't they see I'm trapped?

The bullets rip into my back.

A distant voice says, "Your punishment is that you will *not* die."

Manic laughter follows.

The dream wanders off, and I somehow coax my brain into a deep sleep.

# 6

# AXTON

The wind screams as I rocket backwards out of the pod. It attacks like a swarm of crazed mosquitos, but I ignore it. My face contorts wildly with the incredible force. The ground looms closer. I press a button and the slimline chute bursts open. Now I'm floating.

It's a strange sensation. For the small amount of time it takes to reach the ground, I am one with nature. All struggles forgotten.

The designated clearing is approaching fast. On target. I bend my knees to brace for impact. I hit the ground and rip the belt off, initiating the decomposition process. Ten seconds and it's as if the chute never existed. I scramble through the green towards the Compound, thinking through the plan. I focus my entire mental energy on it. And on how I'm going to get them out alive.

I remember my father's words: "Axton, *shut it down however you can. Save the children. The rest doesn't matter.*" Then they shot him. He dedicated the last part of his life to this rescue mission, and I'm not going to waste his sacrifice.

I sprint towards the entrance and whip a counterfeit card out of my pocket. Some guy named Bob Stewart. I press the card to the touchpad on the door. The light goes green.

*Good job, Bob.*

I try the handle, but it won't turn. I flash the card again. Green light. Still the handle won't budge. Then I remember the code: 1 . . . 5 . . . 3 . . . 6. Stress does strange things to you. I shake my head and run my hands over the door. I latch onto a flap and pull it open. There's the keypad they told us about, but there are no numbers printed on the buttons. There should be numbers. I repeat the code in my head, desperately trying to see if there's another angle to this. They warned us that things are upgraded all the time, but this is next level. What use is having a code if there is no way to input it?

I'm wasting too much time. The others are probably

already in. I decide to go old-school. I visualize the keypad as an old-style cell phone, punch in the code, and breathe a sigh of relief as the door slides open.

I'm in.

# 7

# CARLA

I WAKE, THANKFUL THAT TODAY IS A REST DAY. It's a loose term because we are still required to do chores; they are just supposedly less physically demanding. We head to the laundry. The guard motions us inside. The huge room is awash with buckets, water, and massive baskets crammed with guards' dirty uniforms. I swear there are hundreds of them. Saved up for the entire week. But at least we haven't drawn bathroom duty. Then we'd stink for the rest of the day.

The guard motions us inside, and we get to work. After hand washing some thirty uniforms, I begin to drift off, and a boy in our unit has to nudge me. We push on. The pile doesn't appear to change. Soon my fingers are raw from scrubbing and detergent, and the seconds tick by in an agony of sluggishness.

The mountain of dirty laundry gradually diminishes.

*　　*　　*

We are hard at work when a harsh voice blares from the speakers that line the roof.

"Unit 14, report to MR." Over and over in a monotone. I used to cover my ears during the walk to the Monitor Rooms, but these days I barely notice it.

I recall my first time in the Monitor Room. I was afraid, but Theo seemed calm. Nothing fazes him. We became friends the instant we met. Perhaps because we're close in age—I'm only a year older than him, and the oldest in the unit.

Apparently the great Commander only chooses to enslave young teens and children. Our unit is close in age, but I've seen lots of children as young as five at Assembly. Maybe their delicate fingers are perfect for extracting the tiger's eye from the rock without damaging it. Regardless, I can't figure out what on earth is so special about this gemstone to make it worth this much effort and misery. It's a pretty stone, but there are plenty of gems that are more expensive. And more rare.

We assemble in a ragged line. On the guard's command, we walk quickly, taking great care to stay ahead of his black boots; their steel tips can crush bone. Theo and I used to joke that they sounded like high heels. Out of earshot, of course, in breathy whispers.

In my old life, I hated walking around barefoot. Every little pebble felt like agony. Here, we are forbidden to wear footwear because tiger's eye is easily scratched. Weeks of walking across rocks and concrete has certainly toughened my limbs. And admittedly, callouses and rough feet do make the perfect accessories to our one-size-fits-all pillowcase garments.

Right now, the concrete is burning hot beneath my feet. No one dares to complain. Discipline is what keeps us in line, our footsteps in a steady formation; no one risks creating a syncopated beat. We don't speak, we don't move out of line, we don't protest.

Eventually, we arrive at the Monitor Rooms. Twenty rooms huddle side by side, made entirely of aged concrete, almost like bunkers. We know the drill by now, but the guard bores us with a lecture.

"This is a very important time," he says, his tone harsh and emotionless. "Soon you will enter a deep sleep. Tests will be performed, and you will dream. What you dream will indicate whether you are ready or not."

This area shrieks confinement and strips us of what makes us human. Yet somehow, we exit still intact after each monitor session. They cannot tame us. Other units have not been so fortunate. I've seen some come out like blank canvasses. If you smile at them or wave, they won't or can't respond. Empty and vulnerable. Like shells at the beach that have been deserted by crabs upgrading to a bigger home.

Every time, they say we are not ready. But they never tell us what we're supposed to be ready for. Theo has his theories, as usual, but I don't believe any of them. They are too far-fetched. But I do agree that whatever it is, it must be awful. Why else the need to strip us of our humanity?

One by one, we file into our individual rooms. Theo strides in first, head held high. I watch him lie on the clinical bed. I head to the next room, where an identical bed awaits me. The digital, robotic voice repeats its usual mantra.

"Lie on the bed. Put your arms by your side."

Once I'm settled, the bed pivots and moves into a small enclosure, almost like the CT scanner I once saw at a hospital.

"Clear your mind. Relax all of your muscles."

Are they kidding? I try, but my muscles are stiff from stress and physical labor. I guess it doesn't matter because the machine begins to fill with blue gas anyway. Somehow, the gas forces you to dream. I breathe deeply. The faster I fall asleep, the less scary it will be. I close my eyes, consumed by an overwhelming need to sleep.

I drift into oblivion.

*　　*　　*

The pure smell of fresh air tells me I'm at home. I can hear the familiar clanging of pots and pans as Mom cooks. My bedroom seems normal—bed made, mint-colored bean bag perched perkily near the open window, and clothes neatly hung. My beloved bookshelf is overflowing, and a half-eaten packet of Lay's potato chips lies on the carpet.

I push myself sluggishly off the edge of the bed. I float across the room until the bookshelf zooms close. My fingers run softly against hundreds of paperbacks until they catch on an odd book, its spine sticking out over the edge of the shelf. Slowly, I tug it free. The cover is encased in rich, dark satin. I gently stroke the surface. The title is *The Truth*. Strange. I turn to the first page.

"Carla." A rough, childish voice.

I spin around to face the doorway.

A small boy stands very still, his smooth, innocent face displaying concern. I feel my expression soften.

"Rory." I smile and drift over to him. I reach out to touch his dark, wavy hair as happiness floods my being. His face remains still as he pushes my hand away.

"No, Carla. Concentrate." He pronounces the last word slowly, trying each syllable out, to make sure he has the right one.

I frown and try to understand. I stretch out again to touch him.

He shakes his head. "Carla. You need to come back. I miss you."

I nod as tears run down my face, but I'm still confused.

He continues, "Just find out—"

His voice is overridden by a harsher one. "Run, Carla. Run!"

I am in the open, the wind on my face. I search for the source of the words but find nobody. A train track runs beneath my feet. I can sense it vibrating and turn to see a train looming closer. I'm about to jump out of its path, when I see her. Mom. Standing on the tracks just ahead of me. The train is closing in on us.

"Mom!" I scream. She turns around, her golden hair floating in the wind, framing her face. She's dressed in clothes I've never seen her wear before.

"Mom, get off the tracks! The train is coming," I yell. She doesn't flinch. Doesn't seem to hear me. Doesn't even seem to see the train. Instead, she stares at me. Then she speaks.

"Carla. I need you to find out. Discover the truth." She stares at me desperately. "I need you to understand. Listen to me, Carla." She becomes hysterical. "Promise me, Carla! Promise me!" And then she is shouting, and the train is approaching. I run at her and lift her by the waist, forcing her off the tracks. No time for me to jump. She tumbles down, but before reaching solid ground, she disintegrates into dust. I turn around just as the train slams full-force into me.

The world turns black.

*　　*　　*

My eyes flutter open and I hear the robotic tone. "Carla, your dreams will be analyzed and results available shortly. Stand by."

The bed slides back out of the enclosure, and I sit up. I walk past the screen where the results will display, not even bothering to glance at it. I stand at the door, but it doesn't open. I spin around, confused. A look back at the screen gives me the answer. In red. Written in the middle is: *'TECHNICAL DIFFICULTIES. WAIT.'*

Wait for *what?*

I sit on the bed. This shouldn't be happening. Does this mean I have turned out like the others? The ones I've seen come out of here . . . emotionless? I mean, I don't think so. I still feel the same.

I touch my face and run through some emotions to see if my face reacts. Happy? Yep, mouth curves upwards. Surprise! Yes, my jaw drops. Sad. My forehead crinkles. I still care about my family and about Theo. I'm good.

I sit by the screen and wait.

After five minutes, I begin to worry. Why hasn't it printed out my ticket? Out of nowhere, I remember Dad's old trick of kicking something if it stops working. I half-heartedly kick the screen. Dads are awesome, but not this time. Throbbing toes are the only result. I wait again.

Eventually the screen changes to green. The machine prints a script that says, "Carla, you have potential." Business as usual.

Gee, thanks.

The door opens and I exit. Outside, my unit is waiting for me. Everyone else is there, except Theo. The guard is facing the other way, so I take the opportunity to peek into the neighboring rooms. Still no Theo. I even check inside the small storeroom. Nothing.

My heart begins to race. What if he has become emotionless?

Suddenly the guard appears in front of me. He glares at me.

"What are you doing?" he booms, and I flinch.

I avoid his gaze. "Uh," I say. "I thought I left something . . ."

"Follow me to your unit," he barks, clearly not bothered to delve any deeper.

I line up with the others. I still don't know where Theo is, and it's clear the others don't either. But no one would dare ask.

The guard doesn't seem to notice Theo's absence. Where could he be?

*   *   *

We reach our room as the food arrives. I am not hungry, but I force it down so Theo won't be disappointed with me. We clean up, and everyone falls into bed as the siren sounds.

I'm desperately sick with worry about Theo, but at the same time I feel like I haven't slept in days. Somehow, dreaming is exhausting.

I can't stop yawning, but I can't drop off to sleep either.

I know I won't make it in here without Theo's calm presence and quiet confidence.

Nina, the girl who sleeps on the other side of me, leans towards me. She's only fifteen, and normally very reserved, so I'm surprised when she speaks. Especially since the siren has already sounded.

"Hey, Carla," she whispers.

"Hey," I say, perching on my elbow.

She continues sheepishly, "I know you're worried about Theo, but you should try to sleep."

"Thanks, Nina," I say. "I will. Are you feeling tired after today?"

She bites her lip. "I don't really mind. It's missing my family that hurts the most."

I agree.

"I miss Mom," she says, tears already welling. "I really miss her."

"I miss mine too. What's your Mom like?"

"Mom's the nicest person on the planet. She's always smiling; she has such a beautiful smile. She's my best friend."

"She sounds like an awesome mom," I say.

"I wish I could talk to her. Just once."

"I know it's hard to imagine now, but I'm sure we will make it out of here."

"Yeah," she says. "I hope so. Good night, Carla."

"Good night, Nina." It feels nice.

I roll over and try to get to sleep.

My muscles won't quit groaning. Work today was especially bad. They directed our unit to a hardcore location in the mines. One that they had identified as potentially high yield. They seemed very pleased when we discovered a mother lode of tiger's eye, rich and gleaming.

Since it is forbidden to leave any of the gem behind, we were forced to shovel for hours and hours. Back-breaking work that wore out even the strongest. Our carts were overloaded. How I hate the sight of that orange-brown gem. It glows in the dim light like a tiger's eye with a hint of orange. Hungry eyes. Predatory eyes. Death eyes.

Eventually, I sink into a dreamless slumber.

# 8

# AXTON

I step inside, ducking my head. It's not a particularly small doorway, but I'm a particularly tall guy. I enter, and am immediately surrounded by concrete. There's a bleak grey hall, exactly as expected, but I wasn't prepared for this intense, suffocating sensation. I almost expect the walls to start closing in on me.

I shake the doubts and turn left, as I have in each of our training runs. I follow the sequence. Left, right, past the fire hydrant . . . then right at the first chance I get. I dash straight ahead before reaching a dead end.

I spin to the right and stoop through a doorway before sliding into a side passage, just before a guard in a black uniform speeds past. I let him go and quickly glance in both directions before sprinting off. I quicken my pace until I can barely keep my footsteps silent. In the distance, I can see a door. I don't know if I've made it in time. Beyond that door, my brother is waiting for me.

I hope he's still alive.

# 9

# CARLA

I wake, and Theo has reappeared. I do a double take and raise an eyebrow to ask where he's been, but he shakes his head. Either he doesn't want me to know, or he can't tell me here. As we exit the room in single file, I notice something else strange. It is only a flicker, but there's something about the way the guards are moving that puts me on edge.

My instincts are confirmed when our normal mining routine is interrupted, and we're instructed to head upstairs to a large cavern. The rumor is that it's near the surface of the Compound.

Numerous other units arrive, and we are herded like

nervous cattle towards a lengthy convoy of strange vehicles with drone-like propellers. They look like something out of a sci-fi movie; maybe some type of hovercraft.

"Load them up," the guards command.

From nearby storerooms, we collect boxes of food, water, guns, and advanced military equipment I'm unfamiliar with. I try to take the food boxes because they're the lightest. Not because I am lazy, but because if I injure my back—like Dad did when he was shifting the TV—I'll be sent to medical. And that's a guaranteed one-way trip.

We trudge back and forth between the vehicles and the storerooms without speaking, avoiding eye contact. No one wants to be picked on by the guards.

I want to ask Theo what he thinks all this is for; he seems to have a better clue of what's going on. But I don't dare risk it. It's clear that we're preparing for something. Perhaps an expedition for the guards. But why the weapons?

I entertain my brain as much as I can, in order to numb my body from the monotonous labor. I recall books I read long ago and songs that Mom used to sing to me. And I think about my brother. I would do anything to get out of here just to see him again. I miss him so much.

Finally, all of the strange vehicles are packed, and we file back into the great hall. They make us sit on the concrete in tight clusters with our units, and we don't get much of a chance to even look at the other children.

The Commander stands before us in complete silence until everyone is gathered. "Our recent analysis of your dreams provided much insight, and we believe that all of you are ready. It has taken longer than we thought, but you are now prepared for the task ahead."

I hear myriads of gasps and groans around me. My stomach clenches, and I am stricken with terror. I glance at Theo, who merely raises an eyebrow. How does he manage to appear so calm? Isn't he scared?

I don't even want to imagine what our task could be. Then I have another thought. What if they separate me from Theo? No, I couldn't survive. I have no one else. If they try to make me, I won't do it.

The Commander continues, "You must all be wondering why we have brought you here to the Compound."

*No, not at all.* Why would we want to know the motivation behind our kidnappings? The reason for forcing us into hard labor like war prisoners? For starving us and threatening us with death?

"You have been selected because we see your individual talents. We believe that you are the best the world has to offer. We understand that you have loved ones that you've left behind. But you are now fighting for a cause.

Keep the image of your parents, siblings and friends fresh in your minds. This will maintain your focus for the battles ahead. We have chosen you, the strongest among us, to form a rebellion against an army that is threatening to take over your home cities. We have done what we've had to do to prepare you for battle. You are now mighty, and it is up to you to protect your loved ones. And in return, each of you is destined for greatness."

He actually seems to think that we see him as a reasonable human being. I'm no genius, but I fail to see how digging up stones and being starved has prepared any of us for so-called glory.

"Together, we will fight against evil. Together, we will save our loved ones. And together, we will conquer the world."

The Commander lifts his pitch at the end, as if he is expecting a round of applause. Which, to my surprise, there is. Children are cheering in the front. Everyone is clapping. Smiling even. Are they falling for this? Are they that desperate for some hope, some meaning to all this, that they'll accept such a blatant fallacy? How is everyone so blind? The guards are not good people. They have deprived us, humiliated us and frightened us. Besides, where are our weapons? I don't see how bare feet, dirty dresses and filthy nails can overpower anyone.

"We understand that you may have some doubts. We had no choice but to bring you here. Don't worry, your parents know where you are. They are so proud of you. In fact, parades are being held in your honor as we speak. The world is depending on you. Our world is in danger, but together we will overcome those who wish to cause us harm. You will be amply rewarded once we are victorious. It will be worth it."

I don't know what to think. Our families have been told? What if he is telling the truth? Maybe our families are in trouble. What if the only hope of stopping those who are threatening our families lies with us? I can't help reevaluating everything we've been through. I wonder what Theo is thinking. I glance over at him, but his expression reveals nothing. He is staring intently at the Commander.

"We leave at dawn in two days," the Commander says. "Do not be afraid. You have what it takes."

*     *     *

I'm opening my mouth to ask Rory what he wants me to find out, when I hear Theo's voice.

"Get up, Carla. You have to get up now."

My eyes flash open. I was dreaming about Mom and

the train again, but this time my dog was there too. And the train didn't actually hit me.

Theo is leaning over my bed, frantically shaking me, and the other miners are waiting. I'm lying on the hessian bag, my skin freezing. I am so tired of being woken up.

"You have to get up. Can you hear me, Carla?"

He pulls my arm. I guess it's morning. I stay still. Theo continues to wrench me. The intense look in his eyes grabs my attention.

"What's wrong, Theo?"

He growls, "Would you hurry *up*, Carla."

I startle at his sharp tone. Highly unusual for Theo. His eyes are bright, and I wonder for a second whether he's okay. He sighs.

He beckons me closer.

"Now's our chance," he breathes. "Our planning wasn't wasted."

I stare at him. Surely, he can't be serious.

"Are you out of your mind?" I say.

He shakes his head. "Be ready."

"Theo, don't! Just do as we're told," I warn him.

"You have to trust me," he says. I want to protest, but he quickly adds, "I'll tell you everything soon."

He pulls me up. "We've already wasted too much time," he mutters.

Everyone else is awake and as confused as I am. What on earth is Theo doing?

"Line up," he says firmly. What is happening? Is he one of *them?* One of the guards? I hesitate. What if he's been spying on us this whole time? Using me. What if he isn't Theo? My Theo.

"Oh, don't look at me like that, Carla," Theo says. "Just trust me."

He grabs my wrist and yanks me towards the door, lining up behind the others. Jackie, one of the strongest girls in our unit, stands at the front. "The guard will be arriving soon," Theo whispers to us. "Stay calm."

We remain silent, listening for the sound that will alert us to the guard's arrival. We don't have to wait long before the heavy footsteps resonate down the hall. My heart is pounding.

The solid door slides open. Outside stands a tall figure. I begin to tremble. He's not our guard. In fact, I've never seen him before. The first thing I notice is his messy brown hair, totally abnormal for a guard. They *always* have a buzz cut. His thick boots shine despite the poor lighting, and his hands gently caress a gun. He strides through the doorway and plants his feet directly facing us.

He glares at each of us in turn before reaching out,

pulling me out of line, and pressing the barrel to my temple.

I gasp and hold in a yelp.

*Don't shoot, don't shoot, don't shoot.*

"A deed was performed this week." His soft tone is chilling. "An unforgivable deed."

I shiver.

The gun digs further into my temple.

"And what do we do to such people?" Silence. "What do we do?" he repeats icily.

Nobody moves.

I don't answer him. I won't obey him. I can sense his hot breath on my face as he whispers the next word.

"Carla."

I shake my head.

His free hand lifts my chin, forcing me to turn and look at him. "I hope you've enjoyed your time here."

I squeeze my eyes shut and think about my family as his fingers close over the trigger.

The bullet never comes.

The sirens do. They scream like a thousand fog horns. Smoke oozes from cracks in the walls. The lights go out. He releases me. Everything slows down, as if I'm in the stage between death and life, being dragged painfully out of consciousness. It is completely dark, but I know I'm not dead when I feel Theo's hand grasp my wrist.

"There you are," he breathes, his voice sounding strained. I look around for the guard, but I can't see anything. Theo tugs me along what I hope is the hallway out of here. He pulls me harder.

"Run," he says.

I push my legs harder, run faster. How can he see where he's going? My vision is completely obstructed by the blackness. I cling to his hand. My heart is pounding at double speed. I'm panting. Fast.

Then Theo says, "Look."

I have no idea what he is talking about. Until I see the light. I burst ahead of Theo. A heavy glow fills the hall further away. I have to squint as we get closer. Finally, I can see. I spot a flight of stairs just beyond the single bulb hanging from the low ceiling. I turn to Theo to beg for a break.

Then I rip my hand away and sprint up the concrete stairs.

He's not Theo.

# 10

# AXTON

I SEE IT IN HER EYES. The realization. I reach out to stop her, but her filthy smock has already disappeared. Not surprising. I *was* just holding a gun to her head. I scowl and dart after her. It doesn't take long; within a few seconds, I'm a stride behind her.

"Carla, stop."

She pauses. I know I've got her now. "I'm here to help you."

She takes two more steps, and slowly turns to face me. She squints into my eyes, trying to read my soul. I don't think she likes what she sees.

"Get away from me," she yells.

"No, Carla," I say. Ugh. It's going to take a while to build her trust. I have to convince her that I'm not one of them.

"What are you going to do to me?" She demands an answer.

I hold my hands up, palms facing her.

"I'm here to get you out. No time to explain. I'm not a guard. You have to trust me."

She opens her mouth to object, but I raise my voice.

"The guards are already coming for us, Carla. We need to get above ground before the pod leaves without us." I beckon her forwards.

She glares at me.

"I don't believe you," she says belligerently.

I grit my teeth.

"You've got no other option. You stay here, they'll kill you." She glances around. I see the acquiescence in her eyes.

She huffs but runs on. I'm hot on her heels. Eventually, we can see the top of the stairwell. A row of lights is blazing. At the top, a long passageway stretches out. Carla turns back to me, confused.

"I thought . . . we were out," she says.

I laugh. "That's the thing with the Compound. You're never out."

"What's that supposed to mean?" she pants as we continue down the corridor.

"Nothing," I say. "Find the elevator."

Carla spins around at the sound of shouts and heavy breathing spiraling up the stairwell.

I don't need to look to know who they belong to. Change of plans. I grab Carla's wrist and tug her along, urging her to increase her speed. This time, she doesn't complain.

"Stop where you are," a voice thunders behind us. I glance ahead. We are a dozen strides from the elevator door now. I know they won't shoot us. They need us. They need her.

"Get down on your knees!"

Just a few more strides. Our feet hammer the floor. The elevator doors are approaching. We need to hurry. I have to save her.

The mission depends on it.

# 11

# CARLA

I HAVE TO GET AWAY FROM HIM. I don't care what he says, I don't trust him. He nearly killed me, and that's enough of a reason for me. The only problem is, I can't see a way to escape. I hear the shouts of the guards just behind us, and the elevator is approaching in front. Two options, both bad.

Suddenly I see it.

A third option.

There's a small hatch-door low on the wall beside the elevator, with a danger symbol on it. Perfect.

I wrench my hand from his grasp just as he's entering the elevator, and dive through the trap door. It swings freely and I tumble onto the floor inside.

"Ugh." I stifle a shout and rub the side of my arm. The room is tiny. I can't stay here for long. I push on the flap door but can hear the guards' muffled voices just outside. I can't see another way out. A sickening thought dawns on me. *You're trapped. A little birdie in a one-way cage.* If I want to survive, I'll have to save myself.

I hear a foreign sound, almost mechanical. It must be the elevator. Hopefully it's carrying at least one of my problems away. I inspect the small space more thoroughly, and realize that while the room may be small horizontally, there's a giant shaft running upwards. Light trickles in from far above.

Thick wires snake up the walls on the wall opposite the trapdoor, but I can't tell how high up they go; I can't even see the top. Don't tell me I have to try to climb those. Suicide.

A glint catches my eye, and I spot a thin ladder half-hidden to the left of the wires. *Oh my gosh,* I think. *I really do have to climb out of this thing.*

I wonder how much time I've wasted standing here, and the thought panics me. I grip the rungs of the mis-shapen ladder and test the bottom one. It seems sturdy, so I take a deep breath and begin to climb. My limbs soon start to burn. I take a moment to shake my legs out before climbing again. I tighten my grip as my fingers begin to slip on the grease that cakes the rungs. I hear a bang and a shout, and the entire shaft vibrates. I flinch and gasp as my left foot slips. I cling even tighter to the metal.

The sound of voices travels up the shaft from outside. *Oh no!* I think. *It's them.* I need to climb faster. I try to pick up the pace, but the slippery coating on the bars conspires against me.

Where is Theo now? What if he was taken just like I was? How will I find him? He'd better be okay. My arms weaken at the thought of Theo in pain. What if I never see him again?

I can't think about that. It's time for some positive self-talk. I will reach the top of this musty shaft, and then I will find Theo. Then, somehow, I'll get back to my family.

I drag myself up ten more bars and then freeze when I hear something. It sounds very close. Too close. My gut wrenches when I realize it's coming from inside the shaft. *Something is in here with me.*

I whip my head around like an owl on the hunt, searching for the origin of the sound. *Thump, thump.* I look down. Nothing. I glance upwards. A figure is climbing down towards me.

*No, no, no!* I place one foot on the rung below. Then

another and another. I scramble down, barely even holding on, no longer trying to conceal my presence. I need to get out of here, but what can I do? Even once I reach the bottom, there is no way out.

I hear a shout reverberate through the shaft, but my heart is pounding so hard that I can't decipher it. I look up briefly, and see that the figure is gaining on me. I try to descend faster, but my feet are slipping so badly, I'm sure I will fall. I must be near the bottom by now, but what can I do once I reach it? There is no escape.

I squint as I watch the figure descend from above. There's something familiar about the way they move. I'll be able to see them up close if I don't hurry. I can't see the ground, but I don't have a choice. I let go of the rungs, push myself away from the ladder with my feet and mentally brace for the landing. I'm falling.

"Oh, come on."

The words echo with annoyance through the darkness, and only then do I realize I know him. I hit the ground with a thud, and my legs twist painfully beneath me.

"Carla," I hear Theo whisper. He climbs down until he is beside me. Surely my legs must be broken.

He reaches down to hug me and holds me as if he'll never let me go. But then he rather brusquely lifts me to my feet and pushes me back towards the ladder. "Carla, keep moving," he says roughly. "We don't have much time."

"Didn't you see me fall?" I say, momentarily hurt.

"You're fine, Carla."

Why doesn't he care? I scowl, grasping the stupid rungs once again and beginning to climb. My legs, surprisingly, seem fine after a few steps. Somehow, climbing seems easier the second time. I glance below, and Theo is right behind me.

"You found me, Theo," I say. Tears well, and I blink rapidly to keep them at bay. "I had to get away from the guard. There was no other way out."

"I know," he says.

"I don't even know if this ladder goes anywhere. But I had to try. Wait, how did you find me?"

"Axton told me where you were."

"Who's Axton?"

A pause. "My brother."

"What? Theo! Your brother is *here*?" I say. Suddenly I feel a streak of unbidden jealousy. Why couldn't *my* brother be here?

"Why didn't you tell me?" I ask.

"I couldn't tell you anything about this, Carla. It would have put you in too much danger."

"Oh, come on, Theo."

"I couldn't do that to you, Carla." There's a bite to his words, and I know I can't argue with him. It's strange seeing him like this. Normally he saves this part of his personality for talking about things that are important to him. Does he actually care about me?

We don't talk for a while as we climb, but my mind is whirring. What else don't I know about Theo? It's obvious he's been planning this escape. And not told me. But why would he risk his life coming back for me?

We reach a platform stretching out from the ladder.

"I need a break," I whisper breathlessly. Theo stops beside me in the dark.

Then I hear him snicker. "What's so funny?" I ask.

"I can't believe you jumped off. I've never seen you move so fast. Brilliant landing." He begins to laugh harder.

"Oh, whatever," I say. I pretend to be offended, but a small smile escapes.

"You're the only person I know who would go the *opposite way* when someone is trying to rescue them," he gasps, before breaking up again.

"How was I supposed to know who it was?" I protest. He continues to laugh louder. "You could've been a guard."

He's chuckling too much to respond. I've rarely heard him laugh, and now it's happening at my expense. I narrow my eyes and hold my tongue, which, of course, only makes him laugh harder. Why is it so much easier to climb this ridiculous ladder with Theo by my side?

We reach the top quicker than I thought we would, and right above me is a circular trapdoor, similar to those Teenage Mutant Ninja Turtle sewer openings. My brother would love this; he was obsessed with those green karate turtles when he was ten.

The plate looks heavy. I reach up and try to dislodge it with one hand, nearly toppling off the ladder in the process. I turn to Theo to ask him to hold me so I don't fall, but he's already pushing me in place against the ladder. I smile, but I think it looks more like a grimace. I turn back to the plate and plant my hands firmly against it. I push as hard as I can.

It doesn't move.

"Do you want me to try?" Theo says.

I shake my head. "I can do it." I reposition my hands. I push again, and this time I hear it creak.

Theo snickers.

I snarl at him. "What's so funny?" I ask.

He reaches up past me and slowly twists the plate with one hand. It turns easily and he gently pushes it out into the open air. Cue smirk from Theo. Seems like he was into the ninja turtles too.

Light streams into the shaft and warms my soul. I squint in the unfamiliar sunlight, and inhale the glorious fresh air. Theo pushes me through. The brisk morning breeze fans my face as I take in my surroundings. Familiar concrete spans several hundred yards in every direction. But after that, there is green. An unbelievably rich rainforest. It's beautiful.

I can't believe I'm outside. I'm in the real world. I'm free!

"Theo," I yell with excitement, "We're out!" I marvel at the beauty of the outside world.

He begins to speak, but is cut off by the sound of a motorbike, or a thousand motorbikes. I cover my ears, but the sound pierces through my hands.

Someone else, not Theo, starts yelling at us.

"Quick! Get out of the way. It's coming!"

What's coming? We run towards the voice. I don't recognize him until we're much closer. It's the guard I ran from! I yank Theo back and try to force him to turn around. We have to get away. Theo glares at me for a split second before dragging me back to the enemy. I pull back hard. No. I won't go near him.

"Carla, stop. What are you doing?" Theo is yelling.

He isn't quite strong enough to hold me in my desperate state but manages to push me into the man's arms. Strong arms that hold me tight even though I struggle. I try to rip my way free, but I can't. I search for a face to help me—and there's a whole group gathered nearby. But nobody makes any move to assist me. I open my mouth to scream, but am immediately smothered by his hand. The whirring noise becomes even louder.

"Carla! He's a good guy, you idiot." I relax slightly. "He told me where to find you. He's on our side," says Theo.

I growl. It makes sense, but I don't like it.

"He held a gun to my head," I mutter.

The guard breaks out in a grin. "It had to look real," he says with a laugh. "You weren't supposed to get away, though."

Theo says, "Never does as she's told."

"My brother just *had* to go down to get you. I told him you'd find your own way out."

Theo crosses his arms sheepishly. "Well, I didn't want anything to go wrong."

The words sink in. "You're Theo's brother?"

He releases me. "I'm Axton," he says. "Nice to meet you."

I find myself studying him. His smoky eyes are very different to Theo's. He doesn't seem too much older. And he has almost none of the same features. Certainly not Theo's wavy, red hair.

Theo reads my mind. "I take after Dad."

"What's he doing here?" I ask Theo.

"Um, saving you," Axton says.

"He's in the Organization," Theo answers, shooting an annoyed look at Axton. "He signed up for the mission when they found out where you were being kept."

I open my mouth to ask more questions, but Theo cuts me off.

"Pod's landed. Let's get on this thing."

I realize that the whirring sound has died down a little, and now I can see where it's coming from. A giant, black airplane. Well, more like an alien spaceship. Or some secret military project. There are no external blades or propellers to be seen—only some intakes.

A hundred or more children from the Compound huddle on the other side, watched over by other soldiers. I presume they're waiting for the ship, too.

"Let's go, Carla," Theo calls. I realize that he and his brother are already running towards the sleek craft.

*     *     *

The inside is even more sophisticated: silver furnishing

and gadgets I don't recognize. The chairs are strange and angular, and they don't appear at all comfortable.

I choose a seat at the front next to Theo and sink into unbelievable luxury. I am surprised when the chair automatically molds to my body. I relax even further and it responds. Truly one size fits all. Axton sits beside me. The others enter the craft, and the soldier leads them past us to a back room. I wonder why they didn't send me back there.

The ship prepares for takeoff, but it doesn't move forwards at all. It simply *lifts*. It rises as gently as if we were floating on a marshmallow. I stare out the window, watching the Compound shrink as we rise.

It is only when Theo hands me a silver pillow that I realize how exhausted I am.

*    *    *

I don't open my eyes right away when I wake. I moan as my joints creak. Don't tell me I've overslept again. The guards will punish me. Us. They will work us longer and harder. They won't give us food. It will be my fault again.

I hold my breath, because something seems wrong. Then I realize that I'm awake, but nobody is shaking me. It's the first time in a long time that I've woken naturally, and it's an incredible feeling. Everything comes flooding back to me. I'm not in the Compound anymore. I am free. All thanks to Theo's brother.

In fact, he's staring at me.

# 12

# AXTON

I realize I'm staring at her when her eyes lock onto mine. I look away instantly, but I know my face is turning a shade of red. She looked so peaceful despite everything she's been through. I'm still trying to figure out who she is. She's not what I expected after reading her dossier.

She flicks me an indecipherable look, so I decide to gaze out of the window. It's the safer option.

The soldiers let me know that the other team didn't succeed in shutting the Compound production line down. Frustrating, since that was supposed to be the easy win. My team's mission was to rescue the children, yet we didn't even get all of them out. Seems like neither group achieved their aim.

A flash of black passes by the window. My heart races, because I know exactly what that means. I speak into my microphone to warn the pilot. I look at Carla and am reminded that my group succeeded in the most important part of the mission. I promise myself I will at least keep these ones alive.

"Carla," I say. "They're coming."

"Who?"

"The guards."

"What? How do you know?" she asks as I tug on Theo. He begins to stir, but is clearly in a very deep sleep. Justifiable, given that he spent the entire night awake, preparing for the rescue.

"I saw their pod outside. They'll try to shoot us down."

"What are we going to do?"

I shake Theo again. "Come on, Theo. Get up."

He sits up. "What's going on?"

I glance back at Carla. "We have to perform some evasive maneuvers. But you need to be prepared in case we have to exit."

Her eyes widen but she says nothing.

I shake everyone else awake in the front room, while Theo heads to the back to stir the others.

I open a small storage compartment at the back of the pod and haul out black packs marked *Autochute*. I sense Carla's breath on my neck.

"Are you crazy?" she says. "We can't jump out. Can't we . . . isn't there another option?"

I guess there's a harsh expression on my face because she doesn't object again.

"Help me hand these out," I say.

Before I've even finished the sentence, Carla begins to toss autochutes to everyone in the pod. Many of the children have come out to the front room to see what the fuss is about.

Terrified little faces bravely open the packages. I see determination beneath the fear. Carla turns to me.

"How do these work?" She seems alarmed by their tiny size.

I take one and place it along her back and pull the green tab. The chute self-wraps around her neck and waist.

She still seems hesitant. "And this is supposed to save me?" she says, pointing to the thin black webbing. I guess it doesn't look like much.

"Press the red button when you hear a loud beep," I say. "It auto-opens if you forget, but better not to."

Carla nods and turns to help one of the other children. I attach my chute, then begin to check on everyone else.

I reach a tiny girl who must be about five years old. She shouldn't be here. She's too young. What hurts me the most is that tears stream down her face, but she doesn't make a sound. She gazes at me with wide, frightened eyes as I kneel down to her height.

"Hey," I say softly. "It's going to be okay."

She scrutinizes the chute in her hands. "I don't want to." She locks her expression solidly. I can't imagine what she's been through in the Compound.

"Hey, hey. What's your name?" I ask her. Her big, blue eyes latch onto mine. I just want the tears to stop.

"Sapphire," she whispers.

"That's a nice name. Like the gem, right?"

The hint of a smile forms on her lips. A split second later it has vanished.

"It's easy, Sapphire," I say. "All you have to do is press this button when you hear a loud buzz, okay?"

"I know. I heard," she says gruffly.

"You can do it," I say. "I know you can."

She shakes her head slowly, studying the button. Then she turns away, finalizing our conversation. I don't have any more time to spend with her.

I glance out of the window and spot the enemy pod again. It is positioning itself directly opposite to get a precise shot, and is weaving to avoid our targeting radar. The

pilot warns everyone to sit down, and the seatbelts automatically activate as if they're alive. A perfect fit.

Suddenly the pod hurtles in multiple directions. We
bounce around in a desperate dance. A boom signals
the enemy firing. We duck and weave. It's on our tail.
Sparks fly outside as their shots contact the pod's protec-
tive armor. A back section rips off, and I hear children
screaming. But these pods can handle a lot of damage,
and we maintain control.

More shots hit the craft, indenting one side. A volley
smashes through the wall over our heads, and I instruct
Carla and Theo to keep their heads down. Luckily,
nobody is injured.

Despite that, it's clear we are in trouble. The pilot
sounds the emergency alarm.

"Evacuate. Evacuate. Evacuate."

A deafening sound splits the air as another round
strikes the craft. I unbuckle and leap to my feet.

"Everyone to the rear of the pod. Now," I order. They
need no urging. Within a few seconds, everyone is assem-
bled.

"Get ready to jump," I shout. "Go on my command."
I pull the lever and the door thrusts open. The wind buf-
fets my face as I peer down. I can't see water below, nor
any buildings. We can proceed.

I yell above the whirring. "We've got to jump quickly. Every second we wait means a longer distance between each other when we land." Their eyes are wide with fright. No time to repeat it. I glance down at terrain whooshing terrifyingly fast down below.

"Jump," I yell. No one does.

Theo steps forward, "I'll go."

Carla seems shocked for a second before lunging in front of him. "No, I will."

"Hurry up, one of you," I say.

Without another word, Theo pushes Carla aside, salutes us, and leans out into the turbulent slipstream.

Another boy steps forward and leaps out. Greg and the other soldiers help the rest of the children from the Compound jump one by one, less than a second apart.

Soon, only Carla, Sapphire and I are left. Carla steps forward and waves at us, her face impassive before leaning out. She screams something before jumping, but I don't quite catch it.

"Sapphire, come here," I say.

She doesn't move.

I reach out to her. "I'm going to jump with you," I say. I pick her up, and thankfully she doesn't object.

I lean out, holding her tightly as the wind beats against my back. She tenses as we drop, but she doesn't scream.

The trees below us grow larger, and I get ready to press the button. My chute will be able to lower us both.

A loud buzz disturbs our free fall.

I punch the red button, and a streamlined paper-thin chute billows above us, slowing our speed dramatically. I drift down, Sapphire a rag doll in my arms.

Soon my feet impact the ground. Thanks to the auto-chutes, it appears that our entire group has landed mostly without injury. I am beginning to think this is going to be okay.

Then I hear the explosions. I dive over Sapphire's body to form a barricade between her and the shrapnel, which burrows into my back and shoulders like dozens of little knives trying to burrow their way to my vital organs. *Well,* I think, as the explosions die down, *that's the end of our pod.* I hope the pilot made it out alive.

My ears are ringing, but I doubt there's permanent damage. Whew, that was a little close. I turn to Sapphire, but she hasn't moved. I lift her chin so I can see her face. She isn't breathing.

I unstrap her from the chute and shake her softly. "Sapphire."

No response. No rise and fall of the chest. I check for a pulse in her neck. There isn't one. My own heart rate picks up. I begin CPR, but after four sets of compressions and breaths, there is no movement. I keep pumping for what seems like forever. They told us in training that CPR is exhausting after even a short period of time, and I can confirm they're right. Sweat drips down my face from exertion and stress. Time crawls by, and after an eternity, my watch points out that twenty minutes have passed. Normally at about this time we decide to give up. But I don't. This little girl has to live.

I am vaguely aware of the sound of footsteps through the thick underbrush. I can only hope these people are on our side. I decide to risk shouting. If they're guards, they will find us anyway.

"Carla," I yell. "Theo."

Nothing.

I am seriously fatigued, but I can't stop. I won't let myself.

Then, with no fanfare, Sapphire coughs.

"Sapphire, can you hear me?"

She inhales loudly and bolts upright.

"The jump wasn't so bad," she says.

"Thank goodness," I grin. "We'd better get out of here. The enemy pod will come searching for us and I don't want to be here when they do."

I scoop her into my arms and begin to trudge through the light jungle in search of the other children. I've only taken a few steps when my watch lights up, indicating another soldier is trying to contact me. It's Eric, my close friend.

I speak into the watch. "Axton."

"Eric. Greg and I have a group of children. The others have some too."

"Okay. Glad you made it."

"Watch out for pods," he warns. "We're all taking different routes. If we cross paths, great. If not, keep moving."

"Okay."

"You have Carla?" he asks.

"No. But I haven't had time to search yet."

"Roger that. Good luck. I'll see you at the meeting point."

"Roger. Out." I hang up.

I straighten my shoulders. At least some of the children are okay. Now I have to find Carla.

*Please, Carla. Please be all right.* My father drilled into me numerous times the importance of making sure Carla is safe. But I'm not sure that's the only reason I care.

"Axton?" I hear a shout. I stop and turn around. I know that voice.

"Carla." I can just make her out through the thick foliage. Another blur of a body is beside her on the ground. "Wait there. I'm coming."

I race over and spot Theo lying on the ground. At first glance, I can't see any injuries. No blood or twisted limbs.

"Axton," he says, "I'm glad you're okay."

"What happened?" I ask.

"He had a heavy landing," Carla says. "I think he's sprained his ankle."

I sag with relief. That's not so bad.

"Can you walk?" I ask Sapphire.

"I think so," she says, and I set her down.

"We have to get out of here," I say.

Carla points at Theo. "But his ankle . . . " she says.

"I'll walk." He sounds resolute, but by the appearance of his swollen ankle, I don't think it'll be easy.

I shake my head. "Let us help you."

"Don't be ridiculous," Theo says, leaning on his elbows to prop himself up. He puts his weight on his good leg and stands, wincing as he tries to step with his other foot.

"Let me help you, Theo," I say. "We've got to move quickly. Away from this place. How is everyone else?"

"A few minor injuries, but everyone seemed mobile. They left with Eric and the others," says Theo.

"All right, then. Let's go," Carla says. She grasps Sapphire's hand. I hitch Theo up and put his arm around my shoulders. We half-limp, half-jog through the grass.

"Who are you, anyway?" I know Carla's talking to me because of her harsh tone. She doesn't talk to anyone else like that. "I mean, I know your name is Axton and that you're supposedly Theo's brother . . . "

Theo speaks up. "He is."

Carla turns to Theo. "Well then why did you *never* mention him? And if he is your brother, then why did he come to save *me* instead of *you*?"

"Because I knew the rescue team was coming, so I didn't need an escort."

"What? Why wouldn't you tell me?"

"Come on, Carla. It was top secret and I swore I wouldn't tell anyone."

Carla squints at both of us suspiciously. I'm going to have to tell her everything sometime, and I'm not looking forward to it.

*　　*　　*

After several hours, we are moving through the jungle at a decidedly slower pace. The foliage is now so dense that Carla has to hack through it to force a path. Luckily, my laser-machete makes fast work of it, and we progress with good speed. I check the compass every now and then to ensure we stay on course.

We haven't spoken in a while. To my surprise, even Carla is staying quiet. I hold back the branches of a stinging tree and let the others pass. So far, I've counted more than sixty of them and even more viper vines. And we've only been walking for an hour.

"Do you even know where we're going?" Carla says, breaking our non-speaking streak. Her breath is jagged. Exhaustion is evident in every nuance of movement.

I open my mouth, but she cuts me off. "How can I even trust you? I don't know you! I don't know where we are, Sapphire is too young to die, and I have to get back to my family . . . " She trails off and bursts into a sob.

I stop and look her dead in the eye. "We're traveling to a small town, where we will be safe. It's one of the places of refuge in the backup plan."

She wipes the tears away. "Really? How do you know which way to go?"

I hold up my watch. "Built-in compass."

My body is struggling under Theo's additional weight. His face appears pale, and I know he can't go much further, either. At the next clear area, I place him gently on the jungle floor. His ankle has already started to turn red and blue, and is even more swollen.

"We should be far enough away now, so I'll treat you here."

"What's the matter, Axton? Don't tell me you're tired?" Carla says, teasingly.

"Yeah? How about you carry him from now on?"

She gives me a black look, then laughs. I narrow my eyes and swing the pack off my back. I set it on the ground. Inside are medical supplies and enough non-perishable packaged food to last me eight weeks. With four people, that means only two weeks. Maybe three if we ration it.

I need to work quickly. I pull out an XtremeCool pack and place it snugly around his ankle. The heat-activated self-adhesive holds it perfectly in place. Its auto-regulation means it will run cold for twenty minutes, then normal temperature for twenty minutes. And repeat for the next forty-eight hours. Perfect first-aid for promoting rapid healing. I should have applied it earlier; icepacks work better if you remember to use them.

"All done." I pour some water into Theo's parched mouth, and hand him a protein bar. I pass another to Sapphire and Carla. They wolf them down.

"Thanks," Theo says. "I think I'm okay to walk on my own now."

"We'll try it." I lean over and pick up a stray branch. "This can be your cane, but take it slow."

Theo stands up and I measure the stick against his

side, snapping it to the right length.

Sapphire's soft voice pipes up, "I'm still hungry."

I glance at my watch. It's 4:10pm. "We need to start finding shelter. Then we can eat again. Okay?"

She agrees reluctantly.

"Where's Carla?" Theo asks.

I realize I haven't seen her for several minutes. She had offered to scout ahead along a little track to see if it appeared promising.

"Wait here," I tell the others.

I scour the shadowy bushes and spot a broken branch. I follow the path swiftly. I haven't gone far when I nearly bump into her, hiding behind a thick tree. She motions for me to keep quiet and points ahead.

In front of us is a sizeable clearing. Several small log cabins surround it. A campfire sits in the middle and wisps of smoke trail upwards, dancing in the balmy breeze. A village. I reach out to grab her, but she shoots ahead before I can stop her. She flattens herself against the wall of one of the cabins. She glances back at me, and I make a motion to urge her back towards me. She rolls her eyes and moves carefully to peer into the doorway.

I breathe heavily out of my nose before walking swiftly towards her. Before she can cast her shadow into the structure and alert the occupants, I grab her and drag her back to the safety of the trees. She nearly yelps, but I cover her mouth with my hand.

*She's so impetuous*, I fume. She nearly put us in a very dangerous situation. These people don't know us, and we don't know them. Trust nobody.

"They are not our friends," I breathe harshly in her ear. "Don't let them see us."

Then a head pokes out from the slit of a window in the next cabin. Carla gasps in shock. Intense eyes capture us in an instant, and a horrifying grin smears across his face.

"Run," I say. I grab Carla's hand and sprint hard back in the direction we came. We hear shouts of alarm behind us, but we soon reach the others. I release Carla, haul Theo onto my back, and clutch Sapphire's hand. We run through the trees, vines grabbing us from every direction, until we are a safe distance from the village. I finally slow down.

"Don't ever do that again," I call back to Carla.

No reply.

"Carla?" I stop and turn around.

Sapphire brushes her hands on her dress, then looks up, her eyes shining.

"Carla isn't here."

# 13

# CARLA

Without warning, a powerful hand grabs my arm and yanks me backwards.

"Help!" I yell, struggling furiously, but my mouth is smothered by a hand that smells of soil and rotten fish. I watch Axton sink deeper into the jungle, oblivious to the fact that I'm no longer right behind him.

I'm lifted up and hoisted effortlessly over a shoulder. My head bounces on rock-hard muscles for an eternity as blood pounds in my ears. I feel a headache coming on. I hang limply in defeat before being dumped unceremoniously onto the ground like a bag of rocks. I struggle to catch my breath.

Many pairs of eyes bore into me. I'm in the doorway of one of the cabins that Axton and I had seen earlier, which seems even larger from the inside. Dozens of people rest on huge logs lining the perimeter of the room. I scramble into a more dignified sitting position and glare at my captor. He's not much older than me, but far larger. His messy hair flops over his eyes. His muscles are prominent beneath a mud-stained shirt.

He points to the log closest to me and motions me to sit. I notice that his walnut colored eyes are very large, and almost beautiful. I perch tentatively on the log. There must be twenty people in the space. All of their eyes are on me.

A woman sitting opposite me speaks first. Everyone seems to defer to her, and I think of her as the leader of this unusual-looking group.

"We know who you are," she says, gesturing towards the number on my wrist.

What on earth is she talking about?

"There are others like you, and we know what you've done. But we won't let you harm our people anymore."

"I haven't done anythi—" I say, before she cuts me off.

"Do not speak."

I'm not afraid. Yet. I force myself to take a breath and gather my wits. I need to find a way out. But how can I when these people are watching me like a bomb they're eager to deactivate?

The group begins to squabble about my fate. I wait for what seems an eternity, until there's silence. An old man claps his hands.

"Your future rests on your next words. Consider them with care. Should you choose to help us in our endeavors, we might return the favor and choose not to harm you. Or your . . . allies," says the old man.

I reply recklessly, "Or else what?"

He slips a knife from his belt and throws it effortlessly into the log I'm sitting on. No one flinches, except me. I may have screamed. I look down and spot the blade wedged firmly between my first and second fingers. I lift my hand slowly and inspect it. Not a scratch. I place my hands gingerly in my lap to disguise the tremors.

"Why are you doing this?" I say. "We've done nothing to you."

"Your people have attacked our villages, destroyed our homes and killed my children. Is that reason enough for you?"

That's terrible. But what does he mean by 'my people'? Others from the Compound? Does he think I'm a guard?

He strides towards me and levers the knife from the wood. I inspect the notch left behind. The log is covered in identical markings. I shiver involuntarily.

He relaxes on his log again, and his gaze pierces right through me as if I'm fogged-up glass masking something important.

"You will stay with us. You will help us. But first, you will tell us where the rest are." He fingers the knife's wooden handle absent-mindedly. "*All* of them."

I stay silent. Speak no evil, and just maybe I'll see no evil.

He snaps his fingers, and two men strut over to me. One seizes my arms, and the other my legs. I don't argue, and instead search frantically for a way out.

The leader rises too and steps outside the cabin first, her head held high. She seems very pleased with herself. I am carried behind her to the rear of the biggest cabin. I inhale the fresh air, and notice how beautiful the trees are. She stops abruptly and turns to whisper something to the men holding me. Then she gives me a decidedly sinister sneer and steps out of the way. She watches me for a reaction. I don't know what I should be reacting to.

Then I see it. The heap. It towers higher than me. At a glance, it's just a pile of metal parts and thin, silver wires. Irregular pieces poke out in every direction.

Looks like your average scrap heap.

They whisper to each other. I catch one of them

saying, "She's not scared." They seem worried that I'm not afraid. Afraid of what? I scan the mound to see if there's any electricity connected to it that could give me an electric shock, but it's clear that there's nothing. Just a dumb pile of stuff. These people are straight up crazy. Maybe they're so out of touch with the civilized world that metal is something amazing or obscure, just as I would view a pile of the latest iPhones, or a twisted knot of cobras.

I don't say anything, and they seem annoyed. The leader speaks, and they haul me onto the very top of the pile. Metal edges jab me, but I pretend not to notice. Then a couple of scraps tumble down under our weight, and the others spring to safety. I'm left alone on my steel castle. It doesn't feel stable. My kingdom could crumble at any moment.

They surround me. Makeshift swords and assorted weapons are aimed in my direction. One man has an axe. I feel decidedly vulnerable as the weapons are drawn back, ready to strike. I wonder vaguely where my friends are; I hope they aren't searching for me. Theo's going to be mad. My curiosity has gotten me into trouble yet again.

The woman speaks. "Where did you come from?"

I turn to her. "I'm sort of in-between homes right now. I'm just trying to find shelter."

One of the men thrusts his sword in my direction, which spurs a chain-reaction from the other men, who each poke their weapons at me, hard enough to hurt but not enough to break the skin. I am at serious risk of morphing into a human pincushion.

"That's not what I asked," the woman grunts. "You will only make it worse if you don't give us what we need. Now where are you from?"

I frown in frustration. What does she mean?

"Well, I used to live in Chicago." For some reason, I decide to lie about my home town.

"We want the truth."

"I'm telling you the truth. What do you want me to say?" I yell.

"Your kind have been haunting us for over fifty years."

Again with 'my kind'. Maybe others have escaped from the Compound?

She continues, "You come into our camp claiming to be regular folk. But we see through that. We can tell."

To be honest, a part of me is flattered that somebody in the world doesn't consider me boringly normal. I've certainly never excelled at anything, although I can play the piano reasonably well, and plank for six minutes. But somehow, I don't get the vibe that these are the skills they value.

"I don't know what you're talking about . . . "

"We need answers, and you are not helping us," she accuses. "Where is your next target?" Her callous eyes bore into mine like a drill.

It makes no sense. I take a breath. I think fast. "I'm not supposed to tell. They'll kill me." She leans forward. "But . . . okay, it's Texas. San Antonio." I am lying, of course, but they can't prove otherwise, so I figure it's worth a shot. I've never been there, but it seems like a place that would be worth fighting over.

She huffs. "San Antonio."

I look back as innocently as possible.

"How are they going to strike?" she says doubtfully. "And when?"

"I . . . I don't know exactly," I stutter. I did always enjoy drama studies, so I really go for it, hands shaking with fake fear. "On the evening of the fifteenth of . . . " I hesitate. I don't even know what month it is right now. I'm in trouble.

"Yes?" she says, honing in like a snake on its prey.

"Of next month," I blurt out.

A couple of the men around me gasp. I pretend to agree with their shock. But the leader seems unmoved.

"They've been preparing for a long time, you know," I continue. "They want to defeat San Antonio, then Austin and Houston, so they won't attack this area for quite a while." Shakespeare would be proud of me. I'm half believing my own lines. I'm a proper thespian! When I get back home, I'll have . . .

The leader nods to the old man, who steps forward.

"Interesting." He rubs his hands together again, one of his habits. "We were seeking your help." I bow my head, as if attempting to appease the almighty powers-in-charge. "However, you've proven to be rather less helpful than expected," he accuses. Somehow, I don't think he's fallen for my performance. How does he know?

He gestures.

The spikes dig deeper into my sides. It really hurts. *Come on. Think*, I tell myself. *You can't outmuscle them; you'll have to get your rusty brain firing.* I decide to try something.

I take a breath and muster what little courage I have. "I would like to go along with your little plans and help you. But really, I've had enough. I'm bored."

The woman scrutinizes me, confused.

"It would be best if I returned to the Compound." I lift the front of my collar up a little to my mouth, like I'm talking into a miniature walkie-talkie. I've seen the Compound guards do that hundreds of times, except they were never as fashionably attired as I.

"This is Carla, reporting for duty. I request immediate pick-up. GPS coordinates uploaded from my current location. Over." I turn to the leader. "Since you've revealed your location to a Compound agent, we can now set the bombing coordinates and target this location. If I were in your shoes, I would consider a rapid evacuation."

They appear startled. Scared even. Ha! Shakespeare would have given me a role if girls were allowed. The woman turns to the rest of the men, and they whisper to each other. The swords don't move.

"Carla?" the leader says slowly, as if she's heard the name before. She mutters something to one of the others holding a sword. "Could it really be her?" He whispers something in return.

This is great. Apparently, Carla is some famous person in the deep jungle. I'm glad this mystery gal shares my name. Want my autograph? The price: my freedom.

"You're lying!" I hear the leader shout. "You are too small to be the one they've told us about."

I stop. What? They dispute the only thing I'm telling the truth about? My name? I'm a little insulted. Just because I'm on the small side doesn't mean I can't be the renowned, legendary, glorious Carla they speak of.

"I'm her. I'm Carla," I declare, with as much confidence as I can muster. "Let me go, and I will call off the attack."

They pause, and the swords loosen a little.

"You have one minute to release me." Just then, a whirring sound erupts, and I look up to see a dark aircraft crossing overhead. A pod. It's *them*. Of course they would have seen me, exposed as I am, king of my metal castle. Inside, I shudder, and my blood turns to ice.

On the outside, however, I remain calm and wave to the aircraft before smiling back at the leader. The atmosphere instantly changes. The men lower their swords and back away with terror in their eyes. Ignoring me, they focus their attention on the pod, huddling and pointing.

An opportunity. I skid down the mound, trying not to yelp as sharp edges claw into me, and run at top speed back into the dense jungle.

I half expect a throwing knife in the back at any moment. But they don't even call out. I don't matter to them anymore. I risk a glance back, and they are glued to the terror in the sky.

Sometimes, what strives to kill us is the only thing that can save us.

*　　*　　*

I run as long as I can in the direction that I think I came from. Somehow, I don't get tired. Adrenaline, no doubt.

Compared with what I've just been through, running is a pleasure. I welcome the slap of plant leaves in my face, keeping me focused and reminding me how lucky I am to be alive.

But thoughts bounce around with no chance of stopping. What was all that metal? Why was I supposed to fear it? Have they seriously heard my name before?

I need to find Axton. He has the answers. And so far, he's told me none. After an eternity, I begin to recognize the shape of the track, with its dense undergrowth and peculiar white foliage. I can't risk shouting. And I can only hope I don't come across any jungle predators.

"Carla," an urgent voice cuts through the vegetation. I freeze. I'm almost sure it's Theo, but his voice sounds tense.

"Stay where you are," I call out. I lunge behind the nearest large tree.

Finally, a reply. "Okay."

It's definitely Theo's voice. Something's wrong, but I run towards the source anyway and gasp with relief.

Theo stands directly before me.

Held up by the tree-trunk arms of the village brute.

Have I somehow managed to run in a huge circle?

"You might have scared the rest of them. But I'm not afraid of you. Come any closer and he's just a memory."

He jabs a knife threateningly toward Theo's face.

I put on my nonchalant persona and shrug. "And why should I care if you do that?"

"Enough of your games, girl."

"I don't know him. I mean, I would prefer if this didn't result in the murder of innocent individuals, but . . . " I trail off.

"Nonsense. He—"

I cut him off quick smart. "I knew the moment he spoke that I didn't know him."

"Really? I know you two are together."

I hang my head, because he's right.

And then something crazy happens. Muscle boy drops Theo onto the ground.

And he runs away.

I quickly scan around for anything that might have frightened him, but see nothing. Theo's eyes are wide too, but then he laughs.

"What happened?" I ask. "Why'd he run away?"

Theo points, and I follow the direction of his arm. Axton is standing under a tree with an absurd expression on his face. Sapphire is on his shoulders holding a little knife. They both have mud smeared on their faces.

"Smart play, Axton," says Theo.

It makes no sense. Axton and Sapphire look cute, not

terrifying. Why did he flee? What is Theo talking about?

Axton appears unrattled, just pleased. Then he lets Sapphire slide down to the ground. She runs over and hugs me.

"We thought you were gone," she sobs. "Dead."

"I'm okay," I assure her. "But you weren't going to be, Theo. How did you get separated from Axton?"

Theo answers me. "When we realized you were gone, we ran back to the cabins. We saw you but there were so many of them that we didn't have a chance." I frown.

"So we hid. We were going to create a diversion when it seemed like they were going to kill you, but then you performed your little deception. Nice job, by the way."

"I thought you were stupid to try something like that," Axton chips in.

I scowl. "I made it, didn't I?"

Theo gives a broad grin. "Did you come back? Or did you run in a circle, like everyone does without a compass," he teases. "You were very lucky that the pod came by." He pauses. "Well, lucky as long as they didn't see you. Or us."

"But that's unlikely," Axton says. "We should get moving."

I raise my eyebrows. "You still know the way from here?"'

He rolls his eyes. "North is always north, Carla."

Axton heads off in the desired direction, and we follow. I decide it's time for an interrogation. I need answers.

"Axton?" I say.

"Yes, Carla?" He sounds exhausted. Maybe because of me.

"You know everything about the Compound, so you know why we were put there in the first place, right?" I ask.

"I've told you everything I can," he says carefully.

"You haven't told me anything," I say matter-of-factly.

Theo says, "Just tell her, Axton. She deserves to know."

*Thank you, Theo,* I think. *You're the only one on my side.*

"Fine," says Axton, holding a branch out of the way and letting us pass. "The Compound is not just a tiger's eye mine. Its hidden purpose is to build an army. A very powerful army of, um, of special fighters. They are planning on taking over our territory."

A trained army of guards? Horrific. Having them take over the world? Beyond horrific.

He opens his mouth to add something, but thinks better of it. Then he says, "I can't tell you anything else about the mission."

"Are you serious?" I say.

"Of course I'm serious. It's a serious mission."

"A serious mission that *I was part of.* I need to know what's happening." I formulate a question. "Why was I put there? And Theo? What makes us so special?"

Axton looks to Theo for confirmation. He nods. "Theo wasn't put there. He snuck in as a spy so we'd have tech help on the inside. He was working with us the whole time."

"With you?"

"The Organization. Our goal is to dismantle the army and shut down the Compound."

Theo butts in. "And my mission was also to find you and get you ready."

"All this time, I thought you were my friend," I say. "But really, you were babysitting me!"

"Carla, I *am* your friend!" Theo says, annoyed. "Of course I am. Everything we did was done to save you."

"Me?"

"You were the mission. The whole mission."

*　　*　　*

We walk in silence. My mind is whirling. Axton and Theo are trudging along, staring at the ground. Only Sapphire seems happy.

"So, what does this mean for me now?" I finally ask, even more confused. "What is my purpose?"

Axton and Theo exchange a glance, as if my question is a grenade.

"To help us. And the children," says Axton, choosing his words carefully.

"But . . . how?"

Theo jumps in. "By unblocking the emotions of the children who were brainwashed."

"How am I supposed to do that? I was brainwashed too, you know."

"Ha!" Axton laughs out loud. "You're funny."

I glare at him.

"Don't know yourself very well, do you?" he smirks.

"They gave up trying to brainwash you long ago," explains Theo.

I am lost. What is happening here? A private joke between the brothers? Why do I have a sinking feeling that the joke is on me?

"We believe that with your help, we can stop the army," says Axton solemnly. "The Compound needs the children, but the children are also what it fears most."

"Right," I say. "Scary children." My tone drips with sarcasm.

"And you," adds Axton. "Especially you."

Nothing makes sense anymore. I have so many questions, and these answers make no sense. The more questions answered, the more that emerge. It is nearly dark and I'm tired, and my brain can't take any more of this absurd conversation.

"Can we just find somewhere to sleep?" I ask, yawning.

The others agree. We stop at a small clearing, and Axton hands us water and packaged food. Beef stew, apparently. He apologizes, acknowledging chicken curry is better. We eat in silence. It doesn't taste that bad, actually. Far better than what we had in the Compound.

We scavenge some branches and leaves to lie on. Hopefully we won't come across any dangerous wild animals.

Or scary children.

# 14

# AXTON

I NUDGE THE OTHERS AWAKE AT SUNRISE. We'd better start moving, or we won't make it to civilization before we run out of food. We've already wasted enough time between Theo's ankle and Carla's shenanigans.

Theo groans. "What time is it?"

"Time to get up," I tell him bluntly.

He answers with something unintelligible.

I hand everyone another package of food and keep one for myself. That's eight we've used already. Carla reads the label out loud.

"Beef stew." She raises her eyebrow. "Again?"

"I can take it back if you don't want it. Maybe you

can find a fern to eat," I say sarcastically, gesturing to the plants around us.

She places her hands on her hips. "They're all beef stew, aren't they?"

"Would you prefer nothing?"

She rolls her eyes and opens the sachet, peering inside to get a better look. I can't help but laugh as her face turns sour.

"Haven't you eaten worse at the Compound?" I tease.

She scowls. I find my bearings while everyone else finishes their food.

"Right," I say. "Let's get moving."

We kick the leaves to cover our tracks, and I shove the breakfast trash in my bag, leaving no trace that we were ever there. We don't want to be followed.

"Oh, man," Theo says, his gaze sweeping the forest floor. "I've lost my cane."

I find another stick that should do the trick. He tests it and declares that it's perfect.

We head off as the sun begins to rise higher.

I take the lead, followed by Carla and Sapphire. Theo brings up the rear, and we walk for several hours in silence. The pace is still rather sluggish because of Theo's ankle, but at least we're moving. The silence is broken only by Carla comforting Sapphire whenever she complains she is tired or hungry. Which is fairly often. I'd give her some food, but we need to ration it.

"How much further now, Axton?" I hear Sapphire's small voice waft from behind me.

Carla beats me to it.

"Shouldn't be long before we take a break," she says pointedly.

"Yeah," I say, picking up her cue. "Very soon."

"Oh, good," Theo says, grimacing. He must be in a lot of pain. I've almost never heard him complain since we've been here.

I glance at my watch: it's 11:28. We can have a quick break.

"Next flat patch we find," I say. "Only for a couple of minutes."

"Yay!" says Sapphire, her energy immediately picking up.

Carla laughs.

"What about there?" She points ahead. We gather in the shade and Sapphire flops onto the underbrush, gazing up at the leaves. Carla scolds her mildly for getting grass in her hair.

"It's not like we *slept* on grass last night," I tell her.

She flicks her hair in response.

Sapphire shrieks. "What is that?" We look up. Peering

down at us are two curious yellow eyes. Attached to a small monkey. That smiles at us. Is it wearing clothes? It takes a second for my mind to register. Sure enough, the fur ball is wearing a tiny jacket.

"Get up," I say to the others. "Move slowly."

Because this is no wild monkey. He is clearly a pet, and I don't want to meet the owner. We move out of the clearing with great haste. *Please don't follow us.*

We cover the next mile quickly, despite our fatigue.

I hear a yell. "Oi!"

Sapphire gasps, and I stop in my tracks.

"Turn around. Yes, you. The tall one."

I figure he's talking to me. I slowly spin around to see a teenager, maybe fifteen years old, wearing pants crafted from leather and some leaves. No shirt. Some muscle. He is holding a knife that appears handmade. The monkey is perched on his shoulder.

"Where are y'all headed?" he asks, strolling closer.

"Just out for a walk. To get some fresh air," I say. He tilts an eyebrow.

"Raffie, check him out," he says, pointing at me.

I see some movement. The little monkey jumps onto the ground and wanders over to stand at my feet. I pre-pare myself for an attack.

"Stand still," drawls the boy.

The monkey, whose name is apparently Raffie, scrambles up my pants and pats me down. Then he reaches the backpack and I stiffen. He can't have our food. If he takes it, we won't survive.

"Don't worry, he won't hurt you," says the boy, misreading my apprehension. I can hear the monkey sniffing the bag. Then the zip moves, and I'm about to reach around and swat the monkey.

Carla reads my face and yells out.

"Raffie, down," the boy orders and the monkey leaps, barely disturbing the leaves on the rainforest floor.

Before any of us can object, Sapphire squats down to Raffie's height and says with a beguiling smile, "Here, monkey."

The scruffy but well-dressed monkey bounds into her outstretched arms. She picks him up and cuddles him, his large, brown eyes wide with delight. She strokes his brown and white fur, and he shivers.

We all stare at her in amazement, even the boy.

"Raffie," he says angrily, "they are not your friends." The monkey simply stares at him with innocent eyes before returning his attention to Sapphire.

"Can we keep him, Axton?" she pleads.

"No," the boy and I say simultaneously.

Sapphire frowns at us and hugs the monkey tighter. It snuggles back.

"Put it down," Carla says calmly. Sapphire doesn't move. "Sapphire!"

She kisses the monkey directly on the head between his ears and reluctantly places him on the jungle floor.

Then the boy drawls, "Didn't mean to scare y'all. I thought y'all were *them*."

I avoid his gaze. We *are* them. People from the Compound. Well, at least the others are. Luckily, the monkey only checked me. I now realize what he was searching for.

"It's fine," Carla says, but the way she says it makes me think she doesn't mean it.

"What's your name, anyway?" I interrupt.

The boy hesitates. "Levi," he says.

"I'm Axton."

"Who do you mean by *them* anyway?" Carla asks, lifting an eyebrow. I know what she's thinking. If he's scared of them being here, then we should be too.

Levi says in a sinister tone, "I'll show you."

# 15

# CARLA

Levi leaps through the jungle, climbing skinny trees to use as vantage points. He's so light on his feet that the leaves barely rustle, and the branches sway beneath him with a natural rhythm. He's almost as agile as a monkey himself. Raffie alternates his means of transport between scampering on his feet and clutching Levi's neck.

In contrast to their deftness, we trudge heavily through the jungle, snapping almost every twig on the rainforest floor.

Every now and then, Levi waits for us to catch up, leaning nonchalantly against a tree. I don't know how I feel about trusting him so soon. Axton says we have no choice. And he's right, I guess.

I glance behind at Sapphire's small figure. Her usual hyper demeanor is gone; all that's left is a bowed head and dragging feet. She's exhausted. My own stomach growls—it must be time for lunch.

I lean towards Axton, who's walking beside me.

"We should stop to eat sometime," I murmur.

His body stiffens as he halts. "I don't think that's our major concern at the moment," he replies, not making eye contact with me. He locks his arms around Sapphire and I. I look around to see what the fuss is about but don't spot anything.

Except eyes. Gleaming yellow eyes.

We all stop, and Levi melts into the thick foliage with Raffie.

"Hey!" Theo calls out. "Where are you going?"

I don't think Theo has seen the monkeys.

"Theo," I whisper. He turns around and his face registers shock.

Monkeys surround us from all angles; some hang from the trees above us. Axton reaches down to pick up a sturdy stick. Theo backs up until he's practically pressed against Axton, holding his makeshift cane like a sword. The shape of the monkeys' mouths makes it seem like they're smiling. They begin to close in on us. It was a trap.

"Axton?" Theo whispers. "What do we do?"

"Be quiet." Yeah, great help he is.

"Hey, don't be afraid," I say to the monkeys. "We aren't here to hurt you."

They respond to my voice, but all I did was redirect their attention to me. Axton steps in front of me.

"Come with me," he says to the monkeys, starting to walk away from us, taking the majority of the monkeys with him. He turns back to us and his eyes are commanding.

"Go," he mouths.

I shake my head, trying to form a decision. I can't leave him. But I look down at Sapphire and know we have no choice. I grab her and Theo, and we begin to run.

A few seconds later, I risk a glance behind me. To my dismay, a few of the monkeys are following us. We've barely run a few more steps before Raffie and Levi leap down directly in front of us. Sapphire shrieks, and Theo yanks his arm from mine.

"Woah, calm down," Levi says. He whistles and the monkeys instantly run to his side. There must be about thirty of them.

"Calm down?" I scream. "What do you mean calm down? You just incited an attack by your crazy monkeys."

The monkeys squint at us mischievously. Levi smiles condescendingly. I scowl.

"Silly girl. It was a joke."

"It wasn't very funny." I turn to the others for support, just as Axton rejoins us.

Axton rubs his hands together. "I think it's best if we continue on our own."

"Sorry. Guess y'all can't take a joke," Levi says. "At least let me show you what you're up against. The—"

"Don't worry about it, just leave us be and we'll be on our way," Axton says lightly. But there's an edge to his tone.

Levi laughs. "I don't know why you're afraid of me. I'm not the enemy." He points directly through the trees and underbrush. I follow the direction of his arm. "*They* are."

*　　*　　*

I gasp. I hope with all my heart they're not what I think they are. People. *Dead* people. Levi swings through the last few trees before jumping down. An inch to the left and he would have connected with a person's head. I shudder. I cover Sapphire's eyes, but it's too late. Can't be unseen. The bile rises in my throat, but I force myself to look again.

Thousands of bodies. Mostly men, some women, and some teenagers, and even a few smaller children. The area has obviously been cleared as a graveyard. No shrubs. No grass.

Levi beckons us. I notice with some relief that his four-legged pranksters have retreated into the jungle. Except for Raffie, who's attached to his shoulder like a barnacle on a boat.

"There's nothing to be afraid of," he says in a way that opposes his very statement.

"Who are they?" I ask no one in particular.

"Come here, and I'll show you." He sees us hesitate. "Don't be afraid. They're dead for sure, now."

Axton turns to Theo. "Recycler," he mutters.

"Solar," adds Theo.

What are they talking about?

As I'm pondering this exchange, I notice that there's more to see. There's not only one pile, but two. The other one is far away in the distance. Not bodies, though. Gleaming metal parts. Like scrap metal, but shinier than a junkyard. It's hard to focus on anything other than the bodies, though.

A quarter of a second before Axton moves, I see the determination on his face. It takes him several strides to reach the pile of bodies. I don't move, and neither do

Theo or Sapphire. He kneels down to a body, lifts the eyelid, and gazes directly into the eye. His lips press into a thin line.

He turns to me. "It's safe. You can come over."

There is no way I am ever coming any closer. And only a sick soul would want a little girl like Sapphire to see that up close. Thankfully, I don't think she understands much of what's been happening. Not that I really get it, either.

Trying to avert my gaze, I notice a machine further away. It seems similar to our pod, except its side boasts vertical engine slots. And it's very tall. A flying crane? Secret military mining machinery? Or was it used to kill people in some horrible way?

"Why?" I ask Levi. "Why kill them?"

Levi frowns. "I didn't."

"Who did?"

Then he begins to show the first real signs of emotion since we met him. His shoulders shake and his nostrils flare. "They did."

"Who?" I whisper.

He glares at me. "*They* did. For fun," he spits. "Maybe they thought it would scare us. Oh, and it did. Very much. We ran away; we tried to hide. We knew that whoever— whatever—was killing these people, was going to kill us next."

# 16

# AXTON

I reach the edge of the rainforest where Carla sits in the shade of a large tree. She is staring at the pile of bodies lying not far from us. I can imagine what she's thinking, but if she asks me anything about this, I can't answer. I can't afford to tell her anything right now.

*　　*　　*

We decide to continue walking towards town, with the help of Levi. We leave the pile of corpses behind us and make our way through the thick jungle. Progress is slow, but faster than before. I'm relieved that Theo's ankle is almost completely healed.

Levi tells us that his family was taken. He's been alone for a decade.

"Except for the monkeys," I say, and no one laughs. What a unique life he must be living. He clearly hasn't seen the news or surfed the web in a while.

It becomes quiet, and I notice that Carla hasn't spoken the entire time, which is unusual. I thought I would enjoy the day Carla stopped arguing with me, but I can't stand it now that she's gone radio silent.

The silence extends for another half an hour, until Theo suggests to Carla that we take a break. She refuses, insisting she's fine, so we have no choice but to continue.

That's why, when she utters her next words, I know something is very wrong.

"I have to sit down," she says, weakly.

I rush to her. "Easy, Carla." Theo and I lower her to the ground.

"Give her some water," Theo says urgently. He turns to Carla. "I told you. We should have rested earlier."

She doesn't say anything, and instead slumps back against a tree and closes her eyes. She groans softly.

I swing my pack off my back and rummage around

for some water. I unscrew the lid of my bottle, handing it to her.

"Here."

Theo helps her into a sitting position. She squints and takes the bottle, lifting it to her parched lips. I don't mind if she drinks the rest of our water supply, as long as it keeps her alive.

She drinks in small sips, mumbling that we shouldn't waste any more time; that we should keep moving. We hush her.

Sapphire brings some soft moss to place under her head. Raffie climbs a tree, snags a banana, and peels it for her. I haven't seen a real banana in a long time. Levi approves, touting the high energy content they possess. As the monkey hands Carla the fruit, I notice that it's peeled from the bottom up. I wonder if monkeys always peel bananas like that.

We wait five minutes, twenty, thirty. Carla's condition doesn't improve. In fact, it deteriorates.

"How do you feel?" I ask her gently. Possibilities fly through my mind—heat exhaustion, dehydration, heat stroke—not that these things should really be possible.

"Do you think you can keep moving?" asks Levi.

Theo and I both send him our most withering glare.

"Are you crazy?" says Theo.

"She can't even sit up," I say.

Levi ask, "Do you think she needs a doctor?"

I object immediately.

"No," I say. "We don't have time." More importantly, a doctor would have to examine Carla. Don't want that. "Let's keep moving."

Levi looks at me quizzically. "Anyway, there isn't a doctor around here anymore."

Theo speaks soft, soothing words to Carla, who says she thinks she can keep going if she takes it slowly. We help her stand up, but she would have toppled over if I hadn't grabbed her arm in time. Theo and I stand on either side, stabilizing her, as Levi leads the way.

Sapphire scoops Raffie up in her arms and picks berries and low-hanging bananas to feed him along the way. This keeps her entertained, but my hopes aren't high that it'll last long.

Gradually, Carla's steps slow down and her feet start to brush the jungle floor. I'm about to call for a break, when I walk right into Levi. He has come to a complete stop.

"I'm afraid this is as far as I can take you. Good luck, and I hope you don't come across any of *them*."

I wish he could help us more, but I know there's no point protesting.

"Thanks for your help," Theo says. "We appreciate it."

"Good luck to you, too," Sapphire pipes up. "Hope you don't come across any of them, either!"

She says it with a grin, but clearly has no idea what she's talking about. Raffie is perched on a branch, just low enough for Sapphire to give him a pat on the head before returning to my side. I'm fairly sure she whispered something like 'good monkey' to him as well.

"The buildings are through there," Levi says, before sinking into the jungle. A hint of movement in the trees and the lone banana peel on the ground are the only tell-tale signs they were ever here.

Sapphire stares at the trees that were rustling mere seconds before. When she turns around, her eyes are wet.

"He said we're nearly there," Sapphire says, blinking quickly to hold in the tears. "That's good."

Then something not so good happens.

Carla drops to the ground.

# 17

## CARLA

I am drifting in and out of consciousness, but I can distinctly hear Axton's voice. The side of my body aches as it presses into the dirt and grass.

"Carla, can you hear me?" Theo says. I can, but I can't speak.

Everything seems wrong. I can't do this anymore.

"Carla," I hear Axton say, firmly. "You need to stop this."

Why is he blaming me?

"Carla," he says, even more firmly. "You have control over this. This is an emotional reaction and you, of all people, have the power to control your emotions."

Even in my current state, I inwardly roll my eyes. Controlling emotion has never been my strong suit. As if he doesn't know that by now.

Axton might not, but Theo certainly does. Why isn't he defending me?

"Carla," says Theo. "You can alter your thoughts to fix this."

What on earth is he talking about?

Suddenly Axton yells loudly, "Sapphire is hurt! Real bad."

My eyes jerk open and I sit up, only to find Axton and Theo squatting next to me, staring intently. I spin around and see Sapphire sitting quietly; she's totally fine. Simply watching Axton and Theo with confusion.

Axton's face radiates relief. "See, Carla? You're fine." He walks away.

"Yeah," I say, surprised, mostly to Theo. "I'm fine. Much better, actually."

I stand up and shake out my legs. "All right," I say. "Let's go." I take a step and Theo rushes to my side.

"Are you sure you can walk?" he says, putting his hands out as if I might fall. "Don't you want to rest for a spell?"

"I'm fine," I say. "Let's keep going."

"Well, then," Axton says, picking up his backpack. "Let's go. Stay on high alert."

We stumble through the jungle until we reach an open expanse. We cautiously creep to the edge and spot several buildings. The town! But my excitement wavers as I realize these structures are rundown and crumbling. There's no sign of life.

"So much for the backup plan," says Axton. "Clearly, the army has been here. Our intel hasn't kept up."

We head to the buildings and search for anything that might be of use. But dust and debris do not interest us, so we find nothing of value.

"These houses are so old-fashioned," Theo says, mainly to himself. He gazes bemusedly at the buildings. I don't say anything, but I'm confused because they seem ultramodern to me.

"Hello?" Theo's voice booms in the dead silence. No reply. It's as if the town is in a void, all sound and movement sucked out of it. All signs of life erased. No birds. No flies.

"Where are the people?" I ask.

"Dead," says Theo flatly. "Or fled." He smirks at his own rhyme.

Axton is walking ahead of us. As we trudge deeper into the town, he begins to slow.

"Watch your feet," he says dryly. I look at the ground, and am shocked by what I see. Bones. Fragments of human bones. This time, I gag. Haven't we seen enough of this already?

"This town was recently attacked. No survivors, I guess," says Axton.

Sapphire runs toward us, her skirt billowing in the faint breeze. "What did you find?" she asks Axton, excitement in her voice.

I watch as Axton grabs hold of her hand. "Isn't the sky incredible here?" he says, pointing upwards, and I realize he's distracting her from the human remnants beneath her feet. Axton must have noticed my hesitation to let Sapphire see the bodies back at those strange piles.

I try to walk in a line that avoids the gruesome street decoration as much as possible.

After a few minutes, Axton stops. Sapphire stops too, her hand still in his. She looks up at him.

"There's no one here. Let's see what supplies we can find inside," he says, letting go of her hand and heading to the nearest building.

I take Sapphire's hand as Axton tries the handle and finds the door unlocked. We venture inside, and it's obvious that the house once had a beautiful interior.

"Lights," Axton calls out. One light dimly flickers before blacking out.

"Yeah, control center is working somewhat," Axton whispers, turning back to Theo, Sapphire and I. "Don't say who you are or refer to each other by name. Don't discuss anything important. You don't know who's listening."

I stare at him incredulously. What is the control center? Is this some weird version of Siri or Alexa?

Theo agrees with Axton. "We'll take what we need and go," he whispers. "Don't say a word," he says to me. "We don't want it to pick up your voice."

I obey him. I wonder if maybe the enemy has a thing against teenage girls.

At the entrance there is a huge flight of stairs, made from a substance resembling marble. We head upstairs and locate the kitchen. I am so shocked by what I see that I forget my agreement to remain silent. "Where are the stoves? And ovens?"

"What?" Axton says frowning. Then he shrugs. "Oh, there's none of that. They would've had their food delivered to them, and all they had to do was heat it in the thermo-blast." He points in the direction of a small device that reminds me a little of a microwave.

I frown. I always loved to cook with Mom. She taught me everything I know about food. Yet here, it appears no one cooks at all, and not because they're lacking advanced technology. Mom would love these gadgets. I'll have to get her some when I go home. Just the thought of her makes tears well painfully. I wipe them away.

We search the cupboards, finding little more than a few suction-packed plastic food sachets. No expiry dates. No identification. I grab them anyway. As I place the last of our findings in Axton's backpack, a siren begins to scream. Its insistent shrill consumes the room.

"What is that?" I shout as I reach Theo. I cover my ears, but it barely helps.

I look down to see Sapphire cowering on the ground and covering her ears. Axton tries to talk to her. She doesn't respond, and instead begins to roll around in an attempt to distract herself from the sound. I release my ears as it becomes evident that there's no point. The siren is too loud. Actually, it seems horrifyingly familiar, but I can't place it. Where did I hear it? The next blast triggers my memory.

"It's them!" I yell. "The guards." I grab Axton's arm and try to pull him, but he stays motionless. I stop still and join Sapphire, jamming our fingers in our ears.

Sheer terror overwhelms me as I picture heading back into the depths of the Compound. I don't want to go back there. I can't! Someone strong grabs my arms and pins them to the ground, preventing me from protecting my ears.

"Carla." I can barely hear him over the piercing sound. "It's just the control center alarm." Hopefully, the control center can't pick up voices over the sound.

Axton leaves the room. Finally, the alarm stops. The silence reveals something we couldn't hear before: the sound of a thousand roaring motorbikes. Sapphire covers her ears to block the new noise.

Theo stops, his body frozen in place. "*That's* not the control center."

Axton peers out the window, and turns back with a grave expression. "Okay," he says. "That's a pod. And not one of ours."

"What do we do?" I whisper to Axton, who has now entered what I call Soldier Mode. He looks upwards towards the sound, and clicks his tongue with a disappointed scowl.

Theo leans out of a broken window and scans the sky. He stares for a few seconds, before his entire expression transforms.

"Unmanned pod. Recon only. We got lucky," he says.

Axton looks relieved, but only for a second.

"They'll send an attack pod next. We've got to separate from our signal."

He turns to face me.

"Hold still," he says. "This has to be done."

He pulls out his knife and moves to cut my wrist. I yelp, yanking my arm away and scrambling towards the door.

"Are you crazy?" I blurt out. I've completely forgotten I'm not supposed to speak.

"Carla, don't be dumb," he says, exasperated. He's obviously forgotten, too. "I'm cutting the tracker out of your wrist."

"Tracker?" I shriek. "What tracker? Shouldn't you have mentioned that earlier?"

"Don't move," Axton says.

"No, Axton!" I shout, pulling back further.

"Do you want them to find us and kill us?"

"No," I whimper.

He brings the knife towards me again. I shake my head in fear.

"Uh," grunts Axton. "Fine."

He rummages around in his pack and brings out a small case. He opens it and tips a white pill into his hand.

"Painkiller," says Axton. He holds it out. "Swallow it."

I study it skeptically for a second, before downing it. I don't have much choice.

He waits a few seconds. "Shouldn't be any pain now."

I frown and reluctantly hold my arm out for his blade. I don't want to watch, but it's like a car crash—impossible to tear your gaze away. The sharp metal touches the skin, then slices through. Surprisingly, there's no pain. A small amount of blood oozes out. The growling sound coming from outside grows stronger as he digs around in my flesh. He finally yanks out a small electronic component with a tiny light.

Axton rips a piece of fabric from his shirt and ties it gently around my wrist. I suddenly notice how close he is to me. I wonder if he is as aware as I am.

"All done," he breathes and smiles down at me. I notice he has a perfect smile. I can't help it. I smile back.

He reaches out and I take his hand. His firm grip makes me feel safe, and he easily brings me to my feet. I don't want him to let go.

Axton strolls over to Theo, and I trail along.

Theo presents his hand to Axton.

"Tracker suppression must be failing," says Axton. He holds the pill bottle up with a wry grimace. "Want some?" Theo shakes his head, teeth gritted.

Why won't he take a painkiller?

Axton pauses. He seems more reluctant with his brother than with me. He grasps Theo's wrist.

Theo shrieks as the knife punctures his skin, and

normally I would have teased him for the somewhat girl-ish sound.

Axton wraps the wound, and heads towards Sapphire, who is resting on the bare tiles. She startles at the sound of his footsteps. Axton hides the knife, but Sapphire doesn't need to see it to know she's next. Her gaze lands on my makeshift bandage stained with blood, and she shivers, hiding her arm behind her.

"N—no," she says, a little too loudly. Axton kneels next to her and spills another pill. She shrinks away.

"Sapphire, it's okay," he says. "Just swallow this."

She shakes her head rapidly and shuffles away from him. I reach down and hold her hand.

"It'll be quick, Sapphire," I say.

"No!" she squeals.

"It won't hurt," I say. "You'll be all right."

Axton backs me up. "We've got to do it to keep you safe."

"You don't want to go back to the Compound, do you?" Theo pipes up. I think it's kind of mean, but it does the trick.

She gulps the tablet, and calms down long enough for Axton to make the initial cut and ease the tracker out in one swift movement. She doesn't even wince. He's getting good at this.

Axton holds the three stained trackers in his hand like precious jewels. He turns to me and says, "I'm going to lead them away from us. Buy us some time."

No. He can't just leave us.

"What do you mean?" I say. "You're the only reason we've survived this long in the first place!"

"Well, it's the only way I can hope to keep you safe."

His tone tells me there's no changing his mind. He embraces Theo with a loud pat on the back and mutters something I don't quite catch. He turns to me.

"Stay here until it leaves," he says, handing me his watch. "Then head north. Not in a circle," he jokes. "Due north is where our pod was taking us, and where I was supposed to take you if anything went wrong."

How are we supposed to make it on our own?

"Can't we smash the trackers instead?" I ask.

He shakes his head. "No good. Then this would be the last area where they would detect the signal. It would be too close to you."

"But . . . "

"Two days and you'll be there."

"*We'll*," I say.

"What?"

"Two days and *we'll* be there," I say emphatically. "Because you'd better come and find us."

He frowns. "Be strong," he says, holding his backpack out to me. "Good luck."

Theo shakes his hand and whispers something in his ear.

Axton turns to leave and sadness strikes me. I'm not even thinking when I run up and embrace him. To my surprise, he squeezes tight, holding me a little longer.

He loosens his grip and heads off, giving us one last wave. I watch as his striking figure disappears down the stairs.

No one says anything until the sound of the pod fades to a hum. I don't like Axton's plan, but I have to accept that it's the smartest move for now. I will be brave for everyone else. Theo takes the backpack from me and lifts it onto his back, which makes me smile a little.

Whatever sadness I'm feeling about Axton's departure must be nothing compared to Theo's. To lose him twice must be horrible. But surely Axton will catch up to us.

Besides, there's nothing else out here for him.

# 18

# AXTON

With the trackers tucked safely in my pocket, I run in the opposite direction to where Theo and the others will be headed. Once I'm far enough away, I will destroy the trackers. I'll toss them into a river or over a cliff so it appears we have perished.

I slow to a jog after what seems like hours of trees racing past my vision. I lift my arm to check the time, but my wrist is bare. For a second, I wish I had my watch, but I know it is serving a bigger purpose. Saving my brother and his friends, who are, it surprises me to think this, my favorite people on earth.

I find myself hoping I'll see a monkey, indicating

Levi's presence. But I know it won't happen. He's gone and wants nothing more to do with us. And if that's what he wants, he won't have any trouble making it happen. That boy could hide from a bloodhound.

I'm on my own now. It's not a question of whether I'll survive—that's not possible. Even if I evade them for a while, they will eventually catch me. They'll inevitably follow the trackers directly to me. The only thing I care about is how much of an advantage I can give Carla and Theo and Sapphire.

I come across a banana tree and quickly strip it, stuffing the sugary fruits into my pant pockets. I left all of my packaged food with Carla, so I need to stock up. There's no telling how long it will be until I'm tracked down, but in the meantime I might as well stay fed. Energy will keep me running and give my friends more time to get away.

The green rushes by, every tree the same. Once, I think I catch a glimpse of a monkey's tail, but it could have been a branch. No time to investigate.

Every now and then, I take the trackers out. They are still flashing, so presumably the enemy is still scanning them. That means they know where I am. They could just get it over and done with and find me. No doubt the only reason they're holding off is that they want to find out where we are headed. I'm amused to think that they'll end up at a random point in the jungle, far from their true prey.

I slow down to eat a banana, before building back up to speed. With all our training, it shouldn't be a problem to run thirty or forty miles. However, the heavy jungle terrain does make travel significantly more difficult. Every few minutes, I stumble on a root, or a heavy branch whips my face.

After another eternity, I check the trackers and they are no longer flashing. Finally, some good luck! They aren't tracking me anymore. Perhaps the jungle is too dense for the signal, and they aren't able to get a visual on me.

However, I mentally prepare myself for the possibility of a pod appearing, loaded with an army of guards. No doubt they'll torture me for information about where Carla, Theo and Sapphire are. Mainly Carla, though. They want her.

Because she has something they utterly, desperately need.

# 19

# CARLA

WE HURTLE DOWN THE STAIRS OF THE HOUSE. The pod has long since disappeared, but that doesn't mean it won't return. We move as fast as we can through the town and into the jungle, using Axton's watch as a guide. 'Head north' is what Axton told us.

I hear a labored breath behind me. I glance around, expecting Sapphire to be struggling, but she's doing well. The bandage on her forearm is holding firm. Then I spot a tear running down Theo's face. He wipes it away quickly and I turn back without speaking. I don't want to embarrass him.

We keep moving. I check the watch every now and

then to make sure we're heading the right way. I clutch its sturdy weight and hold it close. It's as if I have a piece of him with me.

"Hold up," Theo says suddenly. "I need a second."

I look back, and he still seems to be in pain. He's clutching his injured wrist.

We slow down, and Sapphire complains that she's hungry.

"We've got to save the food, Sapphire," I say.

"Okay." Her little head droops, and I feel terrible for not letting her eat.

I check on Theo.

"We can keep going," he says. "I'm good."

He clearly isn't, but we continue to move through the jungle. Roots and low branches make progress frustratingly slow. Eventually, Theo falls behind, so I put his arm around my shoulder. Sapphire tries to insert herself under the other arm, which elicits a huge laugh from Theo and I. She's not much help, being the size of a couple of foot-long subs.

"Wait," I whisper urgently, interrupting our laughter. "Listen."

We freeze. There is intense silence until the sound emerges again, this time much louder. A rustle. Leaves crunching. Theo clutches my arm in alarm. Footsteps. There is definitely more than one pair of boots stomping through the dry undergrowth. These people are not making an effort to hide.

Theo pulls both Sapphire and I behind a large, leafy bush. The foliage is thick, but if they move the right branches, they'll spot us immediately.

A voice emerges from a loudspeaker, booming threateningly in our direction. "Stand down. We know who you are."

It must be the guards. Axton took the trackers in vain.

I shrink down, and Sapphire cowers behind Theo. It's no use trying to run away. Theo, as usual, doesn't seem afraid. He stares directly ahead. Motionless.

The rustling ceases. I peer through a gap in the leaves and see that a dozen guards have stopped just short of us. One of them strides towards us with a wide gait.

I hold my breath and hear Theo and Sapphire do the same. The other guards appear uncertain, and they call him back. He turns to leave. I cheer inwardly.

Then something terrible happens.

Sapphire sneezes.

The guard whirls around and pounces on our hiding spot. He thrusts through the foliage, revealing our pathetic, huddled group.

He spots me, and an evil grin slashes his face. He stabs out his hand to grab me.

I dodge out of the way and he stumbles. That wiped the smirk off his face. Then his eyes rise up to meet mine. I expect an expression of anger, but instead his lips break into a sly grin.

"If you want to kidnap us, I'd do it soon," I say with as much sass as I can muster. "Sapphire's getting hungry."

Her stomach answers with a grumble.

"Missed breakfast did we, Goldilocks?" he drawls, reaching out to tug a strand of her curly, blond hair.

She hisses.

More guards appear and surround us. Theo maintains his dignity in silence. They move in to grab us and I struggle, but I know my efforts are futile.

"Where is the fourth one?" a guard asks roughly. "We know there are four of you."

We don't say a word.

"Speak!" he says. "I know *you* can, Feisty."

Ha. Ha. Good one. I ignore him. I won't give him the satisfaction of hearing fear in my voice.

"Fine. Take them away."

They lead us along a track, pushing us roughly through the brutal terrain. Sapphire whimpers.

Then I hear a shriek. And another, drifting from above. I look up.

Monkeys drop from the trees, screaming in shrill

voices. They land on the guards and claw at their faces. The guards release us to protect themselves. Everyone knows monkeys can spread disease, especially if they draw blood. Thankfully, the monkeys focus all their attention on anyone in uniform, so we are ignored.

A wave of rage takes over me and I swing my fist at the guard who was holding me. Somehow it connects, and he falls to the ground. I stare at my fist. I've never properly hit anyone before. I never felt I could, and never really wanted to. The months in the mines have made me stronger.

The monkeys scratch at the guards' necks and screech in their faces. The guards are in a world of monkey trouble.

"Get outta here, guys." I spot Levi perched lazily on a branch. He doesn't need to say it twice.

We turn and sprint back along the track, pulling Sapphire along with us. As we run, I keep watching for Levi. But there's no sign of him. I hope his monkeys are safe.

Suddenly Theo holds his hand out to stop us. He puts his finger to his lips. We freeze.

"You'd better come with us," a gruff voice says. A man emerges from the cover of the trees, blocking our path. He has a gun.

At first glance, I think he must be another guard. But

I quickly notice that he's wearing camouflaged overalls instead of a guard's outfit. It doesn't make sense.

"There's no need to run," he says with a brilliant smile, reading my mind.

"Run," I say to my friends. But no one moves. We stand still, waiting to meet our fate. I don't think it will be a good one.

Suddenly there's a rush of wind as Theo runs up to the man and grabs him in a friendly bear hug. What in tarnation?

"Greg," he exclaims. "How did you find us? Axton said he couldn't reach you."

*What?* Am I in an alternate universe? Who is this guy?

"This is Greg," Theo says. "He's on Axton's rescue team."

My fists are still clenched, so I don't shake his hand. A grunt is the best I can do. I turn to Theo.

"Why didn't Axton tell us?" I blurt.

I feel like I'm always asking the same thing.

"He couldn't get through to them at all, so he didn't want to get your hopes up."

I shake my head. *That man,* I say to myself. But I am sagging with relief.

I can't help but stare at Greg. He has thick, grey stubble covering most of his face. As he draws closer, I realize he must be over six feet tall. His biceps bulge heavily through his shirt sleeves and his legs resemble tree trunks. The span of his broad shoulders is probably equal to Sapphire's height. He's a giant.

Two other soldiers emerge, wearing the same camo gear. They turn out to be women with braided hair and friendly faces. As they come closer, I can see that their facial layout is similar, almost identical. I realize with surprise that they must be twins.

Greg says, "We'd better hurry and get to the pod before we debrief. The others are waiting."

We still can't hear the guards, but it won't be long. We race after Greg, and soon a pod appears in a gully, flanked by large trees and heavy boulders.

We pour into the open door. Squealing and laughter fill our ears. Roughly ten children—ranging from Sapphire's age to teenagers—are having a pillow fight with seat cushions. Other children are staring at the screens of strange electronic devices. Most quieten down instantly when they spot us, but a few children take a couple of seconds to figure out what's going on. Then they resume whamming pillows at each other's faces.

The door buzzes closed behind us, and I get the sensation of being in a flying daycare. A beautiful one, at that. The chairs are a stunning shade of blue, and silver detailing crowns every surface.

Theo finds a spare seat among some older boys, and Sapphire sits on the floor with the youngest children to play a pretend game with antique teddy bears.

I decide to take a seat beside a girl who is reading a book. She seems slightly younger than me, with deep red hair that falls past her shoulders in huge curls. I'd be amazed if it was her natural color, but I can't see any regrowth.

She doesn't even glance up from her book when she says, "Where are *you* from?"

"California," I say.

A beat, before she finally addresses me like I'm stupid. "No, I mean what squad?"

"Oh. Fourteen. I'm not sure about Sapphire, though."

"Sapphire," she mutters, returning to her book. "Strange name."

I turn to peer out of the window, and realize I didn't even notice the pod taking off. The pilot must be experienced.

"He is," the girl says.

I'm sure my heart stops. I turn to her, and then realize she's talking to the girl on her other side about some hot boy. The girl with the book catches me staring.

"What?" she says haughtily.

I shrug, my cheeks heating up. "I just . . . where'd you get the book from?"

"Oh, physical copies are super rare. But we've got a couple." She reaches under her seat and grabs one. "Here," she says, dropping it on my lap.

I read the title. *The Follower.*

"You've probably read it before," she says, furrowing her eyebrows.

"No, I haven't . . . I've never heard of it."

"What? No way." She nudges the girl beside her. "Oi, Lavender, this girl has never heard of *The Follower.*"

This is embarrassing. I was the resident bookworm of our household. I've read a lot of books in my time. Why haven't I read this one? Or even heard of it?

Lavender studies me. "Serious?" she says, disbelief evident on her face.

"Yes," I say hesitantly. This is very peculiar, especially since all of these girls seem to be raving about it. I've only been in the Compound a few months.

"But . . . how? It's been out for ages. And it's *so* good!"

"Yeah," the girl with the red hair says. "I've read the series twice." She pauses. "My name's Foxie, by the way."

Figures.

"Nice to meet you," I say. "I'm Carla."

"That name's familiar," she says, inspecting me. "Weird,"

is all she says before turning back to her book.

I look over at Theo, who is chatting and laughing, and I feel a strange sensation. Almost jealousy, but there's no reason for it. I decide to go and sit near him. Two girls have taken the seats on either side, so I kind of walk past him, hoping to catch his attention.

The girls notice me and quieten down, almost asking *'What do you want?'* with their eyes. *'He's ours.'* Only now do I see that Theo is quite good looking. Handsome even.

Theo spots me.

"Hey, Carla," he says, frowning. "Are you all right?"

"Just wanted to talk to you, that's all."

He excuses himself and leads me to a quiet area behind the main room of the pod. Eyes like daggers pierce my back. He gestures for me to sit beside him.

"Do you know how they found us?" I ask.

"Yeah. Obviously, they tracked the comm signal." He gestures at my watch. Axton's watch.

Axton!

He's wandering somewhere in the jungle with barely any food. And now we're headed to safety. He took the trackers for nothing!

Theo continues obliviously. "And our team hacked into *their* system to block the trackers. Then we were able to use the same system to track you. When the signals diverged, we chose the closest one."

Finally, Theo pauses and notes my panic. "What is it?"

"Axton," I get out.

"Finally remembered him, did you? Don't worry, they're onto it. I spoke to Bentley. They'll find him using the trackers he took."

I slump my shoulders. Axton's a survival hero-style guy. Surely he'll be able to survive until they can rescue him.

"They hacked the trackers without the Compound noticing?" I say.

"Apparently. Our team only tracked the children who made it out—the ones that evaded detection by the Compound. A lot did, surprisingly."

"You were in on it the whole time?"

"Yeah, who do you think put a virus on their tracker system? And I hacked the WPS of the entire Compound so we had control of the lights and elevators."

We don't speak for a while. This little room barely has space to move. I stand up and try to lean against the wall.

I guess I seem on edge, because Theo adds, "It's okay. You'll see him at the meeting place."

"Where is the meeting place?"

"Not too far away. It's where Axton told us to go. It's a camp."

"What kind of camp?"

"It's the HQ of the Organization that saved you guys from the Compound. Axton and I volunteered to be part of it," he adds.

"You volunteered . . . " I echo thoughtfully.

He shrugs. "Yes. Entering the Compound alone was a high-risk operation. But I was the most capable tech guy in the Organization, so I had to do it."

"At sixteen," I scoff.

"I'm a very gifted teen," he jokes. "Seriously, they knew the rescue would have the biggest chance of success if we had someone inside to gather intelligence and set things up."

"And Axton was always on the team?" I ask, remembering that gun to my temple.

"Of course."

I just wanted to make sure. Then something occurs to me. Why do they care so much about us? I mean, they've gone to an awful lot of effort. There's no reason for them to do this.

"Why are you guys so committed to saving us?" I say.

"Firstly, it's the right thing to do." Theo pauses. "But also because of our father. He and a few friends were the first to find out about the Compound and the work they were doing, and they quickly realized it was ethically wrong."

"Okay," I say.

"The company claimed that they were only working on industrial robots; robots that could work in high-temperature environments to cope with climate change. As a result, all of their projects were approved and they received tons of funding."

He scratches his chin.

"But my father was suspicious and dug deeper, and discovered what they were really doing. The mines, the kidnapping, and the children. He knew something was up, and he persevered until he uncovered the truth."

The pod jerks, and the speakers crackle overhead.

"Prepare for landing," Bentley's raspy voice carries throughout the aircraft. We make our way back to our seats. The pod's landing is slightly rocky, but we make it down safely. Better than my last experience in a pod.

We barely have time to scramble out before the pod lifts off again. In pursuit of Axton.

I hope he's still alive.

# 20

# AXTON

Soon I am panting with each step. I am afraid it will give my presence away to whatever man-eating beasts live in this part of the jungle. I'm alone now, and a much easier target. Cautiously, I lower my speed to ease my heavy breaths.

As I run, my mind drifts to my brother. I never thought I'd lose him a second time. He's just like Dad. Brave and selfless. Sometimes I feel a twinge of sadness, especially when he gives me a particular look with those same unusually green eyes. Theo says I'm more like Mom. That I notice the good in everyone. That I always see people for who they are.

I can imagine Mom sitting in her bedroom, eating dinner alone. When she lost her husband, we lost her too. She pushed away those she loved—relatives, friends, and those she most cared about. She's never been the same since. Too embedded in her grief to be able to risk attachment any more. Now she's lost both of her sons to war. I know she misses us, but sometimes it's hard to see it when her walls are so high.

However, this is a unique type of war; less to do with weapons, and more about strategy. At least up to this point. But if the Compound has their way, it will be a battlefront won or lost on weapons alone. And they have the most powerful weapon of all—an army that feels no pain.

I notice my pace has slowed to a jog, so I decide to risk a quick rest. Four hours of running—pods can cover that in mere minutes. But I have to try. And the jungle will definitely make it hard for them. I devour several bananas to keep my energy up.

I'm just beginning to think that thirst may become an issue, when I hear the sound of trickling water. I'm sure it's not in my head. I follow the sound and duck under low-hanging branches, arriving at a small and beautifully clear pond. It's out of place in this endless green landscape; too calm and serene.

The water is a light blue, and a flower floats in the

middle. Maybe a waterlily, like the pictures I've seen online. I didn't think anything this picturesque existed anymore. I wonder if the pond is man-made. Maybe the waterlily, too.

I greedily gulp handfuls of water. Finally satisfied, I recline on a rock facing the water. I take out the trackers and nearly drop them when I see that they're flashing, this time faster. I am being tracked again. I stand up, take my bearings and sprint as fast as I dare in the rough terrain.

Hopefully I can survive for another couple of hours to give them more time, and create more distance between us. I pick up my pace even more, scanning the ground ahead for trip hazards.

All too soon, the crunch of my boots on dry leaves is replaced with the whir of what can only be the impellers of a pod. I move faster than ever, despite knowing I cannot possibly evade it for long.

I throw the trackers to the side as far as I can and continue my mad dash through the jungle. If I'm lucky, the pod will land next to the trackers, and I will be able to keep going until the enemy works out what's happening.

Unfortunately, luck isn't on my side.

Within seconds, I hear the pod hovering above me, its warning lights flashing ominously. I stop still and wait for it to land. My heart is pounding. Suddenly a ladder drops out of the pod and hangs just out of reach. I square my shoulders and prepare to face a grim fate.

I look up to see a smiling face.

"Climb aboard, brother," Greg calls.

Relief overwhelms me as I grip onto the ladder and float to the top, before hauling myself into the pod.

"Theo," I puff.

Greg grins. "We got him. Carla too. And the little girl . . . Sapphire?"

I am elated. "Thank goodness." I collapse into a seat and Greg drops next to me.

"So, where next?" I ask.

"Headquarters. That's where we're keeping them all safe. Until we figure out what to do with them."

The pod speeds up.

"Take them to their families, of course," I say. Words from my father.

"Yes, that was our first thought. The General, however, has a different idea. She thinks they might be useful. As leverage against the Compound's army."

"What? No!" I object. "These are real children from real families."

"I know—"

"They aren't pawns to be manipulated in a war. You

can't do that! Surely you can see the hypocrisy of it all, Greg."

"Hey, this is war. I don't make the rules. I just follow them."

"But the rules are wrong, Greg." I shake my head. It's no use arguing with him. I need to talk to someone higher up in the ranks. "Take me to the Penthouse."

"Okay," he says, reluctantly. "But the decision's already been made. I mean, you're good, but not that good."

"We'll see."

"Honestly, who cares, Axton? It's not like we can send them back and everything will be normal again." He brushes his hair back with his hand.

"Actually, we can."

He shrugs. "If you say so. But don't say I didn't warn you."

We travel for thirty minutes, and the terrain never changes. Green everywhere.

"Back in Organization territory," Bentley announces from the cockpit. I relax automatically.

Finally, the pod hovers over our secondary base. It's hidden among tall jungle trees—the largest I've seen. The buildings are well camouflaged. On foot, they would be unidentifiable, and even from the air they would be very difficult to spot. There is still a risk of discovery by the

Compound, but even if they discovered the base, they wouldn't dare attack. They know we're undefeatable in our own territory. For now. But it won't be that way for long if they keep building their army.

We touch down in a small clearing that's overgrown with ivy. The door folds out to a ramp, and I wave to Bentley before exiting the pod.

Greg calls out after me, "Once you're done wasting your time, we need you in debrief."

I ignore him and head towards the buildings. I'm not going to debrief until I have convinced the General to take the children back to their families. I can't believe Greg questions why I'd bother to try. Because they are children, and all children belong with their families. Maybe they can catch up on the childhoods they missed out on.

I zigzag through the buildings until I reach the most decorative one. Objectively, it's quite plain, but compared to the others, it is extravagant. It is also the tallest. I climb the short flight of stairs to the front door. Two soldiers stand there on duty; one nods. I grip the door handle and it opens, so I head to the elevator. I enter and press the touchpad labeled *Penthouse*. The mirror reveals my sweat-stained, disheveled state, so I shape my hair roughly with my fingers during the ascent.

The door opens and I step out. I've only been to the Penthouse once before, but I vaguely remember the location of the General's office. After two right turns, the office is precisely where I thought it should be. I take in a deep breath, gather my thoughts, and knock on the white door.

A piercing voice from within, sharp and crisp. "Enter."

I straighten my shoulders and push the door open. The General sits at her desk. Her indifferent eyes glare at me as I approach. She smooths her formal dress, and I am suddenly even more aware of my dirty uniform, covered in week-old sweat, dirt and mud.

"How can I help you?" she asks condescendingly.

"I want to discuss the plan for the children."

"The Compound children, yes? And what in particular concerns you?" She drums her nails on the wooden table.

"We need to return them to their homes. They have families who miss them, and . . . "

"Ah, that is where you are mistaken," she declares. "They are effectively dead. Their families believe them to be dead. It is best if they stay dead."

I open my mouth to object and she tuts.

"Would you want to disturb the peace and tranquility of this territory? The last remaining civilization in the world?"

"But—"

"Ruin their lives? Create an uprising?"

I shake my head. "That isn't the question—"

"Besides, imagine how useful they would be in, say, a battle against the Compound's army. We have weakened the army, yes, but they will build again and come back at us even stronger." She gestures dismissively. "Thank you, Private. It's been a pleasure." With a flick of her wrist, she opens a tablet and starts working.

I take two steps, closing the gap between us. I slam my hands on the hard wood, glaring at the General. She doesn't flinch.

"These children need to go home," I growl. "What's the point of saving them from the Compound just to have them go through the same thing here?" I say, through clenched teeth.

She pauses. "The matter is finished. Remove yourself from my office immediately. That's an order."

"We're supposed to be the good guys!" I blurt out.

She pauses, but doesn't look up. "We are. Here in the Organization, they'll have a life. They'll be regarded as heroes for helping to protect the world. If they go home, they won't be accepted. They'll be too different. They won't *belong* anymore."

"Too different? They're just children. The thought of

going home to their parents is what gives them hope."

Her expression hardens.

"Ignorance," she spits, "is very common in children, especially those who disobey the rules." I don't doubt that her harshness is directed at Carla.

"Carla isn't a child," I say calmly.

"Actions speak far louder than words," she says. "And she *acts* like a child."

"You don't know anything about her!"

"Neither do you," she says.

"I know that you need her. And I could help you." I didn't realize I had come to bargain, but I'll do whatever it takes.

She simply laughs. A shallow laugh that doesn't travel all the way to her eyes.

"What could *you* possibly do that our professionals can't?" Her eyebrows rise skeptically towards black hair swept into a tight bun.

That's easy. "Gain her trust."

She purses her lips. "Why would we need that?"

"She won't listen to you without it."

It's true, Carla is very strong-willed. I don't even know whether she entirely trusts *me*. "And you can't manipulate her. She's too stubborn."

The General pauses, and there is silence. Finally, after

some thought, she says, "Bring her to me immediately, so I can talk to her. Then I'll give you one week to get us what we need. If you do, the children return to their families. If you don't, we go back to our original plan."

I shouldn't accept. Because if I fail, it will ruin all of their lives. They'll never get the chance to be normal again. But this is the only hope they have.

I stare into the face of this despicable woman and wonder how she possibly justifies her choices to herself.

"Deal," I say.

"You are dismissed," she says.

I want to work out details, but she's already back on her tablet. I pry my hands off the desk and march towards the door.

"One more thing," her sharp voice barks behind me. "If you don't succeed, you'll be court-martialed. For disobeying direct orders."

# 21

# CARLA

The soft glow of yellow and orange lights creates a path of calm as a soldier leads us through the main building to the stairs. The children and teenagers chatter happily, some skipping and others holding hands. My heart is full as I watch my friends' faces glow with hope and relief.

Iron banisters lace the stairway as we descend to the bottom floor. The soldier guides us along a sloping hallway with dorm rooms on either side, ushering four children into each room we pass. Soon, I'm left with only Theo, Sapphire and Lavender, the girl from the pod. She scowls when she realizes she'll be bunking with us. I'm not sure what we ever did to her.

He reads our names out even though there are only four of us left.

"Theo, Carla..." His eyes flit up at me as if seeing me for the first time. "Lavender, and Sapphire."

He pulls the door open, and we wander inside. The laughter from the other rooms disappears as he closes the door behind us.

Inside are two double bunkbeds dressed with crisp white sheets, and a small desk and chair.

Sapphire's eyes widen. "I get a proper bed?" she asks. Her expression is so adorable.

"You sure do, honey," Lavender says dryly.

For the first time in a long time, we will be fed and looked after. Most importantly, we'll be free. Maybe not free in the way we used to be, back when we lived at home without a care in the world. But at least free in the sense of being treated with dignity and respect.

During the lecture they gave us just before we headed down, the soldiers highlighted the main features of the Organization's headquarters, including a large communal dining area, bathrooms, and even a pool. I bet everyone is hoping for a swim.

We set up our room, although there isn't much to do. We don't have many belongings between us; I only have

Axton's bag and the novel I'm still holding.

Earlier, the soldiers searched our bags and confiscated my sachets of food. They said that nobody was allowed personal food supplies due to the food shortage. I noticed that Lavender had only a tiny bag roughly sewn from tattered pieces of fabric.

Theo leaps onto the top bunk, yelling, "This one's mine!" The rest of us dump our stuff on the remaining beds. How he still has energy to care about anything, especially sleeping arrangements, is beyond me.

That is, until I notice a bundle of white cloth folded at the foot of my bed. I unravel it.

"Guys," I say, unable to hide my excitement. "New clothes!"

Everyone jumps up at the thought of fresh, clean garments. Sapphire squeals as she unwraps a cerulean blue dress. I rush down the hall to the bathrooms and am only too glad to discard the dirty, ripped attire from the Compound. I pull the new shirt on and my fingers fumble over the new buttons like a toddler.

I return, clean and refreshed. I flop on the bed and bounce a few times. I actually forgot what it's like to lie on a mattress. I realize how lucky I used to be. I had a home and a family who loved me. Now I have nothing.

No, that's not right. I still have a family, don't I? My

parents. And my brother Rory. I can find them; I know I can. And I've got new friends here.

*Bam!* It's as if someone has hit me. Memories flood back. Only short snippets—strange impressions without substance . . . blood, desperation, my mother lying helpless on the ground as blood oozes from her abdomen, famine, houses burning, people fleeing, destruction, gunshots.

The memories disappear as fast as they arrived, but I find my fingers still clutching the sheets of the bed.

I'm shaking, tears pouring down my face. How could I have forgotten everything? I try desperately to cling to my happy memories of beaches and sun and good times. But it's no use. What is going on? Have they filled my head with horrible fake memories? And why am I remembering them now?

I have a family; I know I do.

I realize my eyes are closed, so I rip them open. Theo and Sapphire are sitting beside me with concern on their faces, but I don't care. Theo opens his mouth to speak, but I cut him off in desperation.

"I'm fine!" I scream in his face. He's shocked. I don't apologize.

I leap off the bed and down the hall towards the staircase.

"Carla, wait! Come back," I hear Theo shouting from just behind me.

I take the stairs two at a time. I need to get away. Maybe I can live with Levi in the jungle somewhere, hunting for berries and wild bananas. The thought is a tempting fantasy.

The stairs seem to extend for an eternity. As I emerge above ground, I am shocked into stopping. Yellows and oranges and reds flood the sky like I've never seen before. It seems I'm just in time to watch the sunset. It is spectacular.

I head towards the rainforest—to freedom—at a sprint. Then something rams right into me. Well, someone. Strong arms grip me close. I look up and see a familiar face.

"Oh my gosh," Axton says, staring at me in recognition. "Carla!"

He reads my expression and his eyes soften. He hasn't let go, and I wrap my arms tight around him and press my moist face against his rough shirt. His heart pounds against my cheek. I didn't realize how much I missed him. He holds me tight.

After an eternity, he peers at my face. "Have you been crying?"

"No, I . . . " And just to prove his point, I burst into tears. He sits me down, arm around my shoulder, and waits patiently until the last dregs of water flow down my cheeks.

"What happened?" he asks gently.

"I remember," I whisper. His eyes instantly widen. His arm falls away.

"What do you remember, Carla?" he says harshly.

I'm taken aback. "Why?"

"I just need to know."

I squint at him. "What do you mean?"

"Nothing. It doesn't matter," he says, shaking his head slightly.

I know he's lying. It clearly matters a lot. So I tell him.

"I remember . . . fighting . . . and lots of other awful things . . . my mother bleeding. She was shot. Shot."

He shifts uncomfortably. "Troops raided cities and there was war."

"Why?" I demand an answer. "Why were people fighting?"

"There were world wars. Millions died. Then, after that, the Commander attacked with his army," says Axton. "He wants global domination."

"I never heard about any war . . . "

"You were in the Compound."

"But I was only gone a few months."

"They had you under, um . . . you were kind of in a coma," explains Axton.

"A coma? Kind of?" I say doubtfully. I sure don't remember waking from one.

"Like a coma. Suspended animation."

I highly doubt that. But I ask, "For how long?"

"Um, years. A few years, I think," says Axton edgily.

Years? Could I really have missed years without knowing it? I don't know what to think.

"Take your time, Carla. Breathe."

I shake my head. "I need to find my family."

"I know, Carla," he reassures me.

I lower my gaze.

"And anyway, we're your family," Axton adds helpfully.

I burst into tears again. Why isn't he telling me what's going on? And why is he keeping secrets? It's as if he's protecting me from something. Where is my family? I need to be stronger . . .

"I'm sorry I didn't find you earlier," Axton says. "The medic wanted to treat the wounds in my back. Then I came to find you."

"Me?" I ask. "What about Theo?"

Axton suddenly stands straighter.

"They need you in the Penthouse. Another important job they need you to do. They think you have great potential."

I scoff, "Potential for disaster."

"No, really," he says. "They expect great things from you."

Now he's sounding exactly like the monsters from the Compound.

# 22

# AXTON

I feel bad for keeping things from her. I really do. But I have to remember what's at stake. I need her help. The children need to get back to their families—all of them do. If I tell her what's really going to happen, she won't help me. Or herself. And I can't let that happen. I'm just going to have to take it slow. We'll gradually build some trust.

We wind through the buildings until we reach the one containing the General's office. We enter the lobby and this time many soldiers are gathered. Three of them block my path. Another two grab Carla and drag her towards the elevator.

"Get off me!" she shouts. "Axton!"

"Hey! What are you doing?" I yell.

The closest one grunts, "Doing my job."

"This wasn't part of the plan," I protest.

Carla looks shocked. "What plan?"

"Not now," I say to her. I advance on the soldiers. "Let her go. This is not happening."

Someone grabs me from behind.

"Woah, woah!" I shout. I swing around and fling him against the wall.

More soldiers enter the room. I slam my knee into a groin and the soldier crumples. I take down three more before they swarm and hold me still.

"What's going on?" I shout. I go slack for a few moments until I sense them relaxing. Then I rip my arm free and smash my fist into a soldier's face. He winces. He pounds me back without mercy.

"Stop," I hear Carla say weakly. I turn. Then I see the knife at her throat.

I study the soldier holding the weapon against her flesh.

"Cooperate," he says. He doesn't need to say the 'or else'.

"Big word for a dumb guy," I mutter, keeping my attention on the metal blade.

"What did you say?" he snarls, turning his head

towards me. But I see his grip on the knife loosen.

"You know who she is?" I ask.

"Axton, please stop," Carla pleads. But she doesn't understand. I'm doing this for her.

"Go ahead. Stab her."

Words cannot describe the look that Carla gives me. The soldier stares at me blankly.

"This is *Carla*," I say.

His jaw drops ever so slightly.

"Yes, *the* Carla."

Carla stares at me, confusion and hurt evident in her expression.

The soldier appears shocked.

"You wouldn't want to try to hurt her then, would you?" I threaten. "That wouldn't be very smart."

He lowers the knife but keeps a firm grasp on her.

We aren't allowed to get emotionally involved during this mission. They warned us about helping the children. Think of it as a retrieval, not a rescue, they said. Emotion is for the weak. But they're wrong. These are merely children. And emotions have power.

"I need to know why you're doing this," I say slowly.

"General's orders," is all he says.

"These are not her orders!" I yell, and the soldiers flinch. "I need to talk to her."

One of them murmurs into a mouthpiece, and then gestures to the others.

"She'll see you," he says.

I realize the soldiers are still holding onto me.

"Let go," I snarl.

The guards release me and I walk towards the elevator. I don't trust these soldiers with Carla, so the visit is going to have to be quick. I reach my hand out to press the touchpad, but the elevator door opens by itself. The General marches out, and the soldiers stand taut. A thick silence oppresses the room.

The General doesn't seem to notice me as she moves directly to Carla and leans down to her.

"Carla," she says crisply. "You are appreciated. You will go down in history."

Carla never once breaks her eye contact with me, despite the General's comments. Because she blames me for getting her into this mess. And she's right. It was me. But it wasn't supposed to be like this.

"You liar," I spit at the General.

She tilts her head innocently.

"This isn't what I agreed to," I say.

"Well, excuse me if your little brain didn't understand what I was offering." She stares at me. "A chance."

A chance to what? Destroy my friendship with Carla?

Her trust? Her life? The children need to be returned to their families.

I don't know what to do.

She waves her hand, dismissing me. "You should know that I do what's best for this Organization. You could have provided a great service. But you seem to have lost focus on this mission. You are not the soldier I was told you were."

She snaps her fingers and turns back towards the elevators. Several soldiers follow, carrying Carla like a mannequin. She doesn't even struggle.

"No!" I shout after them. I grasp at straws. "Forget the deal."

I grab the soldiers in an attempt to stop them. Others knock me out of the way.

The General says over her shoulder, "Forgotten." She continues into the elevator.

"Let her go! Wait," I say. "You need me." The elevator door is closing. "I'm your only chance."

Carla's eyes are locked onto mine until the very last second. I can't believe this. The General never planned to bargain with me. She used me to bring Carla to her, and once I was no longer needed, she discarded me. A pawn on her chessboard. How could I fall for that?

I frantically wave my hands over the sensor on the

elevator touchpad, but the doors remain firmly closed. The remaining soldiers eyeball me but don't engage.

I turn away slowly and leave the building. If I'm to have any hope of getting Carla out of this mess, I need a plan.

And some help.

*　　*　　*

Outside again, I sprint between the buildings until I reach the stairs that descend to the bunkrooms.

"Come on, Carla!" I hear someone shout. "Where are you?"

I run towards the sound.

"Theo?" I call.

He spots me and his face lights up.

"Axton!"

He slams into me, wrapping his skinny arms around my waist. But his happiness doesn't last long, and soon his face sags.

"I've lost Carla," he says guiltily. "I did my best, but she ran away and I don't know where she is—"

I grab his shoulders. "I know where she is."

His eyes grow wide.

"She was taken to the General," I say grimly. "I need your help."

"The General? Why?"

"Because I thought I was doing the right thing. It's my fault."

He puts a hand on my arm. "No, it's not. There was nothing you could do."

"No, Theo. You don't understand. I took her there. I made a bargain to get all the children back to their families, and unfortunately that bargain involved Carla."

He scowls at me. "It's not worth it! Giving Carla up for *that*? What were you thinking?"

"That wasn't meant to happen. The General tricked me. I was supposed to help her gain Carla's trust, but now they've taken her."

He shakes his head. "So what do we do, Private?"

I spy a security camera high on the corner of a building. "Not here."

Theo says knowingly, "Follow me."

He leads me through the buildings until he reaches a small storage room. I frown.

"When exactly did you have time to find this?" I say.

He shrugs. "I've known about it for a long time. I discovered it has no security cameras. You know me, I notice these things."

He's not wrong about that. Theo's a tech fiend.

He waves his hand in front of the door, and it slides

open. I slip through the narrow doorway, ducking to fit under the frame.

We sit against the wall, just like we did when we were children.

"We're going to escape," I say.

Well, whatever Theo was expecting, it wasn't this. "What? Axton, you're insane," he says. "We can't leave. You're overreacting. These people are the good guys."

"Unfortunately, I'm beginning to question that. I knew the General was single-minded, but I didn't think she was evil."

"She's not evil," Theo insists.

"Carla's a prisoner right now. In the General's hands."

He turns white. "Why?"

"I'm not sure, exactly. That's what we've got to find out."

"So how are we going to do that?"

I tell him my plan and we go outside.

*     *     *

Five minutes later, we're standing outside the main building that holds the General. And Carla. I glance quickly through a window to check for soldiers and give Theo the signal. He stealthily enters through the front doors.

I creep around the side of the building to wait for his return.

Ten minutes. Twenty. At half an hour I stand up, ready to take down the General myself, and break Carla and Theo out.

Without warning, Theo bursts around the corner with a frightened expression on his face. I rush to him.

"What is it?" I demand.

"You were right. It's not good."

"Tell me!"

"She's strapped down on a bed with wires and cables sticking out of her. It seems like they're trying to get some data out of her brain."

"Was she conscious?" Please. Please don't let her be conscious.

Theo shudders. "Yeah. And she saw me." His face turns red, then white, then hardens with determination.

"Let's go get my gear."

We run back to the dorms. The stairway seems to be hundreds of steps down. We race down the hall until we reach the room, tapping the touchpad on the door. Sapphire is fast asleep on her bunk.

I find my bag on Carla's bunk and grab it. Theo rummages in his pack. He picks up a few electronic instruments that I'm not familiar with.

"Okay," he says as he stuffs them into his pockets. "Let's go."

"Where to?" I ask.

"The powerplant."

I don't know how that'll help, but Theo's the expert.

We bound up the stairs to the exit and march towards a tiny round building. There's a door with the faded words *DANGER ELECTRICITY* inscribed on the front. No touchpad, only an old-style padlock. He picks up a nearby piece of pipe and smashes the lock. The door falls open with a creak.

"Oh man," Theo says, shaking his head.

"What's wrong?" I ask.

He swings the door open wider, allowing me to peer inside. Wires of every color crisscross and take up the entire space.

"Well, that's something you don't see every day," I say.

"My equipment sure isn't going to work on this," Theo replies. "I knew the technology would be old because of the age of this place, but I didn't think it would be ancient. How did it even last this long?"

"I don't know."

It didn't even occur to me that the place wouldn't use WPS. The Wireless Power System is installed every-where now.

"What do we do, then?"

"I just need some old-school wire cutters. Got any handy?"

I shake my head. "No." They haven't been around for the past fifty years. I've only seen them on the internet. I begin to scan around for a sharp piece of metal or a stick.

"I have scissors," a high voice chirps. Theo and I spin around to face a small girl in a blue dress.

"Sapphire?" Theo says.

"What are you doing here?" I say harshly. She stares at me indignantly.

"I didn't want to be alone, so when I heard you say powerplant, I found it. And you," she says forthrightly. Then she swings a pair of scissors briskly in her hand before holding them out to Theo.

"You shouldn't have come here by yourself," Theo scolds. "But thanks."

"Why do you have scissors?" I ask.

She shrugs. "I was doing what Carla said. Getting my bad emotions out using toy guards."

We both look at her. "You were stabbing them?"

Sapphire giggles. "No, silly! Making clothes for them."

"That's . . . um, cool, Sapphire, but you should probably go back to the dorms now."

I glance at Theo. Sapphire shouldn't be here. It's too dangerous.

She nods, but tears begin to well. "Please, Theo. I don't want to go back. All alone."

"You won't be alone," Theo says. "Lavender's your friend."

Sapphire crosses her arms. "Lavender is *not* my friend."

Her moist eyes crumble my resolve. "Okay, you can stay."

Theo winces at my weakness. "You'll have to behave, though."

She grins eagerly. I watch as Theo cuts the thick, red wires in the box.

"Power's out," he says. "Let's go."

I grab Sapphire's hand and we walk briskly to the entrance of the General's building. It's dark inside and people are already coming out. Then I realize something.

"Wait, Theo," I say.

He stops.

"Elevators don't work without electricity."

He frowns and we head to the side of the building. I can hear Theo muttering something as he tries a door.

"The emergency stairwell is locked," he states, annoyed.

I gaze at the top floor of the building.

"How high up was Carla?" I ask.

"Third floor," Theo answers. I still can't see an easy way to get up.

"How about that?" Sapphire asks, pointing at a thin pipe snaking its way up to the top of the building. "I used to slide down ours all the time. To sneak out of my room," she explains with an impish grin. I exchange a look with Theo.

"Looks like it's the only way," he says. "It's a conduit for optical fiber cables. Should be strong enough."

I grab hold of the pipe and shake it gently. It creaks, but we're just going to have to trust it.

"You wait here," I say to Theo. "Look after Sapphire and I'll bring Carla out."

"Nah, I'm lighter. I'll get her," Theo says.

I hesitate. I'd rather get her out myself. Theo probably doesn't have the strength to carry Carla down a rickety pipe system.

I shake my head. "Wait with Sapphire."

Then a small voice says, "I think Theo is right, Axton." Sapphire looks anxiously at Theo with wide, blue eyes. I sigh inwardly.

"All right," I say. There is a fair chance the pipe won't support my weight. I step away from the pipe and stand beside Sapphire.

Theo glances once at me and then at Sapphire. He grabs the pipe and begins to climb. At first, the pipe seems as if it is going to snap. It bends severely to the left. But Theo adjusts his weight, and the pipe straightens.

I grab Sapphire's arm. "Move back," I whisper.

I don't want her to get crushed if Theo does fall. We both take a step back.

We stare up at Theo, who gradually clambers up the wall. Finally, he reaches a window on the third floor. He peers in. I watch as he shudders, then shakes his head. Mustn't be Carla. He gawks anxiously at me. If that isn't her room, it means he'll have to let go of the pipe and walk along a small ledge beneath the window sill.

Hopefully the next room across will be hers.

I give Theo the thumbs up. He knows what he has to do. He shimmies down the pipe until his feet are almost in line with the ledge. Then he reaches one foot down so it rests on the small cement outcrop. Slowly, he puts his other foot out onto the ledge. Now all he has to do is let go of the pipe. I can see his legs shaking from here. I bet he regrets not letting me do it now.

But he presses his body against the wall and releases the pipe. He places his hands flat against the cement and shuffles along the ledge until he reaches the next window. He squashes his nose against it, and his body sinks a little.

He shakes his head ever so slightly. He can't turn towards us, but I know this isn't her room either. He continues along the shelf and peers into the third window. His foot slips off the ledge, and Sapphire gasps. But he grabs the window sill just in time.

Apparently there's no one in the room because he grasps the latch on the window and begins to pull. For a second, panic sets in when it seems the window's locked. But then the glass shifts slightly, and he manages to pry it open just enough to fit through. He swings one leg over and eases inside. He disappears.

I can only hope that he and Carla make it out alive.

# 23

# CARLA

Yellow and orange. Swirls of color—reds and deep purple. Yellow. Orange. A curl of vibrant pink. Blooms of orange in the darkness. Flashes of white. A burst here and another burst there. What is that strange light in the distance? I vaguely wonder where I am, who I am, before the thoughts fade away beneath the colors.

Everything turns green. Something saturates my veins. Where is my body? Who am I? I am just a mind. A wheel of color. An image of green herbs flashes briefly. I remember a dish Mom used to cook, with chicken and coriander. Then it's gone.

An eternity. That is how long I've been here in the

darkness. But also, paradoxically, in the light. A black background flooded with vibrancy. It isn't uncomfortable. Just strange.

That is, until it all goes white. Pain shoots through my body. I can feel every inch of it. Icy white. I am whole once again. An entire being of agony.

The white bursts of brightness are spikes of pain, striking my body from every angle. I can't feel anything, yet every cell of my body is burning. Something tugs at me from every direction. They want to take part of me. What do they want? My brain tells me I shouldn't let them have it . . .

One last blinding flash of white, and the pain disappears. I float for a long time.

*     *     *

In the distance, I imagine someone speaking.

"Carla," the voice says. "Please be alive, Carla."

I know that voice. I force myself awake, and blink.

Without thinking, I try to speak. "Theo." It comes out as a croak, but a wide grin breaks out on his face as he leans towards me.

"Thank goodness," he says. He reaches out, carefully detaches my bindings, and tucks his arms under my body. He heaves me up.

Am I still dreaming?

The pain that consumed me is no more. The people I dimly remember crowding over me are gone. My head feels faint, but I try to manage one more sentence.

"What are you doing here?" I say, as he carries me out of the room and into a long hallway.

Theo shushes me. I relax into him as he takes me into an empty room. I hope this is real. That Theo is real.

"What do they want from me?"

He winces. "No time, Carla!"

We hear a crash and a shout. He pulls us into a closet. It's pitch-black as soon as the door closes. We barely make it. Footsteps and urgent shouts fill the hallway. Although he's panting, I can tell Theo is desperately trying to breathe as quietly as possible.

"We don't have much time," he whispers. "Won't take them long to figure out where we've gone."

The footsteps recede. I wiggle my toes as a test. They seem fine. "I think I can walk," I whisper. Gratefully, he lowers me until my feet rest on the cold, hard floor. I don't have shoes on anymore. And instead of my other clothes, I'm dressed in a hospital gown. Even in the dark, my face turns red at the thought of someone undressing me. What do these people want from me?

I stand for a second and have no trouble balancing.

"I'm good," I whisper. Theo grabs my hand and squeezes it before gripping the handle of the door. He slowly works it open. All is quiet. We squint in the stark light. The path is clear.

Theo confidently guides me to the right. I don't know how he remembers his way around after so long away, but I'm glad he does.

We race down the hallways, and luckily my legs warm up fast. Whatever they did to me, although painful, at least didn't cause any permanent damage.

Suddenly I see the elevator doors. I reach them before Theo, so I press the touchpad. Nothing happens. I push hard at different parts of the door to try to activate it.

"Power's out," Theo explains. "I forgot."

*Oh no. Please don't let them catch us.*

Theo pulls me away from the elevator and drags me back the way we came. Past the closet.

"Wrong way!" I mutter as loud as I can without drawing unwanted attention.

This can't be right. I must be imagining things. But no. He's definitely taking me back to the horror room. What if he plugs me back in? No! I can't go back to that terrifying place.

"Theo!" I yelp. "What are you doing?"

He quickly covers my mouth. I try to shake out of his grasp, but to no avail.

"I'm not going back!" I shriek.

"Shh, Carla," he says harshly. "Can't you stay quiet?"

I stop struggling, and finally we reach the room again. I drag my feet, my hands shake, and my heart is beating out of my chest. Theo doesn't seem to notice. He shoves me towards the window.

"Quick, get out."

I look down. It's a long way.

"I can't do it," I say. No way.

"Carla, now's not the time," Theo says with frustration. "Get out there!"

And that's when I hear the footsteps. Barreling down the hall. An earthquake of boots. I can see the thin metal bedframe shake. Soldiers. Lots of them.

I slip through the window and out into the hot breeze. Down below, I see Axton and Sapphire. Axton is pointing to an old pipe. He gives me an encouraging sign. *No!* He got me into this mess. It's his fault. He betrayed me.

"What are you waiting for?" Theo says.

"This is *his* fault!" I say.

"He didn't know what he was getting you into, okay? You have to trust me."

*Trust.* A strange thing, so easily broken. Who can I trust anymore?

Sapphire waves at me from below. I take a deep breath. I begin to inch along the thin platform, and remember people saying that you shouldn't look down. So I focus on taking one step at a time.

I start feeling faint. Oh no. Not the throwing up. Then I realize I'm holding my breath. I add breathing to the list of critical actions, and keep moving until I reach another window.

Theo is right behind me. A few steps behind him, peering out of the window, are soldiers. The ledge begins to creak as one of them climbs onto it.

"They're coming!" I say to Axton.

"Don't move or we'll shoot!" shouts one of the soldiers.

I stiffen. Then Axton calls, "Carla," in a low, warning tone. "They won't shoot you. Come towards me."

I glance back at the soldiers, praying that he's right. Apparently, I have something that they want, and if they want it that badly then they can't kill me, can they? But Theo! I hurl myself down the pipe and shimmy towards Axton. Theo throws himself onto the pipe behind me, sliding like a fireman on a pole.

Suddenly I'm falling. Too high. I scream.

The ground smashes into me. I hear an awful sound, and savage pain in my feet makes me cry out. Surely my left ankle must be broken. Theo slides off the pipe almost on top of me.

"Run!" yells Axton.

"I can't," I say. "My ankle!"

"Your ankle is fine," yells Axton as he starts moving. "Run!"He glances at the soldiers and back to Sapphire. "Looks like you're coming with us."

He grabs her and swings her onto his shoulder next to his backpack. It doesn't look comfortable, but she sure doesn't complain.

Didn't he see me fall? Hear the crack? Listen to me scream? What a heartless monster. Theo is running after him. They're not even waiting for me. I glance up. A soldier is at the top of the pole, weapon aimed at the others. I hold my breath, but they reach the temporary safety of the forest.

Fear drives me. Adrenaline rush. I stand up and take a tentative step. My ankle holds. My heart is pounding so fast that I feel no pain. I jog, then sprint, favoring my good leg.

I overtake the others, and together we race along a path until we reach the edge of a clearing. I realize we are on the opposite side to the main entrance. I risk a glance behind us and see that the soldiers are catching up fast.

We need to run faster, but Theo is slowing us down.

"Keep going," he yells, barely jogging.

"No!" I shout. I grab his arm and pull him along to

get him moving faster. My ankle doesn't hurt at all. With this much adrenaline, I feel I could keep running forever.

Soon, the rainforest surrounds us again. Anger consumes me. They shouldn't have risked their lives for me. Why didn't they just leave me behind? They don't need me. They could have let the soldiers do what they needed to do to me, and saved themselves. What a waste. Now we'll all be punished because of me. Again.

Then something tries to literally smack the negative thoughts out of me. What seemed like a wall of leaves is actually solid rock. I have slammed right into it. I touch my nose tentatively, but it seems okay.

Axton reaches into the leaves and pulls something. The leaves separate, creating a doorway. It's a pod. Camouflaged in the jungle. Of course, Axton would never try to rescue me without a solid plan! I soften a little towards him.

Axton leaps aboard and drops his backpack on a chair. We follow closely behind, with Theo dragging Sapphire up the steep steps. The door closes behind us just as the soldiers approach. Axton rushes into the cabin. Bullets pummel the side of the pod. Harmless.

Without warning, the ship lurches upwards, throwing us off our feet.

We made it.

I can hardly breathe for a few seconds. We have a ship. A pod. That means they can take me home. All I ever wanted was to escape the Compound and get back to my family. Finally, it's possible.

Sapphire is sitting on one side of me, and Theo on the other. Sapphire's breathing is deep, and her head is lolling. I don't know how she fell asleep so fast.

Theo picks up a tablet console attached to the wall and begins scrolling through the news. I'm idly looking at his screen, when I see something that shocks me.

"Wait," I say. Theo quickly scrolls past. "What was that?"

He looks up guiltily. "Nothing. It doesn't matter," he says. "I was researching old news stories. Go to sleep."

"No, Theo. I know what I saw," I say. Bodies covered in burns and welts. Piles of bodies.

Maybe I don't want to know.

"You said I have the right to know."

Theo acquiesces reluctantly. "All right. I'll tell you."

"The Compound's secret aim was to build their army. And they did, during the world wars, and then afterwards they began destroying cities. These are some pictures from the places they attacked."

"We need to help," I say. "There are children there."

"These are old file photos." He pauses. "But we are doing everything that we can to stop it happening again. That being said, now that we know the Organization has the wrong motives, things are going to be more difficult. I think Axton is figuring out a new plan."

That reminds me. I need to ask Axton what they were trying to do to me in that room. I leave Theo to his horrors.

"What was that all about, Axton?" I demand, bursting into the control room of the pod. I decide he can handle the distraction. He's an experienced pilot.

He frowns. "I'm sorry, Carla. It was a mistake to take you to the General."

"You think?" I say sarcastically.

He ignores me and continues. "The Organization doesn't care about anything except armies and weapons. When my father was in charge, it wasn't like that. At all."

"So, what were they trying to do to me?" I ask. "You said they wanted me to help the children unlock their emotions. But then they did that weird stuff to me. Why?"

"Just searching for a shortcut, I guess," says Axton.

"It was awful. Like the Monitor Rooms again."

"Well, they all want the same secret sauce." Axton shifts in his seat. "That special Carla recipe."

I glare at him. I'm not a condiment. But I try to calm myself. I need to control my surging emotions.

I can see I'm not going to get any real answers from Axton. Maybe I'll just sit out the ride and chill until they drop me home.

"How long until we get there?" I say, casually.

"A couple of hours. Not too long."

"Who's getting dropped off first? Me or Sapphire?"

He pauses for a beat. "What did you say?"

"I'm happy either way, but are we going to my house or Sapphire's first?" It's a pretty simple question.

"Carla," he says, rubbing his head behind his ear. "We have a few things to do before we . . . before we can take you home."

I try to stop emotion from taking over, but there isn't much I can do to hold back the torrential rain that bursts from my tear ducts. Axton seems alarmed at the sight of more tears.

"Please take me home, Axton," I whisper.

This time, there is answering moisture in his eyes. "I'm sorry," he says.

"I want to go home, Axton," I say, the volume rising. "Home. All I ever wanted after I escaped the Compound was to go home to my family. My family who loves me! Take me home!"

Theo clicks on a page labelled Rory Grayson. It loads and he skims through the information while I look away.

I hold my breath.

Theo's eyes widen.

"What is it?" I question him. It can't be good.

"Oh . . ." Theo utters.

I'm scared. Surely it can't be even worse than I could have imagined. Surely. "Theo," I urge him. "What's wrong?"

"I don't think you should see this." He shakes his head and wipes one hand on his shirt. His eyes remain plastered to the screen. "Rory was . . ."

"Rory was what, Theo?" I raise my pitch and sit up. "Tell me!"

"I don't . . . " He hesitates. "No, it's nothing. It's just too much. Don't worry, Carla. I'll show you some other time."

"What are you talking about?" I say harshly as I stand up. "I'm sick of all of you treating me like a child. Stop keeping me in the dark. I deserve to know whatever's going on!"

"All right, Carla. Calm down." Theo puts a hand on my arm. "I just care about you, that's all."

I realize I'm shouting when I look over and see that Sapphire is awake. She stares at me in shock. She's never heard me raise my tone like that. I want to apologize to her, but the words won't form.

I can't take it anymore. I storm over to the sliding doors, slamming the green touchpad. The doors light up, allowing passage into the next cabin. It seems like a storage room with old bags of things from previous passengers and outdated uniforms. I wonder if this pod was stolen? Axton and the others don't seem to have the funding to buy something like this. It appeared difficult enough to find the money to organize enough autochutes for the rescue.

I find a seat on a small sofa and realize I'm holding my fists in a tight ball. I unclench them and tell myself to calm down. Suddenly I feel tired. Us centenarians tire quite easily, you know. Not a very funny joke. What I *am* tired of is the secrecy. They won't tell me everything. I don't know what is going on in this world, a century ahead of my own. They can't expect me to sit mutely and not ask questions.

I need to know what happened to Rory. At least if I know for sure he's dead—if I see the words with my own eyes, I won't have to question it anymore. I will know he is dead. And how. It hasn't hit me yet that my family isn't alive. I still picture them somewhere out there on this earth. They are there, and alive. Yet they are not, and the sooner I accept that, the better.

Then another thought dawns on me. No one I've ever known is alive anymore. I let that thought sink in. Literally everyone is gone. I can't dwell on that too long. I'll have to leave it for another time. It's not exactly a calming thought.

I wince, thinking back to my reaction earlier. Losing my temper won't get information out of people. It only shows them that I'm not ready to hear it. Which, perhaps, is correct. But I want to know. I need to know. What did Theo see in Rory's file? I need to hold a piece of him again. He's gone. And he's never coming back. I feel the tears well up. Such immense sadness. It has seeped into my very core. Longing. Plain longing. A sensation that can't be eased.

A tear slides down my cheek. I hope that I can do the right thing. For my family. I have to stay alive and strong for them.

I need to apologize to Sapphire. And Theo. I stand up slowly and wipe the smear of salty water from my face. I hope I didn't scare Sapphire too much. I press the touchpad and the sliding doors spring open. I hang my head, then remind myself to be responsible for my actions. I stand upright. Theo is now sitting on the chair beside Sapphire and whispering. I'm sure he's reassuring her that I'm not a bad person, and that I didn't mean any of it. Which I didn't, really.

I sit down beside them. I'm sure I catch Sapphire flinching, and my heart aches. "I'm sorry for yelling, Sapphire."

She doesn't look at me.

"I didn't mean it. Everything is fine."

She leans closer to Theo. Great, now I've become Carla the Child Scarer, like James P. Sullivan, the character from *Monsters, Inc.*

"Don't you get scared sometimes?" Sapphire nods. "Well, right now I'm scared, but there's no reason for you to be scared, and it also doesn't justify me yelling. Okay?"

Her large, blue eyes study mine. A hint of a smile flickers on her lips. "It's okay, Carla," she says, gently grasping my hand. "I get mad, too."

I smile at her. "Thank you."

"Especially those mean guards at the Compound. I wanted to punch them!"

She bunches her little fingers into a fist, and I stifle a laugh.

I turn to Theo. "I'm sorry."

He shrugs. "No big deal."

I don't want to pressure him, and I don't want to rock the boat any more than I already have. But I do want to know. The tension I've caused is whirling in raging torrents around us.

I decide to avoid sleeping tonight. I will not surrender myself to nightmares of my own family's deaths. Because I have to know.

"Theo," I say calmly, "I just need to see an image of my brother. To know that he's died. Then I will have to accept it."

"This is not something you want to see. I only have the one photo. You'll regret it."

"I have to face it, Theo."

Silence. He knows me. He knows I won't stop.

"Okay," is all that he says.

He brings over the tablet and swipes across the screen until he finds it again. He pauses before placing the tablet onto my thigh.

Theo was right to hesitate. It is a truly awful image.

It is immediately clear that this is a picture I will never be able to forget. A horrifying depiction of the most terrifying end to a mortal life. A tortured body. A face contorted from the most unspeakable agony of the last moments of existence.

Something else is very clear.

It's not Rory.

"I just can't, Carla!" Axton says, his tone a tangle of emotions.

"Why not?" I say quietly. "It doesn't make sense, Axton."

He shakes his head, regrouping. "We've got important things to do. You don't understand."

I shake my head, tears dripping onto my shirt.

"I'm sorry, Carla," he says. "It'll be okay. We're here for you."

"No, you're not," I say. "You don't care. You're not my family. You don't know anything about me."

"I do care, Carla . . . "

I don't hear the rest. I run out of the cabin, and don't stop until I am past the main room. I find myself in the bathroom.

I wonder if he is lying to me. Is he ever planning on taking me back? I don't understand why they won't just take me to my family! Or at least let them know I'm alive.

My brain is going wild. I can't stop the swirling thoughts. I want to be Sapphire right now—asleep in a sea of peace.

The teenage girl in the mirror does not appear calm. Her eyes are tired and discolored. Bloodshot eyes. That girl needs sleep.

I splash some water on my face and return to my seat,

contemplating the passing clouds. So many of them, all drifting as quickly out of my vision as they enter it. Just like people. So many missed opportunities. So many times I could have told Mom I loved her. Or played one more game with Rory. Or heard one more lame joke from Dad for the tenth time and pretended to find it funny.

I place my hands in my lap. There's no point thinking about it. I will see them again, just not yet. I open Axton's bag, hoping for a package of some food, but instead find the novel, *The Follower*. I shrug. I don't feel like eating, anyway. I decide to read the book. Hopefully it will provide me with some inspiration. Or at least distraction. I open the front cover and flip to the first chapter. I notice that it's in a strange font, very straight and rigid. Even after the first few pages, I can't get into it.

I suddenly wonder when it was written, since apparently it was such a huge hit. I read the bestsellers as soon as they're released, and yet I have never heard of this one. Maybe it came out while I was in a coma. What did Axton call it? Suspended animation?

I flip back a couple of pages to find the print date. The number blurs. 2119. One hundred years from now? It must be a typo. A mistake. That's actually funny. I laugh and flip forward to start reading again. But as I'm trying to read the words, my mind is whirring.

Flying ships that rise vertically like helicopter drones, yet have no propellers. Piles of dead bodies. Gleaming metal.

It's not possible.

Machines that analyze my dreams. Tiny trackers in our wrists. Horrific war images that are simply old file photos.

Surely not.

I look up at Theo. Has he really been keeping this from me? He might not know, I think, and then I laugh at myself. He certainly doesn't seem confused by anything we see or do.

I wipe my perspiring hands on my clothes, then flip through the book for more clues to confirm that the year was merely an oversight. A typo.

But the more I think about it, the more I can't let it go.

I slam the book closed and find Theo, my mind on fire. Please don't let me be in the future.

"Theo," I say. "What year is it?"

"Um," he says.

"Tell me, Theo. What is today's date?"

"Carla . . ."

"Tell me!"

He looks at me silently.

"Please tell me."

"Okay," he says, studying his fingernails. "It is September the 20$^{th}$."

I wait.

"4pm."

I wait.

"Maybe a few years ahead of what you might think . . . " He trails off.

I refuse to budge.

"Okay, okay." He closes his eyes. "It's 2121."

"Okay," I say, turning away.

"I'm sorry, Carla," he says, placing a hand lightly on my arm. "We're here for you now."

Now. As in a hundred years from now.

I was in suspended animation for a hundred years?

Hi, my name is Carla, and I'm not even from this century. I have nothing left to say. There is nothing to say. This is great.

Fabulous.

*　　*　　*

My feet decide to run before I do. I have to get away. Away from this insanity. I need to be alone.

I end up at the hull of the ship and stare out the window. This cannot be real. Theo cannot be real. I am dreaming.

199

That's it! This is just a really bad dream. Calm down, Carla. A nightmare is all it is.

*You're exhausted today, that's why you're having all these crazy dreams, I think. You're asleep in the Compound after a very long day in the mines.*

No, no. The Compound. That's fake too. Thank goodness for that. It's all in my imagination. I'm going to wake up in my nice warm bed at home, and go down to breakfast with Mom and Dad. And Rory.

Today will be an awesome day. My last day of high school. It will be loads of fun, once I wake up. That calms me. I look out the window at all the clouds flitting by. I stare at them and see all sorts of interesting animals and other shapes.

It's funny that my imagination still works in this dream. I can imagine all these clouds, and then I can imagine myself looking out a window, imagining what the clouds look like.

I stare at the clouds, willing myself to wake up. This cannot be real.

I watch the last rays of sunlight disappear as the peachy sky transforms into a navy-blue velvet sheet blanketing the globe. Pin-pricks of light begin to shine through, reminding me of my high school assignment on constellations. I wish that I at least had pictures of my family.

Eventually, the layers of understanding peel away, and I look around. I'm still awake. I'm still at the window. In a spaceship. A hundred years too late.

I'm not dreaming.

Let's think this through. So I'm basically dead. My first life died. This is my second life, and it is a very weird one so far. This is my fake life. The first one was real, this is fake. That at least makes sense.

I wonder if my first family is in the future with me. Could they be? Nope. Not judging by Axton's reluctance, or should I say refusal, to take me home.

I think about my family, back at home. A home that no longer exists, or at least not in this dimension. Maybe somewhere out there in the forever expanding universe there is a parallel world that is a century behind this one. Maybe in that universe, I am still alive and with my family.

But here, in this universe, I have nothing. There is no point in me being here. This is not my life. I died. I am dead. I lived my life; I had my chance. There is nothing here for me.

I go back to my seat. The novel is resting innocently, mocking me. I glare at it. The book smirks back at me. Infuriatingly smug. I decide to kill the mocking book.

I pick it up and tear a few pages out. *Rip.* That's better. I tear a few more. *Rip, rip.*

I want to be with my parents and my brother. But they are dead. *Rip.* They grew old without me. *Rip.* Rory probably got married. *Rip.* He might have had children. *Rip.* Such a strange thought. But not nearly as sad as knowing that I'll never get to meet them. They had to live the rest of their lives without me a part of it. Why? *Rip, rip, rip.*

I scream and throw the book down, having exhausted my ripping capacity, and stare at my feet. My mind slows down as I try not to think about anything.

It doesn't work. At all.

*    *    *

My churning mind reluctantly returns to reality to find Theo watching me.

"I can show you what happened to your family, you know," Theo whispers. The moonlight is surprisingly bright tonight, and some of the rays fall on him, illuminating his face. Maybe I'm not as alone in this new life as I thought I was.

"Really?"

He touches my hand and studies his tablet once more. His fingers fly across the screen, hacking files most people wouldn't even know existed. I look out of the window for a few minutes, trying to prepare myself for what Theo might find.

Streaks of white occasionally fly past: shooting stars. I wonder how our world appears from the point of view of a star. They live for millions of years, while few of us mortal beings make it to age ninety. They must laugh at us from up there. We have been destroying our Earth for centuries. Dumb humans. Shakespeare was right. *Lord, what fools these mortals be.* I used to read a lot of his work. In another life. I enjoyed his morals, and he can be quite the jokester. I vaguely wonder whether I'll read anything written by Shakespeare ever again. As English teachers always seem to ask, 'would Shakespeare be relevant today?' Would I still enjoy it? Maybe too much has happened since then for me to find joy in such fantasies.

A tap on the shoulder brings me back to the present.

"I've got it," Theo says, and I turn to face him. Fear suddenly overwhelms me. I don't want to know. Better to live not really knowing if they are truly dead. Better to pretend they're still out there.

I shake my head. I can't do it. So much for being strong. Theo puts a hand on my shoulder.

"You don't have to," he says softly. I shake my head again. "Don't worry about it."

Theo's right. I try not to think about the gruesome deaths that my family could have succumbed to. But the ogres in my imagination won't allow me any peace. My mind whirs with options. Gunshot wound? Heart attack? Car crash? What about Rory? I hope that he didn't have a painful death. What if he suffered for days? *Please*, I think, *let Rory have died peacefully*. But what are the chances of that in a world of war? My breathing quickens. Panic overwhelms me. How did he die? Was he alone? Were my parents there with him to hold his hand in his last moments? Was anyone?

Most importantly, it should have been me. My parents probably weren't alive for his death. I was supposed to look after him. *I* was! They told *me* to mind my brother. For me to be the one to never leave his side. They made me promise to always be his best friend. Yet here I am, a century ahead of my time.

I am sweating. Theo sits down next to me. We are both silent.

"Please. Just my brother," I whisper. "I have to know." I have to face the truth. It's better if I know for sure. I need to know.

Theo explains, "The only info I can find is from the intel database of the Organization. We have information on every person in the world."

# 24

# AXTON

They've gone quiet in the back, and the only sound I can hear is the soft whir of the engines. It's been a few hours since Carla's tantrum, but I haven't had the chance to talk to Theo about it. I did hear it, though. The whole pod heard. Half the galaxy heard.

No matter the cost, Carla needs to be in the best frame of mind possible when we get there. Theo needs to help me with that.

"Axton," a voice drifts through the door. "I have to talk to you." It's Theo.

"Speak of the devil," I mumble, taking off my headset.

"What?" Theo says.

"Nothing. I was just thinking about you," I say awkwardly.

"Right, well . . ." He opens his tablet and scrolls through some information. He holds the screen towards me.

On it is our intel summary document about someone named Rory Grayson. It has the usual facts about the individual: date of birth, town of origin, nationality. Rory. The name sounds familiar. *Has one older sister.* Carla! He's Carla's brother. I notice that it says he disappeared several months after Carla.

"Carla's brother?" I say, seeking confirmation.

"Yes."

"He was taken by the Compound, right?" I ask.

"Presumably," says Theo.

"And died a horrible death there, too." Bad, but I've seen worse.

"That's the thing," starts Theo. "It's not him."

The comment takes me by surprise. "What?"

"Carla says it's not him. The person in the photo isn't her brother."

"Oh." Now I am thinking. The intel is never wrong. Unheard of.

"I'm not sure what it means." Theo scratches his chin.

"And she's sure? After a hundred years?" I am only half joking.

"She's sure," he says, rolling his eyes. "Eye color is wrong for a start. It's not a hundred years to her."

"No, I know. So why didn't our intel group pick it up?" I ask pointedly.

"Nobody knows what he looks like. We only knew she had a brother. No early photos of her family survived. School photos were lost in the wars. And he was too young to have a softcopy record of his license. No passport. Birth certificates are only text."

"Where's the photo from then? Must be an error."

"Compound hack. Their termination database. Had a corrupted last name in the record, which is unusual, but the biological birthdate cross-matched."

"So it's their error, not ours."

"Yeah."

I can tell there's more, and I know it's going to be nerdy.

"Um, the problem is that this record showed up in the second cache, but not the first. But it should have been in the first because it happened after the date you see in the record. The recycle date. And I remember hearing from the lady on the intel team how surprised the early teams were when they got in twice through the same back door. It was a while ago. You see?"

Clear as the exhaust fumes on a pod with bad hydro.

"In English?" I demand.

"Um, it seems like the Compound record was added much later than it should have been. And they made it easy for us to find."

"Oh."

"They had a sequence of invalid bytes for the last name, so we had to correct it manually. Draws attention. And they didn't change the first name or bio-date, so it cross-matched to her brother."

"With the wrong photo."

"Yeah."

"Makes no sense," I say, pausing. "So you think it's a fake photo? Intentionally?"

"Finally," Theo says with a laugh.

I start thinking aloud. "They wanted us to find it. To think he's dead. But why use such a violent photo? Why not use an actual photo of him? They have him. Or if he's dead and they didn't take a photo, why bother putting in a fake?"

"To extinguish Carla's hope."

He looks at me. "What?"

"To extinguish her hope that her family is alive. They want to remove all emotion, and destroying hope is one sure way to do that."

He smiles with mock surprise. "You *do* say intelligent

things, sometimes. But I don't think that's the only reason."

"Yeah? Go on," I say.

"So . . . " continues Theo. "Face-recognition algorithms. Even back then they were still very good. Give us a false match to the wrong face. Throw off the algs."

"Which means they were worried his face was going to be public. Alive. In the wars. And we know what that means."

"Exactly."

"Still could be an error," I add.

"Yeah. Could be."

"And this is from decades ago, right?"

"Yeah. Several."

"So even if he was alive, anything could have happened to him since then."

"Right."

"Did you tell Carla?" I ask. I don't know whether I hope his answer is yes or no.

"Do you think I should?" he says. "If we do, it might give her some hope. Hope that could end up being futile."

"But she deserves to know," I admit. "It will make her more determined as well. Maybe more likely to help us." I shake my head.

Theo frowns. "I'm not sure about that." He switches off his tablet and leaves the cabin.

*     *     *

I study the map on the screen and realize that we are approaching the destination. I put my headset on again. I grasp the controls tightly and prepare the craft for descent.

The butterflies have kicked into action in my stomach. Not because I'm afraid of landing, but because our next stop is a visit to Mom. I'm a little nervous to see her. Part of her despises our entire plan of saving the children. She wants to help the children, but doesn't want us to risk our lives for the cause. I call that selfishness, but she calls it protecting her family.

After Dad died, my brother and I couldn't bring life back into her no matter what we did. All we wanted was our mother back, but nothing we did made her happy. Eventually, we simply accepted that it was going to take time for her will to live to be restored. In the meantime, we do everything we can to make her comfortable.

A beep from the control panel breaks my thoughts. I push the lever forwards and the craft begins its descent. "Ladies and gentlemen, fasten your seatbelts," I say into the loudspeaker. Although they won't need them. I don't mean to brag, but I'm probably the smoothest pod-lander in all of history. An unsecured egg wouldn't roll an inch.

This descent is going to be perfection.

Even knowing how experienced I am, Mom is still determined to make us quit our association with the Organization. But as much as she is against us being in danger, she recognizes that we have worked hard and would regret it if we didn't try to achieve our mission. Dad's mission. We reassure her that we will be safe, and that we won't take any unnecessary risks. If she knew what we've already been through, she would have a heart attack.

We have rescued a lot of children, but now we've split from the General. We can't go back to our old alliance with her because she isn't doing this to help the children. She wants them for herself, and that is not something I am willing to support. All we ever wanted was to help innocent children, and now we have two groups against us.

I engage the thrusters and we move directly towards the field. It's hard to miss; probably one of the few grassy fields left in this region. As long as they haven't turned it into a sheep ranch, we should be fine. I head for the center of the grass patch, and the ground approaches fast. I pull upwards slightly for the final lowering of the pod. We drift like a feather towards the earth, and the landing is, as predicted, impeccable. I mentally pat myself on the back.

Now all I have to do is steer us to the immense stand of trees on the far right of the field. They will provide cover and prevent us from being detected, at least for a while. It's not perfect, but the canopy is fairly dense.

I lean in to the microphone and announce, "Welcome to my home town." The announcement carries across the entire pod, blasting effortlessly from the tiny speakers. Dad chose this suburb because he said it'd be the last place to be bombed. Seems he may have been right. This place is in Organization territory, so it is still intact.

I exit the cabin and join the others in the main room. They seem excited. I flash them a grin. It's good to be home.

"We're here?" Sapphire asks.

"We sure are," I say.

"Wait, where is 'here' exactly?" Carla pipes up. "This is where you grew up?"

"Yeah. We're going to visit Mom."

"Okay, cool."

"We'll see how she is, eat some food and collect more equipment for the next stage of the operation."

"Sounds good to me," Carla says.

"And me," says Sapphire. "I'm starving."

"Aren't we all?" says Theo.

Only now do I notice the faint grumble in my stomach.

"Let's go." I smile at Theo. "There'll definitely be some food waiting for us."

*     *     *

We head across the grass towards home. My heart leaps as soon as it comes into view. I've missed it so much. We stop before the road. Our house is on the other side. I have a sudden thought. What if something has happened to her? I catch Theo's eye, and he gives me a grin. He seems more hopeful than I. Surely if something terrible had happened, we would have found out about it.

We arrive at the front fence.

Carla gasps. "*This* is it?" she exclaims. "It's so beautiful!" She looks up at Theo first, then me.

I shrug. "Yep," I say. "This is it."

Growing up, I never realized how picturesque it was. It was just home. Now I see that it could be a scene from a book. Perhaps the little cottage from *Hansel and Gretel*.

The fence is overrun by hundreds of pretty flowers, mainly roses. Pink and red and white. The colors of love. The flower bushes are arranged all the way around the fence on the inside, and you can follow them around in a circuit.

"These flowers are amazing! Your mother must enjoy

gardening. So pristine," Carla muses.

I smirk, holding back a laugh. Theo and I share a look. They're fake. Our father genetically engineered them.

Carla soaks up the beauty of the rose bushes.

There's plenty of grass between the flower beds and the house, but we've never had any pets. Not because our parents thought they were too messy or too much responsibility, but because Mom believed it was cruel to keep them like that. I think I agree. Those children in the Compound seemed like trapped animals. There was so much grief in their eyes. I tear my thoughts away from the Compound and open the little gate.

We follow the path to the front door. I knock softly. There is some rustling and shuffling of feet, and finally, the knob turns and the door swings open. The first thing I notice is Mom's familiar, bright red jacket. The second is her beaming smile, which appears the instant she sees us.

"My boys!" she cries with joy.

Theo and I say "Mom!" in synchronization.

She hugs both of us tight for a long time. She checks us up and down, as she always did after school, to search for any bumps and bruises. Sure, we look a little worse for wear, but she seems satisfied. Thankfully, she can't see the shrapnel burns on my back.

Only then does she turn her attention to the girls, who step forward.

"Mom, this is Carla and Sapphire. They're from the Compound."

"It's so nice to meet you. We've heard a lot about you," Carla says.

I can't help but notice the sadness in her face. Sapphire is motionless. Mom gives each of them a warm hug.

"Please, call me Saskia," she says. I hold the door open for everyone and we enter. "Take a seat."

My favorite plush green sofas await us in the living room, and I dive into them. I missed their softness. They never seem to end, molding to every contour of the body. Everyone collapses with me, luxuriating in the richness.

"Can I get you something?" Mom asks, standing beside the sofa. "Electrolytes? Water?"

"Sure, Mom," I say, standing up. "I'll get it."

I head to the kitchen and take out four glasses and an equal number of electrolyte sticks. I hand them out, licking my own and placing it aside.

Carla stares at me blankly. "What is this for?" she says, holding up her stick.

"Just lick it," I say.

She does, frowning, and I take the stick back off her. I place it in a slot in the drinks machine.

"What does that do?" she asks.

"It measures your salt content and calculates the perfect solution of electrolytes for you. Watch."

I place a glass under the opening and liquid streams out of the machine. A few splashes shoot out onto the ground, but the floor absorbs it immediately.

"What on earth?" Carla says, staring between me and the ground. "Did it just . . . "

"Nearly everything here is spill and dust resistant," I explain.

She shakes her head incredulously.

I hand her the drink, and she sniffs it. Sapphire giggles.

Carla takes a sip. "Not bad."

I make drinks for the others and carry them to the coffee table. The drinks are gone in no time.

"More?" I say, and Sapphire accepts eagerly.

I think we're all grateful that we don't have to rely on water from the limited supplies I had with me. At least now we can quench our thirst properly.

I refill all of the cups and we drink those as well. Mom pulls some gourmet chicken risotto sachets from the cupboard. I tell her I'll cook.

"Where will I find the plates?" Carla's words startle me.

"Uh," I say. She's trying to be helpful. "We don't have plates."

She frowns. I hold up the sachets.

"Wait and see," I tease.

I put them in the Thermo-blast, and Carla gasps at what comes out. Five perfect silver bowls of delectable risotto. I explain that the bottom of the sachet turns into a bowl-shape.

"Wow," she says, and I chuckle.

She helps me carry them to the dining table that Mom has already set.

"Dinner is served," Carla announces, and we sit down at the table.

Sapphire's eyes widen. "A whole sachet?" she says. "I can't fit this much in my belly!"

Theo laughs. "I don't think it will be a challenge."

She grins and digs her spoon into the steaming dish.

"Do you like it?" Mom says.

"This is," Sapphire puts her spoon down momentarily, "the best food ever!"

Mom beams. "That's what I like to hear."

Sapphire doesn't waste another second talking. We laugh as she shovels the risotto in, barely breathing between bites. In a few minutes, she's wiped her bowl clean. She leans back in her chair.

"Yummy," she says. "Thank you, Saskia."

"You're most welcome," Mom says. She turns to me.

"So how long do you think you've got here?"

"We can't stay for long," I answer. "We'll have to keep moving."

She knows we are on the run. We are back too early; if all had gone well, we'd still be with the General. Theo tells her a little about how the General has betrayed us.

She knows what that means. They will start hunting us. And they won't take long to find out where Theo and I live. They'll find this house, and they'll find her too. Maybe interrogate her. That's why it's important that we don't tell her where we are going.

"Well, I'm just glad to have my boys home at last," she says ruefully. "Would anyone like dessert?"

Carla groans. "That was absolutely delicious," she says. "But I can't fit in another bite."

And in true Mom fashion, she says, "Of course you can. Just a small slice of chocolate cake, surely." She carries in a stunning cake, its decadent aroma teasing our taste buds.

Sapphire pipes up, "I can. My dessert stomach is so empty." We all agree.

Carla asks, "Did you bake it?"

Mom laughs. "No, no. It comes in a sachet. I wouldn't know where to start." She serves the cake and we dive in. "I'm so glad you're back and safe. You have no idea how worried I've been."

I nod, but we are far from safe. We must head off in the morning.

Mom continues, "You should all go to sleep soon. I'm sure you're tired."

Sapphire gasps.

"What is it?" Carla says. "Are you all right?" She doesn't respond. "Sapphire?"

"Oh my gosh, oh my gosh, oh my gosh!" Sapphire exclaims with joy.

"What?" Carla asks. Sapphire points to the living room.

There's a flash of blue as Sapphire sprints past us.

"Cartoons!" She shouts. "I can watch the Animator."

We burst out laughing. I can hear Carla asking Mom what an Animator is, and Mom laughing.

I collect the bowls and cutlery and take them to the kitchen. Mom gives me a grateful glance.

Carla follows Sapphire into the living room and stares at the screen on the wall. I watch Sapphire's face light up when her favorite show comes on. I think it's about fairies.

"TV!" Carla says, laughing. "It's just a cool TV. Only it seems so real. Such depth!" She joins Mom for a chat.

Carla and Mom are discussing how beautiful the house is. Mom is smiling. Carla has made her happy again, if briefly. Something we haven't been able to do for a long time. It makes my heart leap.

With Sapphire occupied, it's the perfect time to discuss tactics for the next leg of our journey. But I can't bring myself to interrupt, so I sit on one of the kitchen bar stools.

Theo is relaxing on the sofa next to Sapphire, laughing at something she said.

I want to pause this moment, right here. Sapphire giggling with Theo on the sofa; Mom and Carla chatting and laughing. I would have bet money that Mom would never laugh again. But Carla, because she's so full of life and kindness, has made her do it.

*　　*　　*

I'm still smiling when Carla enters the kitchen area.

"Why are you so happy?" she says.

"No reason," I say. "Just glad everyone's safe."

"Yeah, me too." She pauses for a moment. "Have you lived here your whole life?"

"Pretty much," I say. "We moved right before Theo was born. When I was two years old."

"Can I see your room?" she says excitedly.

I frown. "Sure. But it's not very interesting."

I show her to my bedroom. "Ta da," I say flatly.

She looks around. It's a fairly small room. I was always sure as a kid that Theo's room was bigger than mine, but Mom and Dad assured us they were the same size. One day I got the tape measure out, and turns out my parents are liars.

There isn't much in my room apart from my bed and a bookshelf. I used to have a collection of soccer balls, which took up a lot of space, but they've mostly disappeared. You could probably find a few in the neighbor's yard. We were way too terrified to retrieve anything that went over that fence.

I went next door once to deliver the next door neighbor a piece of cake on my birthday. She said she didn't like me or cake.

At least, that's how I remember it. Anyway, the point is that the soccer balls are gone, and they aren't coming back.

"Cute," she says, amused.

She's looking at my comforter—it's blue with stars and a small rocket in the corner. I always wanted to change it, but never got around to it.

I growl.

"Don't worry," she says. "I had a unicorn bed cover for *ages*."

I laugh. "I bet you still do. And you still *like* it." I hesitate. "I mean . . . you still did a century ago," I say awkwardly.

"Ha ha. Very funny." She blushes. "Well, whatever. It was nice and comforting. And it had beautiful colors."

"I knew it,' I say, bursting out laughing. "Do you want to see Theo's room?"

"Sure," she says, still glaring at me. I let out another chuckle.

Theo's room is directly opposite mine. His shelves are filled with gadgets and gizmos. You can tell immediately that he's a science whiz.

Carla runs her fingers over the Einstein and Rutherford posters.

"He's got a few periodic table T-shirts as well," I say.

She laughs, pulling one of the metal spheres back on the small Newton's cradle toy on Theo's bedside table. It clicks away for a while, the spheres swinging hypnotically. I remember Theo once trying to explain to me how it worked. Something about a transfer of energy.

Seeing our rooms again makes me realize how much I have changed since I was here last. I was so innocent then. I remember when Dad first told me about the Compound and their army. I liked hearing about the battles. It wasn't that long ago, but it seems like decades.

He also told me about the tiger's eye mines, but he wasn't sure what the gemstones were being used for. Even then, its special properties were well-known: concentration enhancement, sharper senses, and emotional control. But it was still just a gemstone back then. Dad bought some cut stones and tried to analyze them in the shed, which of course made Theo do some in-depth research into the chemistry of tiger's eye and silicone dioxide.

One day, Dad showed me pictures of people dying— probably similar to the ones Carla saw on Theo's tablet. I was horrified that these things were happening. In my mind, stuff like that just didn't happen.

Before I got into my Dad's project, I was selfish. My biggest problem was trying to pass math. I remember how bad I felt that Theo was so intelligent, while I was struggling to get C's. But what could I do? I was never the smart one. It didn't matter what I did; I simply couldn't enjoy the academic subjects. I like hands-on stuff. That's why I enjoyed the training so much. My muscles turned out to be useful for something other than impressing girls and football, after all.

Then we decided to join the Organization. Theo and I were the youngest by a long shot. They only accepted us because it was Dad who founded it.

I turn and realize that Carla is lying on the bed, gazing up at the ceiling. I see the glow-in-the-dark stars and planets that Theo spent hours attaching while perched precariously on the top of a ladder.

"I forgot those were there," I say.

"They're nice," she says softly. Just then, Theo walks in.

"What are you guys doing?" he says, mock-harshly.

Carla smiles. "Nothing. Checking out your room."

He glares at me. I was banned from his room for many years. I may have broken a few things, but it was always an accident. Ish. Oh well. Not the point.

"We should discuss plans for the next few days," I say, and Theo shifts on his feet. "Obviously, they're going to come looking for us. They want Carla."

Carla sits up abruptly. "Let me go. By myself. You don't owe me anything."

"No, Carla," I say, sitting on the bed. "We can't do that."

"Why not?" Carla demands. "You've already helped me enough."

"Carla..." I say.

"I'll go, and you guys can spend some time with your mom. She deserves that, at the very least!"

"Carla, we can't let you." I shrug my shoulders. "Think about how much time we've invested in saving you, and now you want to run off and get yourself killed? I know you, Carla. You want to turn yourself in. Just to help the children."

I know she would, too. That's why we have to go with her.

Carla frowns and then lies back down on the bed. "Fine. Maybe I was thinking about it."

"Carla, you can't do that. You won't know what to do. We're quite sure the children won't know either. It would be a total disaster. I say one of us goes with you, and the other stays with Mom and Sapphire."

Theo nods. "I've done some more research on Sapphire, and the records say her immediate family is still alive."

"Really?" Carla says. "That's great!"

"Good. We can take her back," I say. "She needs to be with her family."

I hope she's not too traumatized by her experiences in the Compound. I wonder how all of the other rescued children are coping. They seemed to be doing okay in the dorms at the army base, but there's no mother figure to give them the love and comfort that all children need.

"We are going out tomorrow to gather some intelligence," I say. "Who's going to stay with Sapphire?"

Theo shifts his feet. I know he doesn't want to stay. He wants to protect Carla, too.

Carla stands up to face me. "Look, Axton. Whether you like it or not, that's not how it's going to work. You won't let me go alone, so everyone is coming. It's either just me or all of us. We take Sapphire home, where she belongs, and then we keep moving and try to come up with a plan to get the rest of the children out. I won't stop until we save them all. I won't let any more innocent children die in the mines. I can't." She pauses. "I'm not saying I'll give myself up to the General, but I will find a way to do what needs doing."

"And what about Mom?" Theo says softly. "She's going to be under suspicion. They are going to interrogate her."

Carla says, "Okay, I don't have a solution to that," she admits. "Unless she comes with us."

"Don't be ridiculous," I say. But then I think about it. Perhaps it isn't such a bad idea. If she did come with us, at least she would be safe. Definitely safer than here, anyway.

"We could leave her with Sapphire," Theo says slowly. "They don't have intel on Sapphire, because she's too young to be considered of interest."

"Okay," I say. "I think that could work. It's probably the best option we've got at this point."

In theory, that's sorted, but we haven't actually asked Mom if she agrees.

We try to come up with a plan to extract the children from both the Compound and the Organization's military base, but it seems too big of a task right now. I know soldiers aren't supposed to feel tired, but I do. And it's not just me. Eventually, we decide our efforts are futile, and we should get some sleep and work it out in the morning.

Mom helps Carla and Sapphire rinse their teeth with Crest-Restore to fill in any cavities or imperfections created during their incarceration at the Compound. They both borrow some of Mom's clothes to sleep in. We can hear Sapphire's squeals of laughter, which we find out is a reaction to Carla's astonishment at the body-conforming clothes.

I take a scorching hot shower, and it's amazing. Theo and I both sleep in our usual rooms, which feels strange. Only when I lay my head on my pillow do I acknowledge how tired I am. I have barely slept in two and a half days.

Sapphire and Carla sleep in the small spare bedroom. I hope they sleep well, and enjoy their first real bed in a long time.

A century in fact, in Carla's case.

"Axton," I hear Carla shout. "How do I turn the lights off?" The lights in her room go instantly out. There's a pause.

"How did you do that?" she calls out.

"I didn't do anything." I smirk. It's such a primitive robot control. Doesn't even detect sentence structure, just words. Simple voice-activation. It will also switch off if her eyes are closed for more than five minutes.

"Go to sleep, Carla."

She laughs. "Man, that's cool."

I smile. It's hilarious that she's impressed by it.

"Goodnight, Axton. Goodnight, Theo."

"Goodnight, sweet Carla," I whisper to myself.

Sweet, innocent, deadly Carla.

# 25

---

# CARLA

"Don't move, or I'll shoot," shouts the guard. His gravelly voice echoes down the hall. The gun is pressed against my temple. I am going to die. He'll pull the trigger any moment now. I do not want to die. I can't die. I spin around and smack his hand as hard as I can. It has no effect. I am moving through molasses. I try to hit him again, but I can't make my arm move fast enough.

I shout at Theo to do something, but he can't or won't. He's simply standing there. Why won't he do anything? The guard has me in a headlock now. I can feel the gun's barrel against my spine. Bang! The gun fires. My back is ripped open. Searing pain.

I am dead.

I float along in a body that is not my own. Suddenly I am in a room. My brother, mother and father stand in a line before me. A figure enters the room. I can't make out who it is. I see the boots. He has a gun. Bang! Bang! Bang!

Three shots and my family falls to the ground.

"No!" I scream. My shrill cry fills the room. In the mirror I see myself screaming. I continue to scream as loud as I can. My throat aches. I can't stop. Emotion has taken over. I scream for eternity. For my family.

Strong hands grasp my shoulders, shaking gently.

I open my eyes and the last scream escapes my lips.

Oh, it was a dream. It replays in my head.

I am shaking. Sweat envelops my body. I feel like I've been swimming in a sauna. I am panting hard. The dream flashes over and over. I can see the gun. Then my face. Then the Commander's angular face. I wish they would leave me alone. Why won't the thoughts leave me alone?

"Carla, it's okay." I realize that Axton is patting my back gently. "You're okay, Carla."

I shake my head. I am not okay. My family is dead. I will soon be dead. I don't belong in this world.

"I want to go home!" I shriek. "But I can't, because

my family is dead. Everyone is dead. My life back there is *dead.*" I begin to sob. I know there's no point in crying, but I do so anyway.

Axton picks me up, carries me to the living room and lowers me gently onto the sofa. I cry for my family. I cry for my bedroom in my old home. And I cry because I don't belong in this strange world.

Axton turns on the Animator, and we watch some show about a murder mystery. The screen has extreme clarity and realism; it could all be happening right in front of us. But I don't pay much attention to it.

I'm too busy trying to remember the good times at home. I think about my best friend from high school, and how I'll never see her again. All those plans of getting married and living next door to each other are out the window. We would joke about naming our children after each other. Not the exact names, but something similar. We spent forever picking out the perfect house. And selecting ridiculous outfits for each other at the mall.

I think about the times we couldn't fall sleep on sleepovers. We would announce that we were going to sleep, and there would be silence for a maximum of thirty seconds before someone burst out laughing. So, of course, we would stay up until three o'clock in the morning every time, before I would finally freak out and say that I *really* needed to get some sleep. And somehow, miraculously, neither of us would be tired in the morning.

We were in our last year of senior high, almost free from the shackles of school. I was ready for college. I was going to change the world. And then they took me. I lost the rest of my first life before it really began.

My friends would have been devastated. The school probably had a memorial for me and everything. Imagine if they found out that I would still be alive a hundred years later. My history teacher would have been seriously impressed. He might have given me an A.

*　　*　　*

"You enjoying this?" Axton asks, nodding towards the Animator.

It has changed to a cooking show. I used to like them, but this show is nowhere near as good as the ones I used to watch. All of the cooking appliances seem to have become so advanced that the chefs barely need any skill.

"Nah," I say. "You can change it."

He flicks through the channels with a motion of his hand.

"You don't have to stay up with me, you know," I say. "I'm fine."

He shifts in his seat. "I want to."

"Aren't you tired?" I say.

"No," Axton says, yawning. I laugh. He shrugs. "Sleep is for the lazy."

"What's the time, anyway?" I ask.

"Twelve thirty-one." The robotic female voice startles me. Axton laughs.

"How do you possibly live in this house with that robot butting in all the time?" I ponder.

Axton grins. "You learn not to say the things that trigger it," he says, matter-of-factly. "Unless you actually want to darken the room."

The room darkens and I giggle.

"She can do lots of things. She's one talented lady." He pauses. "Hmmm. Come on. I'll show you."

"Okay."

"Quick, lie on the rug and look up," he says, and I do. He dives next to me. He watches me out of the corner of his eye and says loudly, "Stargaze."

Suddenly the white ceiling ripples and transforms into darkness. Black. The ceiling is not the ceiling anymore. It is as if someone has completely removed the roof. As my eyes adjust, I can make out sparkling silver dots. We can see the stars. Why would Theo bother putting up stars on the ceiling in his room when you can see *this*?

"It's beautiful," I whisper. We stare in silence. Even though I know they aren't real, it feels like they are. I even recognize a few of the constellations.

Suddenly I tense.

"Axton," I say carefully. "Are these constellations the same ones we would actually see outside?"

"Yeah," says Axton. "Cool, isn't it?"

"So, where are we? Right now."

"Uh . . ."

"I know these stars," I continue. "This is the southern night sky. Not California. Not anywhere in America."

Axton is silent.

"Are we in South America? Did we fly south? Is the base in Chile or Brazil or somewhere?"

A long pause. Finally, he says, "Antarctica."

I laugh.

"Yeah, right. Like roses grow on the frozen tundra."

"No, really, Antarctica. The South Pole," he states without humor. "We're in Organization territory in Antarctica."

I am taken aback.

"It's the only continental land mass not mostly under water." It sounds like he's reciting something he's learned at school. "The frozen tundra was actually covering elevated land."

"Okay . . ."

"And it was one of the only places still habitable without the need for major cooling appliances," he adds. "California is way too close to the Equator."

"But . . . how?"

"Global warming. The heat melted all the ice, and the oceans rose. The Arctic disappeared. Antarctica unfroze."

"But it's always so hot here," I protest.

He laughs. "Not hot. The poles are just tropical now."

"And . . . trees . . . "

"Yeah. Trees."

"Wow! How fast did that happen?"

"Only took a few decades," he says. "The soil unfroze and seeds blew in on the wind. They grew super quickly from excess carbon dioxide. Trees flourished. Whole forests sprang up. Fast. Took over everything."

I lie back down and view the sky with new eyes.

"I didn't even know that was possible."

"Few people did. The climate got worse and worse. Then the wars. Then the oceans rose and flooding along the coasts got really bad. Then one minute, someone in the government was like: 'Oh. Time to move to Antarctica.'" He pauses. "Anyway, all of that was before I was born."

"So, my house is . . . "

"Underwater probably," he says, matter-of-factly. "It was near the coast, right?"

I am silent for a long time.

*   *   *

After an eternity, Axton says, "I probably should go to sleep. Big day tomorrow."

He seems to understand that I am beyond speaking right now. Long after Axton has left the room, I continue to gaze at the stars. I'm not really watching them. My mind is spinning.

*Please,* I beg the stars. *I will do anything. Please bring back my family.*

The stars callously ignore me.

If only I could go back to that day. If only I hated the bus as much as Rory did. If only the stars would let me rewind back a hundred years. Back to when I had a life. When I had a family. But the stars heartlessly continue their inertia.

I'm not too sure what tomorrow's adventures will entail, but I'm sure they'll be interesting. Understatement of the century. My century. If I'm basing expectations on the past few days, there's no telling what could happen.

Eventually, I go back to the bedroom, but it is impossible

for me to sleep. How can I, when I am in a world that is not my own? Besides, I don't want to have nightmares again. If I stay awake, maybe Rory is still alive. The instant I close my eyes, the images of my family dying will spring back. It is pointless trying to escape them.

If I never go to sleep, maybe I can imagine that everything is normal again.

*　　*　　*

"Lights on," I say as I wake, stretching my arms out over my head.

I glance over to the other side of the bed. Sapphire is gone. I bet she's watching TV. I mean, the Animator. Last night, she mentioned a show about talking chameleons that she found on the cloud repository.

I change into a new set of clothes that Saskia laid out: a sleek red shirt and satin pants. They're not my style, but they sure beat the Organization's hospital wear. Besides, they fit my body perfectly. I am still somewhat freaked out that when I put clothes on, they reshape to my body. Some type of special fabric, Sapphire told me. She used to wear it a lot.

I go out into the living area, and Sapphire is watching her talking chameleons.

242

"Good morning, Sapphire," I say, and she mumbles a greeting in return. "What is the time?" I say to no one in particular. I hope the magical robot responds. Otherwise, I'm going to look dumb.

On cue, she chirps, "Good morning. The current time is six forty-eight a.m."

I didn't get much sleep.

I drift into the dining room where Axton, Theo and Saskia are huddled around the table, talking in hushed tones. Saskia gives me a huge hug and wishes me a good morning.

"You look lovely," she says.

No doubt I'm much more fashionable than yesterday. Cleaner, too.

"I was just making some pancakes," says Saskia.

"Wow, pancakes! You didn't have to do that, Saskia." I feel guilty that I didn't help make the batter. That is, until I realize that it probably came out of a sachet.

"I enjoy keeping your bellies full," she says.

I beam.

Saskia shows me how they make pancakes in the modern world. We stand in front of a special gadget, roughly the size of a toaster with a small hole in the top. She holds up a small cream-colored marble with brown, white and red streaks zigzagging through it.

"What's that for?" I ask.

She smiles. "Just watch."

She places the marble into the machine through the opening, and holds a silver plate beneath it. Within a few moments, three perfectly formed pancakes drop onto it, followed by chocolate sprinkles, whipped cream and strawberries.

At first, I can't form words. I swallow. "How did that . . ." I say, pointing to one of the other small marbles in a container beside the machine, " . . . become *that*?"

Saskia laughs. "It just rehydrates the beads," she says.

I make several more pancakes before Axton interrupts my experimentation.

"We were just discussing our plans from here," he says. "It's not safe for Mom to stay, but she refuses to come in the pod." He frowns. "So she's going to hang out at a friend's house nearby for a while, until it's safe again.

"Then you, Theo, and I will visit a site that the Compound's army has recently attacked. We need to gather information about their strength and numbers. But I warn you, it won't be easy."

We finish all of the pancakes. I thank Saskia profusely afterwards and tell her it's one of the most delicious meals that I've ever eaten. Because it is. I have never felt so satisfied and refreshed after eating breakfast.

Axton suggests that we get some supplies from his father's shed, but he doesn't say it in front of Saskia. He knows it would sadden her to be reminded of her husband.

I know what it's like to lose someone.

*    *    *

As we walk outside, Axton tells me that the shed was truly his father's special place. He did a lot of his work in the little shed. I feel like I'm invading his privacy by entering.

Axton pauses, surveying his father's belongings. He must miss him so much. There is a table and chair stacked with papers, but not in a messy way. More like purposeful randomness. There are a couple of bookshelves filled with books and maps and all sorts of things.

We head to the back of the shed, where there are some big boxes. They are all labelled neatly. A lot of it is long-life food and water bottles, and we stuff our backpacks. Axton says to bring as much as we can so we can be self-reliant.

Axton selects the guns. I am frightened by them. I don't want to put one in my pack. He laughs at me, but what if it fires while it's in my bag? Or what if I try to use it and hurt myself? Or worse, one of my friends? I don't want to have a gun, and I don't want to have to use it. But I guess, if I have to, I will.

Axton hands me a small silver gun that he calls an electrogun. Rory would have loved it. He was into army stuff. Axton says it doesn't fire easily, and reassures me that it can't go off randomly.

"Is the safety on?" I ask. I've watched TV. Axton smirks and give me the thumbs up, and I reluctantly put it in my bag.

Axton also has a small bag for Sapphire, which he fills with food and water. She shouldn't need it though; she'll be home soon. He picks up a few maps as well, even though he has digital ones.

"Just in case," he says.

I agree; you can never fully trust technology. Apparently not even now.

We close the shed doors and go back to the house.

"Where are you going?" Sapphire asks, taking in our loaded bags. She seems about to cry. "I'm coming with you."

She crosses her arms.

"Yes," I say. "You are coming with us."

"Really?" she says. "Yay! You guys can't ever leave me, okay?"

I want to reassure her that we will always stay together,

but that is not a promise we can keep. I nod, but she doesn't know that we will have to leave her very soon.

Saskia comes out with a packed bag. She has filled it with her prized possessions, and a lot of clothes.

"Ready everyone?" she says cheerfully. But I can see the sadness in her eyes. Now even her own home isn't safe.

"Yes!" Sapphire says. "Are you coming too?"

"No, I'll be at my friend's house," says Saskia.

Sapphire hugs her sadly. I think Saskia's the closest thing we've had to a mother in a long time.

We eat lunch, and check one last time that we have all of the supplies we need. We go outside, and I turn back to gaze at the house. I've realized that, a hundred years on from my time, people have reverted back to a style from before my time. Nostalgia in a world gone mad. People were craving the sleek, newest style in my era, and now they're building eighteenth century cottages.

Go figure.

*　　*　　*

We walk silently through the lifeless streets. Abandoned cars dot the roads, but there is not a soul to be seen. Decrepit houses show no sign of movement.

Sapphire is still in the pod. Axton said the people we're trying to find shouldn't see her. I guess it's not safe for children.

Theo and Axton crunch their boots over broken glass from shattered windows. We trudge for what seems like hours, and see nothing but a cat. I want to help it, but the poor thing is scared out of its brain. It doesn't stick around for more than two seconds.

Ten houses down, we hear a noise. A small, scuffling sound. Theo and Axton look at each other and then at me. The sound is coming from one of the houses on the right. Theo puts his fingers to his lips as we approach the building. There is no need. Axton and I are already completely silent.

We stop before the entrance. *Scuffle, scuffle.* Someone, or something, is just inside the door. My heart is beating fast. Who knows what we will find?

Axton tries the handle, but the door is locked. He pushes with his entire body weight against it. The door doesn't budge. Then he shoulder-charges the door. In a flash, he tumbles through the doorway and disappears from sight.

Whatever is in there, Axton is now at the mercy of it.

I rush in, and Theo follows close behind. My pulse is racing.

Axton is fine. He's already on his feet contemplating what he's found. It's a person, but you wouldn't recognize him as such at first. So thin and withered. He's wearing layers of old, stained clothing that seem to have belonged to lots of different people. I check his hands quickly for weapons, but the only thing he's holding is a plush toy that's seen better days.

He was clearly rummaging around for food remnants in the kitchen. Now he is cowering. Too terrified to do anything. He simply stares, eyeballing each of us in turn. He seems to think we are the enemy. I guess his reasoning is sound—why else would we come here looking for people unless we were blood-thirsty guards?

He moves unexpectedly. I catch a gleam of metal in his hand and then his wiry arm is around my neck, holding me in a headlock. The blade of a knife presses into the skin of my throat. My heart races.

"Don't move, or she's dead," the man says hoarsely. He squeezes a little tighter, restricting my breathing. I'm going to die. I can't take a breath.

"She can't breathe," Axton says. "Let go of her!"

The man only tightens his grip. My vision blurs, and I try hard to draw a breath, but he is squeezing too hard. Like a python twisting around my neck, tightening with every coil.

I am beginning to feel faint from lack of oxygen. Can't breathe. Will die. Please.

Suddenly something happens. The blood boils in my veins. I will *breathe*! I grab his arm and twist, slamming his body into the wall in one smooth motion.

"That works . . ." I hear Theo mutter with some surprise.

I take a deep breath. Then I study my arms. Did I do that? Well, he is an old man. But that move. Right out of an action movie! How did I do that?

Theo leans over the man, who seems to be okay, if a little stunned. The man turns to face me.

"You're one of *them*," he growls. "The *monsters*." He spits, snarling at us. "From the Compound."

Everyone is motionless until I speak. "Yes, I'm from the Compound, but I'm not a monster. And I'm not your enemy."

"Don't lie to me! You are evil. Destroying everything: our homes, our towns, our lives . . ." He slumps down on the ground in exhaustion.

"That's not us," says Theo flatly.

"We promise we aren't here to hurt you," says Axton.

He scoffs. "She tried to kill me."

"It was self-defense!" Theo exclaims. "You were holding a knife to her neck. What did you expect her to do?

*Let* you drain the life out of her?"

The man shakes his head. "If you don't want to kill us, then what do you want?" Speaking seems to pain him.

"We want answers," Axton says. "About the army. Their deployments, their numbers, their capabilities."

The man is listening doubtfully, but Axton continues. "We are going to stop the production of those robots. So that they can never hurt anyone again. But we need your help."

"Axton . . . " says Theo in a warning tone, but he trails off, his alarmed gaze flitting from the old man to me.

I can tell the man doesn't believe us. I wouldn't expect him to, either. I mean, *robots*?

I ignore this nonsense for the moment and decide to try something. I rummage through my pockets. Theo and Axton watch me curiously, silently warning me not to do anything silly. I pluck out an energy bar that Saskia gave me. Sharing food is the universal symbol of friendship.

The man watches, breathing heavily like a caught rat. His muscles taut, prepared to spring away. He knows the only way out is the front door, and we are blocking it

I unwrap the bar slowly. The man follows every movement. And furtively watches Theo. And Axton.

I hold out the food bar. "Here," I say. "We aren't here to hurt you."

His hand comes forward. Closer. Tentatively, he takes the bar. Slowly, he brings it to his nose. Sniffs it. A pained expression appears on his face.

The man sniffs the food again. Then it is gone. Not in his mouth. Not eaten. In a flash, he's stashed it in his pocket. And it's clear he wants to run again.

"Aren't you going to eat it?" I ask gently. "You must be hungry."

"No," the man says, his voice rasping.

"I can see that you're hungry," I say gently. "You can eat it. It's good food."

"Yes."

"So why don't you?"

"Later," says the man gruffly.

"You can trust us. It's not poison. You can eat it."

"No," he insists.

"Why not?" asks Axton.

The man just shakes his head.

I'm confused. "If you're hungry, then why not eat it?"

That distressed expression comes over his face again. He doesn't say anything. He doesn't need to. I suddenly understand. It is written all over his emaciated face. He is hungry beyond all hunger, yet he doesn't eat. Because others are hungrier.

His family? His children? He is so starving that he

can taste the food merely by sniffing it. Every codicil of his animal instinct is telling him to eat it. And yet his humanity will not allow it. Others will eat. He will not let his animal selfishness overrule his moral code.

I take another bar out of my pocket and hold it out to him.

"You can eat that one. I've got plenty more for your family. Can you take us to them?" I say.

He snatches the second bar. In an instant, he has devoured it. He moans as the nutritious goodness enters his body. He can't even stop himself. He finds the other bar and gulps it as well. Then he rubs his stomach guiltily. I wonder how long it's been since he ate.

"What's your name?" I ask.

"Winton," he says softly.

"Well, it's very nice to meet you, Winton. And I apologize if we got off on the wrong foot."

He even attempts a smile.

I hold my hand out.

"My name's Carla," I say. "This is Axton and Theo, and we are here to help you and your family."

"Carla," he repeats. He looks at my outstretched hand. After a long pause, he takes it and shakes it. I expect his hand to be weak, but it is firm and strong.

"Will you take us to your family?" I ask.

He knows it is a huge risk; we could be spies or traitors or bad guys. But I hope he will trust us. I remove a few more bars from my pockets to show him. I can practically see the cogs turning in his brain.

"Fine," he says gruffly. He picks up the items from the kitchen that he has collected and exits through the front door.

*　　*　　*

We follow him along the streets, going back the way we first came in. We reach a small building that is almost completely demolished. It's one of the ruins we walked past without even a thought of peering inside. We couldn't imagine anyone living there.

Instead of entering the house, he goes around to the back. There is what appears to be the entrance to some kind of underground bunker; maybe used for protection during hurricanes or tornadoes. We follow him in. The small room opens out into a bigger one, and we go even further underground, into the depths of a tunnel. I realize that we are on his home turf now, and he has the power. Soon, we are in complete darkness. I can't see a thing. Somehow Winton can, and he powers on without hesitation. He grabs my hand and puts it on his jacket sleeve, and

Axton holds onto me, followed by Theo. Eventually, we reach dim light, and I let go. The passageway that we were walking through opens out to a huge underground cavern.

The first things I see are blankets and piles of cloth. They are scattered over the entire floor. Beds. I shudder to recall the hessian bags at the Compound. And then I realize there are people inside most of the blankets. There must be about sixty in this one area.

"Do not be afraid," Winton announces loudly. His tone is commanding and fills the cavern. Some people sit up at the sound of his words. Most remain lying down. They are so hungry that they can barely move. The sight is sickening. "These people are here to help us."

I suddenly feel very guilty. We don't have nearly enough food to feed all of these bellies. What if they go all rage on us? Like Winton did in the beginning.

"Oh yeah?" one woman yells out, her two small children clinging to her sides. "How would you know? Now that you've brought them here, you've risked all of our lives, Winton."

I decide that now is the time to bring out the energy bars.

"Please," I say loudly, "take these."

I hold them out—as many as I can. A pitiful mass rises and walks towards us.

"Wait," Winton commands. Everyone stops. He doesn't want people to swarm around the food. He wants it to be fair for all of them.

"One bar between two, and that is all," he says. They approach us. Only skin and bone. Even the children are scrawny and sickly-looking. I don't want to know how long they've been here.

They come in twos, and take a bar to share. Some people disobey Winton and try to take a bar all for themselves. He notices immediately, and harshly makes them return it. I feel terrible that we didn't bring more food. Searching around, the sole remnants of food I see are tiny piles of bones that I can only assume were once rats. Even in the Compound we weren't that hungry. I shudder at the thought. People pass by, picking up the bars, expressing their gratitude.

One small girl is holding a toy rabbit.

"That's a cute bunny," I say softly to her. She shies away from my words as her tentative hand reaches out for a bar.

"Thank you," she says. Her voice is so tiny.

I want to pick her up and hug her and tell her that everything is going to be all right. And it will be. I'll make sure of it.

Then she says, "His name is Pinky."

I look at the rabbit, and I can almost make out that it used to be pink. Maybe.

She smiles shyly before turning away.

When all of the bars are gone, most people recede to their blankets. Their little sanctuaries. I notice that few of the adults are eating, only their children. It makes me feel worse.

A couple of adults linger, hoping for some more food. Their gaze flits quickly between us, searching. I shake my head, explaining that we have nothing more.

Winton shoos them away with a flick of his wrist and guides us back outside.

*　　*　　*

I blink a few times to adjust to the harsh light as we emerge.

"We are very grateful for the food," Winton says softly.

I shake my head. "It wasn't nearly enough."

He shrugs. "It was something to feed the children at least."

Axton speaks more formally. "We are going to help you as much as we can. Our goal is to stop the entire production of robots. But we do need more information . . ."

Robots? Again. What is this all about?

"I will tell you as much as I know," Winton agrees.

I glance at Axton and he simply shrugs. He's hoping we might be about to receive the answers we need.

Winton scratches his head. "In the beginning, they weren't strong at all; much weaker than an adult and very small, every one of them. We could easily hold them off. They couldn't speak, that I know of, and they were scared. They didn't want to die, and refused to risk their lives for whatever battle they were meant to be supporting. None of us knew what they were here to do, because they were never strong enough to finish their missions."

He's talking about machines. Robots. The industrial robots.

He continues. "Every few months, a new batch would come, each stronger than the last. Then suddenly they didn't want to fight us; they wanted to demolish us. They wanted to take over our towns. Soon they began to arrive every month without fail, and after some time they overpowered us. They destroyed everything. We tried to bargain with them, to reason with them. But they didn't respond. They had no emotion."

"How long since they've been here?" asks Axton.

"More than a month. They couldn't find us, so I don't believe they'll be coming back." He purses his lips. "That's basically everything."

"Thank you," Axton says. "We appreciate it. When they came, did they arrive in pods?"

'Yes," Winton says.

"Did they land the pod or autochute down?"

"Chutes. We think that one pod delivered them to all the different places. We've had contact with nearby towns, and they've been attacked, too."

My ears are wide open. Robot soldiers? Industrial-style robots so advanced that they can see, use parachutes, overpower people?

Suddenly the man says, "Wait, have the big cities in the territory been taken?"

Axton shakes his head.

"They attacked the smaller regions first. We hope to stop them before it gets out of hand."

"Out of hand?" Winton's pitch rises. "As if it isn't already. We've got children and families dying in here, mothers whose babies are stillborn, and the whole town is starving. I daresay it's out of hand!"

I pipe up before Axton can dig the hole any deeper. "He didn't mean it like that. He only means we've got to defeat them as soon as possible. We're already making a move, but we've got to be stronger if we're going to completely annihilate them."

"Well I sure hope that happens before it's too late," Winton snaps.

"So do I." Axton bites his lip.

We walk down a small lane, returning to our pod. As we approach a more open area, Winton hangs back.

"I'd rather not be spotted. It was nice meeting you and I appreciate your help, but I'd best go back now. Good luck with everything."

"Thank you, Winton. You too," I say.

Winton touches all of our hands briefly before scurrying out of view. I wonder if I'll ever see him again.

I have so many questions buzzing in my mind that I hardly know where to start.

"So, who's going to explain this to me?" I demand.

Axton acquiesces first. "Okay. Okay."

"The Compound has an army, right?"

"Yes."

"Of industrial robots."

Theo laughs.

"Kind of," says Axton.

"Kind of what?"

"I guess you could call them industrial robots. Sure."

"Stop patronizing me!"

"Fine. Okay," he says. "Not really industrial. More humanoid. Android. High capability androids."

Suddenly I get it. Industrial robots were a hundred years ago. They have highly functional robots now. Androids.

"What, they walk. And talk?" I say dubiously.

"And fight. You heard."

Dread fills me. An army of huge, walking, talking metal monsters.

"All fighting for the Commander?" I ask.

"Yeah," says Theo. "Only he knows how to make them."

"I've never . . . I hope I never see one."

Theo laughs again. "Tissue infusion. Most of them look human now."

I am picturing awful robots with human faces. A thought occurs to me. Oh no, surely not. The guards? The Commander has a robot army of guards! That is so horrible that I don't want to believe it.

But it must be. And that sure does explain a lot about those guards. Silver Belt must have been a robot! Mean. Strong. Inhuman. That explains everything.

"Wait. Are all the guards in the Compound robots?" There always was something odd about them. But they're so human-like!

"You've seen a lot of them," says Axton. "What do you think?"

I want to throttle him, but don't get the chance. I bump into Theo, who has stopped in his tracks.

"Something's not right," he says, scanning around. As the words escape his lips, four people dressed in rags jump out from behind a rundown house, teeth bared and wielding makeshift weapons. One is waving around a sharpened length of pipe. Another has some kind of knife.

Axton's posture immediately shifts into defense mode. I take up what I hope is a threatening position too, inspired by a karate film I once saw. They outnumber us. I think I recognize one of them from inside Winton's sanctuary.

"Please," I say. "We are here to help you. We will bring more supplies. I promise."

One of them cuts me off.

"Give us the pod, and we won't hurt you," he demands.

"We're here to help you," Axton repeats slowly. The man holding the biggest metal blade takes a step forward.

"That's what they've all been telling us," he snarls.

They are hungry, and not going to give up until they get what they want. The wind begins to howl around us. I realize that I left my backpack and electrogun in the pod. I slowly rummage through my pockets for anything—either a weapon or a distraction. Nothing. Guess

I'm going to be fighting with my fists. Axton and Theo have taken their guns out of their packs, and hold them outstretched.

I can pinpoint the exact moment the strangers turn. For some reason, they don't care about the guns. The guy with the blade narrows his eyes and lifts his weight slightly onto the balls of his feet. His gaze flickers to me for a split second, and I know he will go for me. He lunges, the metal tight in his grasp.

He thrusts it towards my chest, and his eyes bore into my soul. He is determined to end me. I can tell that Axton saw the move coming the same time I did, but Theo didn't have a clue. Why doesn't Axton take the shot?

The man plunges the gleaming blade towards me. Before I can even get over my shock, however, my hand has reached out and latched onto the man's forearm, freezing him mid-motion. It takes almost nothing to hold his arm back.

I twist viciously and his body lifts to teeter on his toes before tumbling to the ground. I feel no strain in my muscles. It was simple, as if I were tossing a bag of feathers. Seriously, adrenaline is amazing.

He stares up at me in disbelief, and his companions' expressions weaken for a few moments before they transform back into snarls. Only this time, there is a sheen of terror behind their bared teeth. The man on the ground rises, and stumbles a little. I give them a small, threatening smile, despite the fact that I am as shocked as they are at the turn of events. They grit their teeth, refusing to give up.

"Do it again, Carla," Axton says under his breath. I frown. A lucky fluke again? Who is he kidding?

He and Theo move towards the others, letting me take care of this one.

I move one step forward, and he reacts swiftly. He plunges the blade into my shoulder and I wince. My face contorts for a second, but the pain quickly stops. I shove him down again and he's struggling, hard. I lift the man right up and prepare to smash him to the ground.

Suddenly I feel a strong vice around my neck. The man has grabbed me. My breath is escaping me, but there's no pain.

With one hand, I rip his grasp off my neck and throw him against the wall. A thud as he makes contact. He immediately leaps back up, but seems unsteady despite the evil look in his eye. I take a step towards the woman with the pipe, her scraggly grey hair half-hiding her gaunt face. I stop. Her feet are bare. She drops her weapon and holds up her hands in terror.

"She's crazy," the woman shrieks. "Get her away from me!"

I've never frightened anyone before. I feel powerful, but I'm not sure I like it.

The man with the knife turns to Axton.

"You're one as well, aren't you?" he says. Axton shakes his head. "Go on, hit me, strike me. Do what you want. You've taken everything from us already. Go on, take our lives as well." I guess they either realize they can't get anything out of us, or that we actually have nothing to give.

"I'm not from the Compound," Axton says in a hardened tone, "and we didn't take anything from you."

He turns and walks away, not bothering to glance back at the four defeated figures.

"We will come back. With more food," I promise them.

They stare at us, and Theo and I follow Axton back towards our pod.

My chest tightens as I think about the children with ashen faces and empty bellies. Did the Compound robots really do this to them?

"Way to go, Carla," Theo says.

"Why didn't you help me back there?" I say.

"You seemed to have it under control."

"I don't even know how I did that!" I protest.

"Well, it certainly did the job," he says laughing. He

sounds slightly shocked. As we walk towards the craft, I can't help glancing behind me to check that those people aren't following us. I don't see anyone, but that doesn't mean they aren't there.

We reach the pod, and the doors swing upwards, revealing the familiar stylish interior. Sapphire is pleased to see us, to say the least.

I sit down and remember my shoulder injury. I touch it lightly and my hand comes away dry. I'm sure I felt blood trickling down before.

"They were so hungry . . . " I think out loud.

"We're not going back there, Carla," Axton says firmly. "The sooner you understand that, the better. There are sacrifices we have to make, and this is one of them."

"But surely we can deliver a few supplies," I protest. "What if they die because we don't help them?"

"Well, then they die. This isn't a game, Carla. You've got to understand the big picture here. If we have to let them die so we can save many more people, then that's what we're going to do. We're not going back."

Clearly, there's no point even arguing. I growl and drop onto my seat. I don't care what Axton says. If he won't let us rescue them, then I'll have to do it myself. I'm going back there. Not now, but in the future. I promise myself that much.

Axton stands near the entrance, and shifts awkwardly. He puts his hands in his pockets and then takes them out.

Sapphire is looking at us both.

"I'm sorry," he says softly.

"Don't worry about it, Axton," I say. He's not sorry. I can't believe we're leaving children in there. The image of the girl and her bunny is plastered to the inside of my brain. Her sunken cheeks in that petite face, her pale lips, and innocent eyes. I feel a tear welling up, but I don't let it fall.

Theo places a hand on my shoulder as Axton moves to his pilot chair.

"It's unfair, Carla. We all know that," Theo says softly.

"Did you see the children in there?" I say, dismayed. "Hungry and dying!"

"Maybe we can drop them some supplies when this is all over."

*Maybe* won't keep them alive.

*     *     *

I try to sleep, but there are too many thoughts ricocheting around my brain. I catch onto one that has just occurred to me. I was brought back into this fake life for a reason. And that reason, clearly, was not so that I would be able to spend time with my family again. It was so that

I could save the rest of the children.

I sit upright.

I am *that* person.

The one in the movies who's supposed to have the hero role. Funnily enough, the thought actually sounds pretty good. Carla the Brave. Carla the Victorious. I can picture the headlines, 'How Carla Cared Enough to Die for Future Generations' and 'Children Reunited with Families Thanks to Reluctant Hero Carla'. Not bad. I laugh at my own musings.

But one thing is for sure. Save the children. That is my purpose.

I lie back in my seat and fall into an instant, peaceful slumber.

*     *     *

The hum of the pod is like gentle ripples on a pond. I have been asleep for quite a while, when Axton rushes out of the cockpit.

"Good news," he says, agitated. "My friends have located the main army. They're deploying soon on a massive mission. When they're gone, we take the Compound."

Being reminded of that awful place is not a pleasant

way to wake. A wave of nausea hits me. There's no way. I thought I could, but I can't.

"I can't go back there," I say softly. "Not even for the children."

So much for being a hero. I can't face the nasty guards and the stench of the rats and bats. The history books will call me Carla the Chicken-Hearted.

Axton pauses, a strange look on his face. "If you can't do it for the children, then do it for your brother."

I stare up at him, my face turning a deep shade of red. I don't know how to respond to that.

"He's dead!" My voice wavers. "He's in the past." How dare he bring my brother up. My body tenses.

Axton shakes his head, his expression firm. My stomach churns. I don't know what he means.

"He's still in there, Carla, in the Compound. It's the only way that photo makes sense."

I suddenly feel very dizzy. The floor seems to disappear from beneath my feet. Could it be true? I can't believe he was in there with me the whole time. I'm going to see my brother! I'm going to see him!

But what if it's not true? I don't want to believe it. I can't go through the nightmare of finding out he's dead for a second time. I can't let my hopes rise, only to be shattered.

I stare at Axton forlornly, shaking my head.

"He can't be. I would have seen him in there."

"The Commander must have hidden him from you. They wouldn't want to trigger an emotional reaction in you."

It's hard to believe they cared about my emotional health and well-being back there in the slave mines. All they cared about was whether those carts of tiger's eye were full.

"It's not a hundred percent," Theo says quietly.

"Yes. But it's logical," Axton says.

"He'd be over a hundred years old," I protest.

"Correct. Same as you," Axton says.

"Suspended animation? For a hundred years?"

"Um, kind of. But yeah."

"He's an old man."

"No, he wouldn't age." I wipe my sweaty hands on my clothes.

"How can you be sure? You don't know if he's alive right now."

He sighs. "Yes, you're right, Carla. We can't know for certain. But I wouldn't be telling you if there wasn't a serious possibility." He puts his hands in his pockets. "There's only one way to find out for sure."

"What are we waiting for, then?" I say, a hopeful tear

rolling down my cheek. "Let's hit the road."

"In the sky?" Theo says, with a half laugh.

"Yes!" I say. "Let's hit the sky!"

*　　*　　*

I think about how some of my worst memories from before I was taken—before I died, really—would be some of the best ones if they were happening now. I recall meeting Jeremy at school.

He was sitting on a small wooden bench by himself at lunchtime, his fingers fumbling absentmindedly over some pastries in a clear Tupperware container. His gaze darted from left to right, as if attempting to determine the perfect piece of delicacy to consume first.

To everyone, he was a nobody. Less than that, he was a nothing. He wasn't a part of their lives; he did not exist in their worlds. To walk past his presence was to saunter by an irrelevant school desk for the hundredth time. The judgmental laughter as they passed didn't seem to faze him.

School children lounged around a table not far from Jeremy, chattering and squabbling, without a care in the world. It was clear he was used to being the backdrop to everyone else's lives. He was the green screen they edited out before the final showing. He happened to glance up, and something in his face made me deviate from my rush.

He seemed skeptical at first when I approached him. Was I going to speak to *him*? Surely I was searching for someone else. But his face lit up as I uttered the first few nervous words.

"Hey," I said with a grin. "How are you?"

We edged gradually into a conversation, and soon his body language opened up. He even let out an accidental laugh, and people began to glance in our direction, wondering why I would possibly be speaking to him. To a social nobody. But talking to him, it was clear that to his family, he was everything.

He asked me about my future, and listened as I told him my dreams and aspirations in a long stream of consciousness. He said, while my dreams were certainly oversized, that he believed I could reach them. We talked for a long time about life and other things. My heart was racing the first time I made him genuinely laugh. His whole face changed, and I realized he was actually an attractive guy. I had rarely met a person with more depth, and the exchange filled me with happiness and satisfaction.

Suddenly I looked at my watch and realized I had to

be somewhere, so I told him he was welcome to come with me.

He hurriedly replaced the lid of the Tupperware container, uneaten pastries and all, and shoved his lunchbox in his bag. He glanced up at me with an undertone of panic on his face, as if dawdling had lost him a friend before.

The second I realized what he was doing, my heart nearly broke.

"No, please, keep eating," I pleaded. "I'll wait for you."

He shook his head and leapt up. "I wasn't that hungry, anyway."

As we walked to class, I was a little stunned that none of us cared to scratch beneath the surface. We had let an incredible person exist like fog that wafts in and out, but makes no impact. In that moment, I vowed to always see the good in people, and to focus on it more than I ever had before.

I'm brought back to the present by the hum of the pod.

I can't believe who I've become. I was once a naive girl who worried about grades, clothes and public perception. Now, I wonder where the next meal will come from. All of my friends and family are gone. Unless, of course, my brother is still alive.

I slump in my chair as a deep wistfulness for my old

life washes over me. My brother had better be in there.

Because I'm coming for him.

*　　*　　*

I've been staring out the window for some time when Axton's announcement blasts through the speakers.

"I've spoken to some of the *reliable* members of my rescue team," he says. "They have good contacts within the intel group. We've got a detailed schedule on when the Compound's robot army will be deployed north. No time to waste, so we'll have to defer our original plan."

I look at Sapphire sadly. Axton's original plan was to take Sapphire home. Thankfully, she wasn't privy to those plans.

"And we've got entry credentials for the Compound, and they assure me that the safest way in is the same as last time. They'll never suspect we would try that again."

He pauses. "Basically, we're teaming up with our fight-ers and making an attack at oh-two-hundred hours on Friday."

"In three days?" I say, standing up. "We can't wait *three days* to rescue them all. To rescue my brother. We aren't waiting. We're going now."

Sapphire looks at me.

I clench my fists, glaring at Theo. He doesn't say anything, simply watches me from his seat. Surely he can see that we have to rescue them right now. I'm not leaving my brother in there a second longer.

"You know what it's like, Theo. We were in there. That's what my brother is going through right now. We can't leave him. We've got to get him out."

"I know, Carla," he says. "We will get him out. We'll get all of them out."

"What do you mean we *will*?" I shriek. "We have to get them out *now*! The longer we leave them in there, the worse they'll get! What if we're too late? What if . . . ?"

"Carla!" Theo says harshly. His unusually sharp tone shocks me into silence.

"If we go in right now, whether we are too late or not, we will fail." His eyes are locked onto mine. It's the most serious I've seen him. "We don't have supplies, we don't have a team, and we don't have a plan."

I sit down again, because I know he's right. But I don't like it. I'm fuming. I don't like it at all. I can't stand the thought of my brother being in there. Mining that stupid tiger's eye mineral with the inhuman guards. Literally inhuman. What I would give to have him be the one who was rescued instead of me. I try not to think about how skinny he must be, or how little they are feeding him, or how long he's been in there.

"Can you focus all of this energy on helping us form the best plan possible and making sure we have thought of everything?" he asks.

I reluctantly agree.

The pod seems to bank and change direction. A few minutes later, Axton walks in. "We've organized a meeting place far outside the territories, and we're heading there now. We will sort out supplies and finalize the plan to get everyone out safely. Any objections?"

Theo shakes his head, and I copy him. "But can I please see the full information on my brother?" I say. "The stuff you found. I need to know everything."

"Yes," Axton says. "There isn't a lot. But we will show you as much as we can."

For once, I'm satisfied that they actually will.

I wonder absentmindedly where the new meeting place will be, but most of all I think about what Rory might be doing right now, what he looks like and whether he's okay. He'd better be.

I lick my dry lips. I might throw up if I think too much. It makes me want to punch the Commander in the face, even though I'm not a violent person. Or at least, didn't used to be. I have a few things to say to him if I ever meet him. Mostly, things I can say with my fists. My mind drifts away, imagining how pleasant that soft crunching sound would be as my knuckles contact the bridge of his nose.

It's my new life. But not as Hero Carla. As Mean Carla. Give me back my brother.

*     *     *

It's a long flight. Sapphire seems to fall asleep. My mind can't let me get there.

As we approach the landing area, Theo leans over and says, "Back there got me thinking. I've been doing a lot of research on you. What I found was quite extraordinary. I think you could be crucial to the rescue of the children from the Compound. Maybe even in taking the entire facility down."

Now he's sounding like the stupid General.

"Two minutes until touch-down," Axton announces.

Theo continues. "I wanted to let you know before we met everyone else on the team, because they might want to use you as well." I shrug. "I want to make it clear that your life may be at risk if you proceed with this mission. But we can't get the children out without you. Are you willing to put yourself on the line?"

It's not a question, really. He knows me too well.

277

"You know I am, Theo."

"Just remember that emotions can help or hinder," he adds. "It sounds kind of weird, but you need to learn to control your emotions better."

I roll my eyes. "What, you don't enjoy my emotional outbursts? Look, Theo, it's been a long few days."

"You're not wrong there," he smirks. "Putting up with you is simply a *joy!*"

He pokes his fingers deep into my ribcage and I squeal. Just like the good old days in the Compound.

"Don't tickle me, Theo!"

"Can't help it," he chortles. "I love undocumented features!"

I see the glint in his eye and I know he's going in again. I brace myself as he hovers, scanning for a hole in my defense.

Luckily, Axton commands, "Prepare for touchdown," and we tighten our seat belts.

I give Theo the death stare, warning him not to tickle me again. Ever.

He grins.

# 26

# AXTON

I ENGAGE THE LANDING CONTROLS AND WE TOUCH DOWN GRACEFULLY IN THE PARKING LOT BEHIND A DISUSED BUILDING. Even after such a long flight, I am on high alert. Darkness envelops us as I kill the engine, and the automatic door lights flicker on like excited fireflies. I open the doors and the three of them gaze anxiously outside to see where we've ended up.

Hopefully we can make our way safely to the meeting point. This was always our back-up safe area, and only a select few in our group were privy to its existence. To be honest, we always had our doubts about the motives of some of the others in our training group. But we never suspected the General would have her focus anywhere other than on the best outcome for the children. How could she go against the goal of the entire mission—my father's dream—of rescuing the children?

We exit the pod and I pause for a second to get my bearings. The first thing that hits us is the foul odor.

"Where are we?" Sapphire asks, holding her nose.

"Some old decrepit town," Carla replies.

"We're in a city that was once called New York. One of the first wars came through here because this was one of the biggest cities. Now only this part is above water," says Theo.

"Will they be able to find us?" Carla says, her brows furrowed. "And where can we go to get away from that smell?"

I open my arms, gesturing to the ruins. "They've basically forgotten about this place now, which is why we're here. Don't worry. Let's go find the others. It won't smell so bad once we get used to it."

I point in the direction we need to go and watch as Carla darts off with a spring in her step.

The buildings tower over us like giants, their walls crumbling and roofs hanging low, threatening to collapse. Our feet scatter glass and dust along the sidewalk.

The hustle and bustle of the city is a mere memory.

Many buildings are barely more than rubble.

We stick to the alleyways, hidden in the darkness and gloom of the ex-city. We zigzag through the streets, and finally we arrive.

"We're here," I say.

Carla scrutinizes the party supplies store skeptically.

"This is it?" she says.

The tiny one-story building is one of the few around with windows intact. Streamers lie partially attached to the glass walls and a closed sign hangs limply from the doorknob.

Carla tries the front door, but it refuses to budge. I knock. Two slow knocks, and three fast knocks. Our code sign.

We peer into the darkness at the back of the store but can't see anything. Then a figure emerges from the shadows.

A man pushes the door open, and I greet him. "Mason."

"Axton," he says, embracing me in a bear hug. "So good to see you, man." He turns to Carla and Sapphire.

"This is my friend, Carla," I say. "And this is little Sapphire."

He greets Sapphire first, then shakes Theo's hand. "Theo, how are you?"

"Not too bad," Theo says, brushing his fingers through his hair.

Mason finally turns to Carla. "We've heard a lot about you, Carla." He holds the door open for us. "Come in."

As we enter, Mason says to me quietly, "She's not as big as I expected."

I laugh. "She's big in spirit."

The lights are dim as we hustle into the party store. Deflated balloons lie scattered on the tile floor with barely discernible messages on them: *Happy Birthday*, *Congratulations* and *Best Wishes*. Mason kicks aside some boxes of miscellaneous party supplies to clear our path. We head left at the back of the store behind the counter and find another door. It opens out to a very large room.

Sitting around a bulky stone table in the middle of the room are half a dozen of my friends from the rescue team. They let out a cheer when they see me.

"How have ya been, Axton?" greets Greg.

"Great to see you," another says.

"Not too bad, it's good to see you all." I introduce Carla and Sapphire, and they exchange handshakes. A few haven't met Theo before, so I introduce him as well. I groan when the guys wiggle their eyebrows suggestively as they flick from Carla to me. But I feel myself blush. In their twenties, some of them, and they still haven't grown up.

They introduce themselves briefly, and we sit down. I notice that their buzzed hair is beginning to grow back. All of them have almost identical hairstyles, apart from Merida, the only girl left on our team. Her vibrant pink hair has been spiked into a fierce mohawk. It certainly won't blend in where we're going. She notices my gaze and gives me a grin, waving a beanie. Of course.

Sprawled out on the table in front of us is a large screen that completely covers the table. Featured on it is a map of the entire Compound.

"What is this?" Carla exclaims. "A giant iPad?"

"iPad?" my friend Eric says, laughing. "Nah, it's just a map."

Carla laughs, but I don't get the joke.

Eric is one of my good friends from training. He is always there to cheer me up if I am down.

Mason, who is clearly the unappointed leader of our group at this point, remains standing at the head of the table.

"I've already explained this to the others, but as you can see, here is the boundary of the Compound," he informs Carla and Theo. "The highlighted blue sections are the areas where the remaining children will be when we arrive, assuming they stick to the normal routine. You can see that they're separated into groups, which means that we'll need to split up and coordinate multiple simultaneous attacks."

I notice that Carla is listening intently. Mason glances at her and continues, "Now, the reason we've decided to include you in our mission despite the fact that you haven't been trained, is because you were actually in there. You know intimately how the Compound works. You know the routines. You have the best information about how things happen."

They sure do.

"They'll be crucial in guiding us through the attack," I say. "Things will have changed since our previous rescue mission, and we will need to adapt on the fly. We can only do that if we have insiders with detailed knowledge."

"Is there a reason we've chosen Friday to attack?" Carla asks. I tense. I notice the change in her body language as soon as it happens. She's about to have one of those Carla moments. I make eye contact, trying to tell her to stop whatever she's thinking. She ignores me.

I kick her under the table.

No response. I give up. If her mind is set on something, nothing I say will stop her.

Mason puts his hands in his pockets. "Friday was chosen because the army will be away attacking the northern territories, which will distract both the Compound and the General, leaving them short-handed. Two hundred hours is when the Compound guards are at their night stations and at their weakest. That gives us the greatest chance of success."

He breathes out heavily, clearly unhappy that Carla is questioning his decisions. I did warn him. Carla clears her throat. Here it comes. I nudge her one more time under the table, almost pleading.

Carla says, "Listen, I've spent way too long in that place. I know their routines. I think that we should bring the attack forward to Thursday."

"Why Thursday?" asks Mason condescendingly.

"It's the one time everyone is together. And Axton said the army will already have been deployed by Thursday. The children will all be in Assembly. Not split out into groups. We can guarantee that we won't miss any."

"It's true," Theo says. "It might make sense to attack then."

"We're not bringing it forwards," Mason says. "The plan is set. No changes." His tone implies the issue is closed.

He wishes. I know she won't stop. Not after we told her that her brother might be in there.

"The guards hang out together at the back of the hall

and will be easy to take out. It's the perfect time to go in," Carla says.

"We don't have enough time to get everything ready. There's barely enough time before Friday to prepare for a mission as big as this!"

"I think she has a point," Eric pipes up. All heads turn to him. "I'm not saying it would be easy, but it does seem that we'd have a much better chance of getting everyone out if we went in while the children were all together."

"Come on, Mason," I say quietly. "We're not giving up the entire plan. Just a date change."

He pauses to consider. "In all seriousness, do we think we can complete our planning and sort the gear by tomorrow?"

"Well, if we hustle," Eric says, shrugging. "This isn't our first time at the rodeo. It's what we've been training for. Either way, I think there's a far greater chance of success if we attack while everyone is together, even if we have less time to plan."

I nod.

"Who supports moving the mission to Thursday?" I ask.

Carla, Theo and Eric raise their hands. Slowly, everyone else does too. Even Sapphire.

Finally, Mason says ruefully, "I guess I've got to be in as well."

He pouts, but I can already see his mind whirring and planning. He's always been like this. No doubt he'll be fine in a few minutes.

I stare at Carla. I can't believe she did this, but she is right about it. She smirks at me, and I roll my eyes.

We begin discussing the logistics of the rescue, including travel and transport. We plan how to thwart the guards' counter-attack and disable any remaining pods. We definitely don't want what happened last time to happen again, where they nuked our pod and we were left to fend for ourselves. Finally, we discuss gear and supplies. Sapphire is starting to yawn.

"We've got a lot of equipment in the truck," Mason says.

I almost laugh. "You guys took the *truck*?"

Mason shrugs. "We figured they'd never suspect ground travel, so why not? Only for the last segment. Taking a pod the whole way would give away our meeting point if we were tracked."

He's not wrong. Nobody would suspect it. Nobody would choose it either, because it takes forever to get anywhere. I guess that's a small price to pay for remaining hidden and safe.

"Let's go through our plan of attack one last time," Eric says, directing our attention back to the map. He points out the entry and exit points, the pathways to the meeting room, and the likely locations of the guards.

"Can I suggest an edit?" Carla asks.

Mason reluctantly steps aside. "Sure. You know how to do it?"

Carla shakes her head as she begins to test random sections of the touchscreen to see how they operate. "Nope."

With Theo's help, she quickly works it out, and is soon busily highlighting sections and drawing in arrows and lines. She circles areas that are the most dangerous, either because of sensors or security cameras. It's clear she knows her way around the Compound. There are some areas she isn't familiar with, but for the most part, her performance is impressive.

"Can I ask," Mason says, "how you know so much about the Compound? Weren't you strictly watched?"

I roll my eyes. As if Carla and Theo wouldn't have been able to slink out from under the watch of the guards. She can talk her way out of almost anything. Even if she got caught, she'd probably be able to convince the guards she was sleepwalking or something.

Carla shrugs. "I like exploring." She glances at Theo. "Sometimes we would go out together."

Mason grunts his approval, and Carla continues making marks on the map, with Theo adding suggestions every few seconds. She moves around the table quickly, zooming in on various sections and indicating secret passages in the vents and other small tunnels she identified while she was there. She doesn't know where they lead, but we figure it out based on the map. Many of her little details don't show up on the maps we use for training. I hate to admit it, but her knowledge is comprehensive, detailed and to-the-point.

At last, she seems satisfied.

"That's all I remember," Carla says.

"I'd say that's sufficient," Eric laughs. "And once we're in, we can split up into groups, each leading a small group out. That way, we'll have more chance of making it out alive. Divide and conquer."

Mason nods. We all lean in to get a better view of the map. Mason works out a more detailed plan. He runs through it a number of times until everyone is clear on each step.

Then he pulls out several small familiar boxes. "Ear pieces, as usual, guys. Same rules apply. Keep them in at all times. Don't mute them under any circumstances. We all know what happened to Sebastian."

"What happened to Sebastian?" Carla pipes up.

"He muted his ear piece," Eric says dryly.

"Ha, ha," Carla says.

"He was a fiery sort, and someone accidentally insulted him over the earpiece, so he muted it. Then he missed the extraction and we had to go back and get him. Nearly didn't make it."

"So the point is, don't mute it," Mason says. "Any mistakes could cost you your life."

He passes out the earpieces and we put them in our pockets.

"Don't *lose* them, either," Mason says, squinting suspiciously at Carla.

I notice her biting her tongue and I hold in a laugh. Mason has picked out the one person who'd probably be the first to misplace her earpiece. In fact, I'd bet on it.

Mason begins to draw in the route of attack through the Compound. I memorize the path, which is similar to the last time I was in there, except there are shortcuts and safe passages that Carla has identified.

Everyone gazes intently at the map, committing it to memory, just as I have. It's one of our rituals before every mission. We all go completely still, practically holding our breaths. One forgotten detail could mean certain death.

Sapphire leans over and whispers. "Why is everyone so quiet?"

I hold in a chuckle. "We're memorizing the map," I

whisper back. I didn't realize how strange it must seem from the outside.

"Oh," says Sapphire, and she begins to stare at the map, too. I have to smile at her intense expression, with her sharp little mind whirring overtime.

When everyone is ready, Mason pairs us up for the mission. I'm with Eric. "And Carla and Theo, you will stay in the control center, which will be Axton's pod. You need to guide us through the tunnels using the earpieces, and take care of logistics."

As soon as he says it, I groan inwardly, anticipating Carla's reaction. I watch her muscles tense, like there's a storm brewing within her. She grits her teeth and I desperately try to catch her attention, but her gaze is set intently on Mason. She's going to explode . . .

"Theo and I know the most about the Compound. We've *lived* in there. We should be the ones on the front line, not shoved on the sidelines." Her eyes flash danger-ously.

Mason sighs as though he were expecting it. "Yes, I understand. You're the most knowledgeable about the Compound, which is why we put you at the head of the operation. You'll be able to instruct *everyone* where to go. If you're out there, the only ones you'll be able to help are yourselves."

I watch Carla pause and ponder this. He does make a good point, and I can tell that she realizes that. But I also know that she is very stubborn.

"That does make sense," Carla says, to my surprise. "You're right. It's best that I stay at the base."

The knot in my stomach grows.

# 27

# CARLA

There's no way they can make me stay at the base. If my brother is in there, I can't rely on anyone to rescue him and get him out safely. I have to do it myself. The second that Mason said I had to stay at the base and be babysat by Theo, I knew I only had one option.

I'm going in.

We finish with the map, and Mason shuts it down. He and Merida lift a piece of granite the size of the table top and start placing it over the screen. Merida grunts under the strain, and her foot slips. The granite begins to slide towards Sapphire's lap, but I react and dive for the slab, stopping it before it can fall. Everyone seems stunned.

Even Axton is impressed with me. Once the slab is properly on the table, Eric tops it off with a dirty-white party tablecloth. Fading balloons and twirling streamers are painted on it.

"All right guys," Mason says. "Let's roll."

We head out, taking the back door this time, which is next to a huge closet filled with dusty props and other once-vibrant party supplies.

Rubble is strewn across the narrow alleys, and small pieces slide across the concrete as we walk. Merida and Axton are helping Sapphire.

"Where on earth could you hide a truck around here?" Theo asks.

Eric, who is walking beside him, answers. "Right there."

We turn left down a little alleyway, and there's an undercover area the perfect size for a large four-wheel drive. Which is exactly what rests there. It is a blast from the past. Such a contrast to the sleek powerful machines—these pods—that I've become accustomed to while living decades ahead of my time. Already, this seems like an unsophisticated and clumsy transport mode. But my father would have given anything to own the latest model like this.

It's an olive-green color, which is a perfect disguise for

the Antarctic rainforest, but hardly effective in any way in the urban landscape.

The ceiling above the vehicle is cracked and crumbling, and I am somewhat amazed that it hasn't collapsed and crushed the truck.

"Let's open her up," Mason says, as Eric presses a button on a key that I didn't see him taking out of his pocket.

"Look how old it is!" Theo exclaims, pointing at the wheels. "The doors open sideways." It's my turn to be amused at his excitement.

We open the trunk, which is crammed full of neatly laid-out equipment. It's strange to see firearms and gadgets from decades into the future inside the back of an old army truck. So shiny and modern compared to the ancient exterior.

I try to focus on Mason's instructions regarding the equipment, but my mind is whirring. The cogs turn as I ponder options and try to think of every possible thing that could go wrong with my plan. My incomplete plan, that is. I have to fill in the gaps before I can attempt to convince Theo. I have to think of everything.

My plan thus far assumes one thing: that Mason won't agree to have me involved in the action. And I know he won't. If he does, my whole plan is unnecessary.

"You coming, Carla?" Eric asks. I jump at his words.

Everyone is opening the doors of the truck, ready to get in. I notice that Theo holds the truck handle a little too long, rubbing his hand over the silver surface. Clearly, they don't make them like they used to.

I clamber into the back seat, squeezing myself next to Theo. I don't ask where we're going, in case they mentioned it while I was distracted.

Turns out, I do know where we're going. My internal compass has never been very good, but right now, it is clear to me that we are taking the path back to our pod. Well, Axton's pod.

Mason and Axton are discussing the logistics of pod travel.

"The coordinates of the Compound have already been programmed into the pod's system," Axton says.

"Good," Mason says. "And the hydro?"

"Half full."

"How good's the machine? How far will that get us?"

"Ten thousand. She's not bad."

I have no idea what units they're speaking in. Do they still use miles? I still know so little about this modern world.

It's a short ride, and Mason parks the truck in between two buildings; out of sight, but within walking distance of where we left the pod. We all step out, and Eric opens the trunk.

"Ah," Mason says, clearly having forgotten something. "Take one of these each."

He is holding a small silver satchel with tiny black bands in it.

"Timekeepers," Mason says.

They are thin, with a uniform diameter, apart from a small section that is slightly wider. I pick one up and stash it in my pocket.

"Let's take all the gear in one trip," Mason barks. We lift backpacks and ammunition onto our backs and jog towards the pod. But as soon as I begin to run, I feel as if I'm going to drop something. Pieces are slipping. Merida sees me struggling and walks towards me. Actually, it's probably more accurate to describe it as gliding. Even though she's carrying a large gun and two massive camo-colored bags on her back, she doesn't break a sweat. She grabs the cartons as they fall, and darts off without saying a word.

"What are you waiting for, Carla?" Axton shouts to me. Everyone has already dumped the equipment they were carrying into the pod and are waiting inside. For me.

The rain begins to pour down, but I can't afford to slow my pace. I wonder briefly whether the equipment is allowed to get wet. Of course they would have water-proofed it. Otherwise what good would it be in the rainforest?

They begin to shout at me from inside the pod's door. I don't have far to go, but the straps on the backpack are killing my shoulders. My back is aching, and I sense a familiar twinge. The same one I would always feel when I was pushing my cart at the Compound. I catch a glimpse of Theo's face at the door of the pod, and am transported back to the mines. My body stiffens, and I want to stop. I have to stop. The gate is closing. They're all yelling. I'm not going to make it! They're going to punish me again.

"No!" I shriek. "I can't make it."

Theo is already inside. My whole team is inside, and it's all my fault. My fault.

"Carla." It is Theo's voice. Suddenly I am brought back to reality. He is always there to bring me back.

I drop to my knees. The weight on my back is killing me. I watch Merida and Eric make their way towards me, but all at once I realize I don't need their help. I am strong. I will not give up.

I stand up easily, as if there is a helium balloon from the party store attached to my back. My legs are made of steel, and my back from iron. I feel no pain. My muscles feel no strain. I run to the transport, and throw my heavy bags of gear into the storage compartment underneath. The others follow.

Everyone is staring at me. With annoyance? Amazement? I don't know.

Eric speaks first. "Okay," he says. "That was cool."

"That was awesome!" Sapphire is on my side, like always.

"It just happens sometimes," I half-explain.

I don't know what to tell them. If I tell them the truth, that I had a flashback, they will know how weak I am. I won't tell them.

But Theo knows.

"I think she remembered something that happened in the Compound," he says.

"Well, I think she unlocked her robotic enhancements for a few seconds there," Merida says.

Several of the soldiers murmur their agreement. Nobody questions her. I simply look at them all. And then at Merida.

"Um . . . my what?"

"Your enhancements. Your augs. Your capabilities."

"But you said robotic?"

"Yeah."

"You think I'm a robot?" I say woodenly.

"You prefer android?"

Merida looks around at all the others and smiles awkwardly at me.

"Carla . . . " says Theo.

"I'm not a robot," I yell. "I just get angry sometimes!"

These people are so stupid. And delusional. They're seeing robotic ghosts everywhere.

Then Mason says, "You lifted a granite tabletop like it was made of air foam."

"It would have hurt Sapphire."

"It was too heavy for Merida and I to lift together."

A pause.

I cast my mind back. Yeah, it was heavy. So what? I've heard of plenty of people having superhuman strength when lives are in danger. Doesn't mean they've somehow morphed into ridiculous robots!

"You should try using your core! I can do a six-minute plank," I splutter.

Silence.

"So you all think I'm a robot, too?" I demand.

Mason shrugs. "Yeah."

Some of the others nod.

"You didn't know?" asks Eric.

"I'm not a robot," I yell. "Are you all crazy?"

They're all still looking at me.

"Axton," I cry out. "Tell them that I'm not a robot. Obviously."

Please for the love of everything that is good in this

brand-new crazy world, please don't pause.

He pauses.

"You, too?" I say, incredulously.

"Kinda," says Axton reluctantly.

"Carla . . . " says Theo again.

"It's so cool if you're a robot," exclaims Sapphire.

I sit there for a while, fuming at the absurdity of them all, my arms folded. Nobody speaks. Theo moves over to me and his hand touches mine.

"But it doesn't make any sense." I suddenly exhale. "If I'm a robot, why do I have skin, and blood, and memories, and . . . why didn't anyone ever say anything about it?"

"Why would we?" answers Mason. "Everyone on the planet knows you're a robot. You're Carla."

I sit there quietly, studying the floor for a very long time. The pod hums and I stay quiet. No more questions. I don't want to hear the answers. Everyone here has gone crazy. Or the world has. Or maybe I have. Or all of the above.

Hi, my name is Carla, I'm over 100 years old and *apparently*, I'm a robot. Or humanoid. Or android. Or whatever stupid name you want to call it.

When I thought that today might be another interest-ing day, this is sure not what I had in mind.

*　　*　　*

I wake after a fitful nap. Obviously I'm not a robot. I mean, robots don't need to sleep.

I look around at everyone. The main area is a lot more packed than when we only had three of us onboard.

Mason sits in the cockpit with Axton. No one talks much, apart from Eric and Theo, who are discussing the transformation of machinery through the ages or something. If he wants to know about the past, shouldn't he be asking me? They're gazing at screens, and seem excited by what they see. They must be gawping at old cars because I hear them name some type of Toyota. Imagine being impressed by a Toyota when you've got pods. I walk over and sit next to them.

It seems that everyone is pretending to forget our last conversation. Maybe it was all just a dream? Like that dream where you forget to wear clothes to school, and everyone is looking at you. Yeah, like that, except in my dream, everyone's looking at me because they think I'm a robot.

Just a bad dream. At least that makes sense.

"Have you tried looking up Ferraris? Or Lamborghinis?" I say, briefly putting aside my worries. "They're far more sporty."

"What would you know about cars?" Theo jokes.

I purse my lips. "I may not be a car fanatic, but I do know a thing or two about the past." Theo smiles at my joke. "And I certainly know that Toyota sedans were not the best sportscars we had back then."

I take Theo's tablet, and ask it to search for 'Lamborghini'. It takes a moment, but eventually a photo of a cherry red Lamborghini pops up. The boys go wild. Some things never change.

I return to my original seat next to Merida, who says, "Let's talk."

This is so annoying. Why won't she let me be? I don't want to talk about robots. I want to yell at her to stop this insanity. But I remember how she helped me. She's always been so nice to me.

She leads me around the corner to a small room with a table and two chairs. She closes the door behind us.

"I just thought we should chat in private," says Merida.

"Don't you need to plug me in first?" I say dryly.

She ignores my sarcasm.

"We've heard a lot about you, Carla," she begins.

I don't understand any of this. She can see that in my face. Why are people hearing about me all the time? Why me? I haven't done anything. I don't even know who I am anymore.

"Even if I'm a robot, which I'm not, aren't there thousands of robots out there?" I say. "Why do you keep saying you've heard about me? How do you even know me?"

"Axton said he's tried to talk to you about some of this, and he warned me that you are very stubborn." She smirks. "He's not always right, that boy, but he was right about that."

I scowl.

"We've heard a lot of different things: rumors, theories, observations, all sorts of . . . thoughts on what you are. But we've done a lot of our own research on you. Not because we like you or want to be your friend, or to get to know you. I mean, sure, we do. But not because of any of that."

"Why, then?" I say, my arms crossed defensively.

"We did it because they are scared of you."

I frown. This makes no sense. I'm not scary.

"They, meaning the Commander and the guards at the Compound. They know there is something different about you. Unique."

Yeah, right, they treated me like I was really special, back in the Compound.

"Some folks in the know said they did it on purpose, as an experiment. But we know they didn't. It was an accident. A fluke in their system. Based on how faulty their manufacturing lines were, I'm surprised more mistakes didn't happen."

"What mistake?" I ask.

"Well, good question. We aren't sure. Was it a mistake with the tiger's eye levels or something special with your DNA?"

At least that makes partial sense. Robots don't have DNA, so that's that. Not a robot.

Merida keeps rambling. "You seem to resist their control. They've had to reset you many times, but you always break free from their command. But also, you've outlasted all other models by decades. And we don't think they've upgraded you much over the years either."

Yikes. Now she's talking about me like I'm a cell phone that needs jailbreaks and updates.

"But the thing that probably scares them the most is that you have the potential to control your robotic enhancements."

She said those same words before, and I still don't understand what they mean. "My what?"

"Your robotic enhancements. All robots are built the same, and have the potential to do a great deal of damage, so the creators don't give them access to any of the control systems. Obviously, they want to control them remotely. They don't want them to be able to do it without the creators instructing them. Robotic enhancements are basically anything you can do outside of your human form, that you wouldn't be able to do as a human."

"What does all of this mean for me?"

"That you can access your enhancements when you haven't been programmed to, unlike all of the other robots, who can only do it under command."

"But I can't do anything like that," I protest.

"Robots are built to think they're human, and can only act human, which is an advantage to the Compound. It means they can control them. The robots don't think they're stronger than the guards. They believe completely that they have human limitations. Except for you. You're different. If you had found out that you have access to your enhancements in the Compound, you could've taken down any guard in that building."

"Except for the robot ones."

"What?" said Merida. "I don't think those guards are robots. They haven't got that working yet."

The guards are not robots, but I am? Sounds backwards to me.

"Of course, you couldn't have fought them, anyway. You had no idea about any of this. But you can learn for the future. You can learn how to take control of it, and use it any time you like."

Merida is speaking so confidently, so matter-of-factly, that I'm almost falling for it.

"How do you know that's possible?"

"We don't . . . but the Compound is always studying you. They didn't just get rid of you. There must be some reason for that, too."

"Maybe they wanted another slave to dig up tiger's eye for the next hundred years," I say, only half joking.

Merida isn't in a joking mood. "Well, yes, the tiger's eye is definitely part of it somehow. It gives you those KF rings in your eyes. And titanium too. And that dinosaur metal. I don't really understand it too well."

There's a sound at the door.

"You guys all right in here?" Eric says, popping his head in. "Want some food?"

I have a million questions for Merida, but food wins. For now.

We welcome him in. He's very lanky, and barely needs to open the door to enter. Trailing behind him is Sapphire carrying a tray of silver tins. He hands each of us a tin of some kind of unidentifiable food. It smells amazing.

"Thanks, Eric," I say. Merida smiles her appreciation, and he retreats from the room.

"Can I stay?" asks Sapphire. "Or is it a secret?"

"Sure," says Merida. "You can listen if you like."

I don't know what to make of Merida. She seems nice, but very firm at the same time. I wonder if she has children.

"I do believe it's possible to control it, Carla. If you put your mind to it."

"But how?" I say.

"There is only one way to truly find out if it would work, and that is if you try it. Are you willing to give it a try? A real try?"

We eat in silence, and the only thing I can identify in the food is chicken. But is that merely my brain trying to connect the flavor to something I'm familiar with? Or is it really chicken? There are no details on the silver can that would indicate either way. I will have to be satisfied with pretending it is.

"Carla?" Merida says as we finish off our meal.

I straighten my back. Of course I will. I have to. I mean, I've done it before, so I know it's possible to use the crazy superhuman strength. I think back. The only way I've been able to do it is under extreme pressure. So, it's simply my adrenaline, right? Maybe Merida has the answers.

"Yes," I say. "I will do it."

At least it'll prove that I'm not a robot.

"Great," she says. "Pick that table up."

I stare at the solid structure, then look blankly at Merida.

"It's bolted in."

She sighs. "The first step in believing you can do any-thing is seeing past the boundaries."

"Fine," I say, skeptically. "I'll try."

I grab the edges of the table and try to lift it a little. It is, indeed, bolted in. My attempt is so half-hearted that Merida laughs.

"Okay," she says. "Now can you give it some real effort?"

I think this entire exercise is silly. Of course I'm not a robot. I grab the table tightly and look to Merida for further instructions.

"Now I want you to think about something that truly angers you."

I think for a moment, but all I come up with is the people who put me in the Compound. And I don't even know who they are.

"Is there someone really close to you?" she asks softly.

Suddenly my brother's face comes to mind. My heart-beat quickens.

"Yes," I say bitterly.

"Can you pretend that person is under there," she says, pointing to the base of the table, "and the only way to save them is by lifting the table?"

I imagine my brother is stuck right beneath the bolts in the table. Picturing him underneath the table makes my face flush. I have to get him out of there.

"Good," Merida whispers.

I lift with all my might, thinking about Rory. Images of his tiny face grimacing in pain flash before my eyes.

I squeeze my eyes shut and heave. For a second, I think it's going to be hopeless, and that nothing will happen, but then I sense the moment my blood turns into steel shards and I can do anything. I thrust upwards, which results in a huge crashing sound.

"You did it," Merida yells.

"Yay," cheers Sapphire.

I stop pulling and open my eyes. I have uprooted the table entirely. The bolts hang loose in their sockets. Axton is going to kill me.

I stand there, holding the table.

Merida laughs. "Don't look so scared," she says. "Come on, I'll help you put it back together."

She pulls out a tool I've never seen before, and I support the table while Merida returns the bolts to their rightful positions.

"That was very easy for you, Carla," she says. "Far easier than I thought it would be."

"It wasn't that easy," I say.

"Yes, but you did it first try. If you keep practicing, you'll be able to summon that power even more quickly."

I am surprised that I actually feel proud.

"Now, maybe Mason will let you go out in the field with your newfound skill," adds Merida.

She stands up and walks out, leaving me to ponder her last words. It's almost as if she's been reading my thoughts. I'm not as devious as I thought.

I leave the room with Sapphire, after one last glance at the table. Sapphire is beaming the biggest grin.

"Carla has secret robot powers. Cool."

*　　*　　*

I resume my seat next to Merida, who is now surfing on her tablet. I can't even begin to understand what's going on. There are snippets of videos and photos flying across the screen, only staying up for a millisecond as she swipes through them.

I decide to watch the sky instead, until Theo taps me on the shoulder.

"What happened in there?" he asks.

"Merida taught me a few things," I say, shrugging.

"Teaching you how to tear buildings down?"

"Pretty much," I laugh. "So where are we going?"

"Some place near the Compound. Close enough that we can prepare, but not so close that they can detect us and take us down before we even have a chance to attack."

"I'm assuming we won't fly above the Compound."

"No, we won't," he says smirking.

The pod jerks slightly, and Theo says it's probably a storm. A flash outside the window confirms this. I hadn't realized before that the pod is completely soundproof. We'd hear intense thunder if it wasn't.

"The pod can withstand it, right?"

Theo nods. "Sure can. Not much could bring this thing down, because of its titanium alloy." He smirks at me like he knows what's next.

"Titanium?" I repeat. "Merida said something about rings or something."

Now Theo is beaming like I gave him a huge ice-cream or something even better. Like ten ice-creams.

"Titanium alloy. It's an aerospace material. Super strong metal but also very light. You haven't heard of it? Well, you should have, considering it's part of you."

He pauses.

"What?" I say.

"Tissue infusion. Your bones. They infused titanium into your bone cells."

"My bones are metal?"

"Basically."

"Don't be ridiculous, Theo!"

He just looks at me, taken aback, as if I dropped his ice cream in the mud.

"Okay," he says, thoughtfully. "Wait here. I'll be back."

*     *     *

Theo returns with a little electronic device in his hand. It looks like a calculator from my high school math class.

"What's that?" I ask.

"Portable MRI," he says. "From the first aid kit."

I frown. Isn't an MRI supposed to be the size of a small closet? He taps a button and the little screen lights up.

"Ready?" asks Theo.

I look at him. "Ready for what?"

He doesn't reply, but simply puts the device up against his palm. Instantly, there's a ghostly image of his hand with different shades of grey. His bones appear more white than the darker fleshy parts.

"Okay," he says. "Your turn."

He holds his hand out toward mine. Something in me wants to scream at him, but he looks so earnest. I reluctantly place my hand in his, and he presses the device against my palm.

313

For some reason, my instinct is to turn away. I don't want to look. Nobody can force me to look.

"See," says Theo.

I hate his tone, but I look anyway. How could I not?

My hand is outlined on the screen. The flesh is almost the same grey color as Theo's. And my bones are clearly visible too.

But they are a stark white. Far brighter than Theo's bones on the screen.

"Titanium," says Theo triumphantly. "White means it's very dense. More dense than bone."

I look again, frowning. Then I remember something.

"This is an MRI?" I ask. Theo nods. "Everyone knows you can't put metal in an MRI."

I feel happy again. Relieved.

"That's iron or steel," says Theo. "They're magnetic. The 'M' in MRI stands for magnetic. This is titanium. It's non-ferro-magnetic."

"Oh."

My throat is dry. I stare at the screen.

White. A ghostly white skeleton of my hand dances on the screen, taunting me.

Why is it so white? How is it possible that my fingers are different to Theo's?

As if reading my confusion, Theo resumes his

explanation. "You know that bones aren't actually solid bone but are kind of fibrous, right? So, at the Compound, they use some secret process to infuse pure titanium atoms into your bone tissue. Somehow you end up with bones with fibrous tissue that is as strong as titanium alloy, but the bones still have bone marrow and produce blood cells and all that stuff."

I hold up my hand to my face and look at it.

"And you knew this? All that time in the Compound, you knew that I had metal bones?"

"Um, yeah," he says sheepishly.

I turn my hand at all angles, examining it with new eyes.

"Might have been useful to know," I laugh. "We were friends. You could have told me."

"Um, would you have believed me? Ever?"

I shrug. "So I'm like a metal dinosaur."

Theo laughs. "Dinosaur? No." He pauses. "Oh, I guess you mean the iridium. That's another metal, like titanium."

"In fossil dinosaur bones?"

"No, no. Dinosaurs just made iridium famous. Iridium is very rare on Earth, but common in asteroids. So that's how scientists proved that an asteroid impact caused the extinction of dinosaurs. Except there's a theory that there's a lot of iridium in the Earth's core because the metal is so dense that it sank to the bottom, um, to the middle, before the crust formed."

I simply look at him.

He shrugs. "Iridium is a dense metal that alloys well with titanium. They only infuse a little of it. Your bones are mostly titanium. You know, as an alloy."

Great. I'm a metal monster. I'm as strong as a pod. And I guess I'm Theo's favorite chemistry experiment come to life.

*     *     *

Axton's announcement booms over the loudspeakers. "Landing in approximately ten minutes. Stand by."

Our seatbelts activate in preparation for landing. We touch down, and I have no idea what to expect outside. No idea where we are, either.

"Trees," Eric says, the instant the doors open. "So many trees."

He's certainly right. We are engulfed in the color green as soon as we step outside. But when isn't that the extent of the scenery here? There's not much ice around anymore.

Actually, the ground immediately below us is a hard

concrete-like substance, and is not green. But we are surrounded by trees as far as we can see.

My heart starts to race, and I half expect to spot a boy and his monkey peering at us through the foliage.

Mason leads us over the rough, synthetic ground towards the back of the pod, where we see a small building constructed almost entirely of the same material as the ground.

"Have you been here before?" I ask Merida.

"This is where we performed most of our training. It's a nice place, once you go deep enough."

Surely she doesn't mean that the majority of these headquarters are underground. I've rather enjoyed not living like a mole rat with no fresh air for the past couple of days.

Mason enters a code on the panel beside the door, then leans forward so the machine can scan his face.

"For those of you who've never been here, there are a few rules. Firstly, don't leave the building without asking me. I'm the only one who can get in, I'm the only one who knows the password, and my face is the only one it recognizes. So don't leave if you haven't told me. Unless you want to be locked out overnight with the rabid monkeys."

Merida shoots a smirk at Axton.

"It was only once," he says defensively, and everyone laughs, before Mason continues with the rules.

"Basically, tell me before you do anything risky that could put you or others in danger. In fact, tell me before you do anything at all."

He holds the door open, which is grey and composed of gritty concrete.

The instant we go inside, the entire atmosphere changes. It is no longer a dull, clinical place, but instead beautifully decorated with splashes of color. The entrance is like the reception area in a hotel. To the left, there are white lounge chairs. Embroidered cushions are arranged neatly on sofas.

What shocks me the most is how old in style the decorations are in here. They're nothing like the modern furniture in Saskia's house, or in the pod.

"Before you go down to your rooms, everyone look at your timekeepers," Mason says. "That's how many hours you have until go time, which is defined as the exact moment you unlock the doors to the Compound."

My timekeeper says 34:28:04. That's less than two days.

"If you follow Eric, he'll lead you to your rooms."

He ushers Axton to the side, presumably to discuss strategy, and the rest of us head in.

*　　*　　*

318

Eric takes over after Mason and Axton disappear.

"You won't be spending much time in your rooms, but I'll show you where they are," Eric says.

The others have been here before, but Theo, Sapphire and I soak it all in. This place is surprisingly large. We step into some kind of elevator and descend deep into the ground.

Eric starts hamming it up like a tour guide as we walk along the corridors.

"And on the left side you will see our executive meeting rooms, where we make all sorts of important decisions . . . like what we should serve for breakfast . . ." He laughs at his own joke. "And on the right side . . ."

I kind of tune him out. I'm not in the mood for frivolity.

Eventually, Eric gets serious enough to take us to our separate rooms, telling us that it's important to remain in our designated rooms so we can be readily found if needed at any time.

My room is dainty, with a single bed layered with an intricate cover.

As I finish spreading my gear, there's a knock at the door. I open it to find Merida standing with one hand on her hip and the other on the doorframe.

"Ready for some more training?" she asks with a smirk.

# 28

# AXTON

Mason leads me around the corner past the small sofas and into a study. He sits in the brown chair behind the desk and gestures to the opposite chair.

"I wanted to go through something with you," he says, resting his battle-hardened hands on the desk. "You see, if something were to happen to me at some point, you would be the next point of call." I don't quite understand what he's talking about. "What I'm saying is, I am appointing you second-in-command."

I hold still in shock. I can't believe his words. My father was second-in-command, before he became first. But he worked nearly his entire life to get there.

"Thank you, Mason."

"Don't get all sentimental. We're a small team now. I've downloaded your face onto the scanning device at the front entrance, so if you ever need to get in, you can override the system and get into the building." He waves me away.

"I have a lot of work to do. You'd better prep Carla and Theo for action in the field. And congratulations."

*     *     *

I head downstairs with a skip in my step and knock on Theo's door. I ask him to join us in the meeting room in ten minutes.

As I approach the door to Carla's dorm room, I hear a crash, then a grunt. I knock, and finally the door opens. A familiar face grins at me.

"Merida?" I say. "What on earth are you guys doing in here?"

"Haven't you heard?" Carla says. "I'm learning how to control my robotic enhancements."

"Carla's a super-strong robot," adds Sapphire happily, her feet dangling off the bunk.

That makes sense. Of course, Merida would be the one to teach her how to harness it. She's been studying the robot industry for decades. She follows all of their pages and is obsessed with researching the way that human-resembling robots function and interact. She probably knows more than Theo about *that*, although he must be one of the world's top experts on the chemistry and properties of the tiger's eye mineral.

"I see. And how's it going?"

"Unbelievable. I can almost summon it whenever I like."

Carla is the most excited I've seen her in a while. The sadness I've detected behind her eyes is far less prominent than normal. I didn't know her before her transformation, but I'm sure it would not have been there. Not when she had a family, and a life. I can't imagine living in a world that isn't my own. Living in one without my father is bad enough, let alone if I lost my mother and Theo, along with everyone I know.

"That's great, Carla."

Merida nods. "She's doing well. Picked it up far more quickly than I would have thought possible."

Carla smiles. "Well, I'd better keep practicing," she says, beginning to close the door.

I hold it open with one hand. "Actually, I'd like to speak to you and Theo."

Her face drops for a second.

"Oh, okay. Sure."

Merida crosses her arms and turns to Carla. "I don't think you'll be needing me anymore. You can keep going on your own if you like, but I think you've got it. Seriously."

"Thanks, Merida," Carla says, and waves goodbye to Sapphire.

*     *     *

"You seem to be coping okay," I open, awkwardly.

"For a robot," Carla says. I guess she's not going to let me off lightly. "This isn't some kind of fun joke you're all playing on me?" she says, plaintive eyes on me.

"No," I say softly.

"So, I'm really one of them? My bones are made of metal. I mean, what on earth?"

She pauses. I don't know how to respond.

"No wonder I didn't break any bones when I fell off the ladder," she says, mostly to herself.

"Yes, but you're still you," I say. I'm not very good at this.

"Yeah, I know that!" She brushes a lock of hair from her face. "But why didn't you tell me earlier?" She glares into my soul as she says it. Of course this would happen.

323

How ironic. I'm here worrying that we've dropped the bomb too soon, and she's yelling at me for not telling her sooner.

"I could have helped to solve the problem somehow. If only I'd known . . . " she says.

"Yeah? How?" I say flatly.

She gazes at the ground. "I don't know. Something."

"I'm sorry I kept it from you."

"No, you're not," she says plainly.

I face ahead. She's not making it easy.

"So, that pile of bodies in the forest. What was that?"

"Um, that was the failures being recycled."

"Recycled?"

"Cheap solar energy used to re-extract the metal parts. From robots that failed for various reasons."

"Like what?"

"Tissue infusion failure. Or the augs didn't mesh with live cells. Or the control was weak. Or maybe tiger's eye toxicity. We're not really sure."

"Tiger's eye what?"

"Toxicity. Blood poisoning. They use it as part of the infusion process."

"Okay . . . titanium bones and tiger's eye blood. Great."

"People have known about tiger's eye powers for centuries. You know—healing, concentration, emotional harmony, lots of things. But it wasn't widely used. Mostly by mystics and alternative healers."

"But you just said it's toxic."

"Well, if you grind up tiger's eye minerals and inject them into someone's bloodstream, they die from liver failure. Quickly. So, the Compound must be doing something special."

"How do you know they inject it?"

"We don't. But Dad managed to get a few blood samples. Massive levels of tiger's eye. And you can see it in their eyes."

"That dead man. You looked in his eyes."

"Yeah. Tiger's eye causes gold-colored rings in the eyes."

She rolls her eyes. "So, I have gold rings in my eyes?" Then she pauses. "Actually, I haven't had a good look in the mirror."

"Yes, you have them. Around your iris. You'll have to take my word for it, for now. Anyway, they're called KF rings. Kayser-Fleischer rings. Humans get them from copper in the blood. Robots get them from tiger's eye."

"So, I would be in that pile if you hadn't helped me escape?"

"No. The opposite. We think they've been having trouble perfecting the process. You saw how many failures they've had. That's one reason why they still need to study you."

"Well, maybe I would have been better off like them."

"You don't mean that."

"Maybe I do."

"Why?"

"Because I'm supposed to be dead. I am dead."

"You didn't die, Carla. It's not like that."

"It's exactly like that."

"Okay, well, it's not. Besides, you should be glad. You don't age," I say. An attempt to lighten the mood. "You've got to admit the technology is impressive. You're one-hundred-and-seventeen, but I can barely see your wrinkles."

She scowls. "So it wasn't suspended animation, was it?" she says accusingly.

"No. It was resets."

"Which is?"

"Factory resets. Somehow they clear most of the recently laid-down memories. Most, but not all."

"Huh," she says, not really comprehending.

"Theory is, you gave them lots of trouble over the years, but they still needed you. So they reset you each time you started to evade their control."

Carla looks concerned. "I've been walking around on *this* earth for the past century and I don't even remember it? Who knows what I've done."

I don't know what to say. There is so much that I could say. But it's not the time. I've said too much already.

"What have they made me do?"

"Don't worry about it, Carla."

She scowls. "I didn't even dream this kind of thing could be possible." She pauses. "More like a nightmare."

I can tell she's had enough.

*　　*　　*

Carla follows me to Theo's room, and we collect him and head to the lounge chairs upstairs. If we're to go through the mission plan, we may as well do so in comfort.

We sit down, and I pull out the tablet that was tucked in my jacket.

"I'm supposed to go over the mission brief with you two, since you'll basically be running it and making sure it goes smoothly."

"Making sure it runs smoothly?" Carla repeats. "It'll run smoothly if I actually get to be part of it. I know what it's like there. I lived there. Theo and I both should be going out."

"It's fine, Carla," Theo says. "I like being on this side of the mission. Remember, I was kind of behind the scenes for these guys in our first rescue mission."

"Behind the scenes? You were actually *in* there!" she protests. "Just like I need to be."

I shake my head.

"It's worth it for one person to die to save the rest of the children," Carla reasons. "Besides . . . I'm not even alive to begin with."

I sigh.

"Come on, Carla," says Theo. "You're more alive than any of us."

"Carla," I say. "We need you to be there for us. If you're on-site you won't be able to direct us if plans change."

"Theo can do that." She stands up abruptly. "I've got to tell Mason that I have super strength. I was going to go about this secretly, but this will make him change his mind."

I know that Mason's pride won't let him, but I let her go anyway.

I turn to Theo. "Where was I? Oh, right. Things will go wrong, but at least if you're absolutely comfortable with what's happening, you'll be able to coordinate attacks. You two are the most qualified for this job because, obviously, you've been in there for an extended time. You know that place."

Carla's voice wafts in from Mason's room.

"I can't sit there and watch from the sidelines," she says.

"I'll be back," I say to Theo, and I head to Mason's office down the hall.

I poke my head around the door. Mason has his elbow on the desk and a stern expression on his face.

He beckons me in.

"I don't see the harm in letting Carla out in the field," I say to Mason. I've decided I'm on Carla's side.

"No, I . . . " Carla protests. "Wait, did you just agree with me?"

"She does have a lot of experience with the layout of the Compound, and she could be valuable out there."

"Far more valuable conducting the mission," Mason interjects.

"Possibly, but likely not," I say. "She's been training with Merida, and she's very strong. She could be an effective asset, as Merida says."

"Let me get this right. You're telling me that she can control her robotic enhancements? Already?" says Mason. "I don't believe that."

"Yes," Carla says, "I can. I know I've got to go out and fight. It's the only way I can truly help."

Mason begins to cut her off, but she ignores him. Even if Carla would be better off helping in the field, Mason doesn't want to admit it.

"I can lift tables bolted to the ground. I went to the basement and lifted an entire vehicle. I can help you."

"Good pitch, Carla," Mason says. "Sincerely."

I shift on my feet. This is Mason's false apologetic tone. He isn't giving in.

"But I know that you're needed even more to oversee the mission."

He packs up his tablet and places it into a pouch, which means the conversation is over. He needs to maintain his authority. Anyone else would have let Carla into the action, because Carla would be valuable as a fighter. Especially because of her past.

Carla stands up, turns to face Mason, and says, "Thanks for understanding." I can tell by her posture that she is holding back.

She does a sassy, one-eighty degree turn and walks calmly out of the room. Her eyes are not calm. Mason appears unaware. I watch her go around the corner.

Mason frowns at me, which means that I, too, am now uninvited.

I leave the room.

I hear a ringtone; he's calling someone. They answer, and their voice carries through the speakers.

It's not a voice I ever thought I'd be hearing again. Nor one I would ever want to hear. The General's.

"Hello, Mason," she says. "I assume that all is going well with your side of the plan."

Mason's reply carries out of the room.

"Everything is on schedule."

"It had better be. You realize that the entire future of the Organization, if not the world, depends on you making this work."

"I know. It is all in line."

"You mustn't let Carla into the Compound. It is imperative, Mason. She would ruin everything."

"Yes, I understand. I took care of it."

"Good. Be absolutely sure that this remains just between you and I. You are in a soundproof area, I presume?"

"Of course."

The sliding door clicks closed, as if he just now remembered to shut it.

*    *    *

My heart is racing as thoughts churn in my mind. How could Mason still be on her side? He can't be. He must be playing both sides.

Or perhaps I don't know him as well as I thought I did.

I head back to the sofas where Carla and Theo are sitting.

"Everything all right?" Theo says as I sit down, his eyebrows crumpled. He's my brother. Of course he can read me like a book.

I try to erase the shock from my face, with little luck. If our team leader isn't on our side, then who is?

The only people I know for certain to be trustworthy are Carla and Theo. Theo because of our father. Carla, because she's Carla . . . and because of her brother.

A tiny doubt inside my head interrupts, questioning me. Carla is happy to sacrifice herself to save the children. But I don't want her to. Why can't I let that happen? She doesn't even belong here. What is it that makes me reluctant to allow her to risk herself? I'm a soldier.

I wonder if Theo would be willing to let Carla die. Probably not. He's known her for longer than I have. But at the same time, he always believed in sacrifice for the good of the people.

I sigh inwardly. I can't let emotion cloud my decisions. Whatever is best for the mission, that is what I have to do.

"Yeah," I say. "Everything's fine. Just talking about logistics. I'm sorry you won't be able to go out in the field, Carla."

I know they won't believe me that nothing's wrong. I can only hope that they think it's some logistical issue. I'll probably have to tell them eventually anyway, unless I figure things out myself.

Carla leans in. "What's going on, Axton? Is it Mason?" she says. I shake my head subtly, hoping she won't ask anything else. She doesn't press further, but I know she's unconvinced.

"I think we should go over the plan," I say. I take out my tablet and open the mission brief.

I turn it towards them and let them read it through. It is relatively simple, and Carla and Theo should be able to conduct the mission successfully, given that all of the rest of us have basically done this mission before.

"The main difference between this mission and the last time we did it, is that this time we don't have the support of the entire Organization. Now we have a team that is experienced but small, and the only external support we have is you guys."

Theo nods, and Carla says, "You know I'm going to find my brother, right?"

I sigh. I have no doubt. I have no doubt that she will do whatever she can to get inside the Compound. Carla will always be Carla. Metaphorically, of course, but she isn't herself literally. She's probably questioning whether she knows who she is. The thought makes me feel guilty that she's found out already. I knew it wouldn't be good, but she'd have to know the truth sometime. Why couldn't it have waited until she had all the information? Then it wouldn't have been such a shock. I wish I could make it right.

"I know that nothing I say will stop you, if that's what you mean. But we will get your brother out if he's in there, even if you don't go in."

"You can't promise that," Carla says. "Last time, even with the whole Organization working together, so many children were left in there."

"Carla . . . " Theo says.

"I got you out," I say.

"And lots more were recaptured afterwards," she says. She brushes a hand through her hair, almost in agony. I can't stand it.

"I promise you that if your brother is in there, we will get him," I blurt out. They always say you shouldn't make promises you can't keep. This could be one of those times, and I know that if that happens, I will certainly lose Carla. My stomach tightens as I realize how much she means to me. They told us no emotion. But when I look at her, I can't see a robot; I see a kind, brave young woman.

She stares at me in shock and surprise at what I just vowed.

"Thank you."

Theo returns the tablet to me as Eric walks in holding a tray of plates. It seems like a long time since I last saw food on actual, real-life plates. Not sure why we'd bother with plates down here, but I'm not about to complain.

"Hungry?" he asks with a big, goofy grin. "I figured you guys would still be working but didn't want you to skip dinner."

"Thanks, Eric," I say. Now Mason has made me wonder whether Eric is on our side or not. I'll be questioning everything from here on.

"We were just finishing up," I say, beginning to stand up.

"Well, then," Eric says with a grin. "Follow me."

This guy never stops smiling.

He gestures for us to head down three levels to the dining hall, but beckons me to stay back with him.

"You guys go on ahead," he says. Carla gives us a small wave.

"Is everything okay?" Eric says under his breath, gazing at me with concern.

"Nothing for you to worry about, Eric," I say. I can't trust anyone until I figure out if anyone else here is in on Mason's plan. As to how I'm going to do that, I'm not so sure.

How are we possibly going to save the children if our new leader and our old leader are both conspiring against us?

# 29

# CARLA

Getting ready for the mission is one of the happiest times of my life. My new life anyway. Life, meaning alive. Not only alive, but alive as a robot. How insane is that? I don't feel like a robot. I still have all of the normal bodily functions of a human being, which doesn't really make sense. Why would they create robots that are exactly like humans? Why not just use humans? I mean, okay, so I'm like twenty times stronger than any bodybuilder, but you get the point.

Merida says that strength is only one of my capabilities. Rapid tissue repair. Also pain tolerance. And I can sense pain, but it's not really in my nervous system.

"Brain pain, not nerve pain," says Merida.

As soon as she said it, I realized I'd never hurt myself since I woke up disoriented at the Compound. That I mined for hours without a scratch. That my wound healed insanely fast after the tracker was cut out. That I didn't break any bones when I fell from the ladder in the Compound. That I was stabbed in the shoulder and forgot about it completely.

That I am indestructible.

*     *     *

The prep time passes in a blur. We pack the pod with more supplies and review the plan. I realize that I haven't seen Axton much over the course of mission preparation. He must be sorting out things behind the scenes.

At last, we are ready to head off.

"Right on schedule," Mason announces.

We are sitting in the pod, final checks complete. Mason will be flying us there, so Axton can jump out as needed. The autochutes are lined up along one side. Theo was nervous when he heard that we'd be jumping, which is possibly why he didn't mind looking after the mission from the control center. I, however, do mind. I haven't fully decided how I'm going to steal someone else's chute, but am sure that I will need to.

Theo catches me gazing at the chutes, and his eyes meet mine.

He shakes his head ever so slightly.

I look away quickly.

As we begin to take off, he walks towards me.

"Don't do it, Carla. I'm begging," he says, under his breath. If there's one thing he won't do, it's snitch on me. He will try to stop me, though. That's something I can't let happen.

I glance up at him and smile. He knows I won't listen to him. I have to find my brother. I can't trust anyone else.

Theo studies my face, and sits back down without a word.

I am sitting pensively when I hear soft footsteps coming towards me. Axton.

"Hey, Carla. I wanted to go over something with you."

I frown. We've already gone through everything in very tight detail.

"We've had a slight change of plans."

I still don't move. He's acting strange.

"Okay . . . " I say, hesitantly.

"Come on, Carla," he says quietly. "Just follow me."

I do as he says, and he takes me around the back of

the pod to a small storage room. It is dimly lit, and Axton leaves the door half-open.

"I need you to go into the Compound."

"What?" I ask. "Why?"

Surely Mason didn't change his mind.

"Things are happening, Carla," he says, "that we need to put an end to."

That told me absolutely nothing. "Oh, don't play that game. You can tell me what's going on."

His eyes won't meet mine. "I really can't. You'll have to trust me."

"You don't trust me, do you? That's what this is."

"No, Carla," he says, exasperated. "If I didn't trust you, I wouldn't have said anything, because I know you'll be going into the Compound anyway."

He's not wrong, and we both know it. Relief washes over me.

"We'd better get back out there," Axton says.

We take our seats again. I'm sitting between Theo and Eric. Neither of them asks what it was about.

Clouds stream past, barely visible through the tinted windows. I glance at my timekeeper, and the display lights up with 189:00—three hours to go.

"It could be tight," Theo says, glancing at his wrist.

Eric nods. "We can always change the time slightly.

But I think we'll make it."

I spend the rest of the journey analyzing and reviewing the mission in my mind, working out the most likely place to find my brother. He'll obviously be in the Assembly room, as long as they don't know we're coming; but I need to know which exit he'll be near, so I can get him out.

I also worry about why Axton suddenly needs me on the field. I'm assuming it is my newfound skill that he's after. What could possibly have changed? Are there more guards? How can I fight if I don't know who, or what, I'm up against?

Animal or mineral?

*　　*　　*

"Ten minutes until we're overhead," Mason booms.

I am wide awake as the craft approaches the Compound, subtly eyeing off the chute I'm going to make a run for. I'll have to grab it, undo the tag, put it on and jump; all before anyone tries to stop me. Which makes me wonder if any of the other soldiers are in on the plan for me to go in.

I don't know if there's a spare chute, or if I'm going to have to become a thief. Maybe I'll be ruining the mission for someone else.

"Five minutes until altitude." Mason sounds appre-hensive. It's the first time I've ever heard his voice waver like this.

Axton comes out of the cockpit just as Mason calls, "Two minutes."

I prepare to sprint, my gaze locked on the chute clos-est to the exit door. I sense Theo watching me, and I'm sure he knows what I'm going to do.

At the one-minute mark, the doors swing upwards. The pod fills with air like a wind tunnel. Theo makes eye contact with me briefly, squeezes my hand hard, and I run. I see nothing except the autochute bag right before me. I dodge Eric, skirt around a chair directly in my path, and snatch the bag. I barely stop to put my arms in the straps, and I'm still doing up the buckle as I step over the edge.

"Carla!" I hear Mason's yell. It is too late.

I am plummeting towards the earth. I grasp the tag tightly; thank goodness it didn't end up tucked in. I didn't have time to think about that, nor to begin worrying about the descent. The only image present in my mind is one of Rory. He made the jump easy.

Around me there is only green, but directly below me is the bare concrete of the Compound. As I hurtle closer, the details become clearer.

The landing is all a blur: tumbling, rolling, smashing into the hard concrete. How did I survive that?

Easily.

Only as I throw the bag to the ground, and press the decompose button, do I notice a nametag on the side. It reads 'A'.

A for Axton. It wasn't meant for me. It dawns on me that this means he's staying on the ship. He gave up his position for me. Surely Mason will know, then, that this was his idea.

I keep moving, trying to convince myself that Axton will get himself out of this mess. He must have a plan.

I hear Axton in my earpiece. "You down?"

The sudden noise shocks me for a split second. "Yes," I respond.

"Head on in." He's all business.

I have to focus on my plan. I hurry towards the entrance, opening up the cheat sheet that I made with a small map of the Compound. It's more of a comfort thing than anything. I know the place like the back of my hand.

I reach the entrance and kick the door down. Don't need a code for that. I am immediately overwhelmed by the distinct musty smell of moist corridors. I never anticipated being back here.

"Move fast, Carla," Axton says in my ear. "No time."

I find the elevator, which is around the corner, and exit on the level directly above the Assembly hall. I haven't seen any guards yet. Presumably, most are in the Assembly hall now. I glance at my folded map and walk quickly to a small room that is barely ever used. We used to go past all the time, and there was never anyone in it. It appears to be a control room and has a tiny window overlooking the hall. I'm careful to stand back from the window.

My wristband buzzes faintly, indicating that everyone should be entering now, including Mason.

"You in?" Axton asks, startling me.

"Yes," I say.

"Find him and get out."

I creep to the window, and my heart is racing as I scan the cavern from high above. Superb vantage point, and I realize that it would be almost impossible for anyone to spot me so high up. Hundreds of children sit below in the large area, and a few guards roam to keep them in line. I've skimmed the room twice now, and Rory's not there. My stomach drops.

"Have you located him?" His tone is becoming agitated.

I rub my hands on my thighs to wipe the sweat off, and blink hard and fast.

"Carla, do you have Rory?" his voice booms, but I can't focus on it.

As I search harder, I spot a dark head of hair in the corner that I didn't notice before. Slightly curled, brown hair; seems possible from up here. He's in the far corner, which adds some difficulty. We had hoped that he'd be closer to this side. "Found him," I say, perhaps a little too loudly, because I hear a grunt from the earpiece.

I race down the stairs, noticing a guard who is standing on the platform at the bottom. I don't slow for an instant. He only sees me when I'm almost on top of him. He lifts a hand to go for his gun, but I grab his wrist, twist his entire body, and throw him to the ground. His head bounces. He doesn't move. I guess he isn't a robot.

I curve around the passageways behind the Assembly hall on the outside, and just reach the entrance closest to where I should be able to reach Rory, when an awful, inconceivable thought occurs to me.

What if he doesn't remember me?

I stop dead in my tracks. It is quite possible, if not likely, that he has already been brainwashed. If he looks at me with those empty, sunken eyes, I don't think I'll be able to handle it.

"Have you got him?" I hear Axton say.

I can't go in there. What if he doesn't know who I am?

"I . . ." I say.

"Carla, what's going on?"

"I can't . . ."

I can't face seeing my brother if he doesn't remember me.

But that's selfish. If I don't go in, I won't be able to save him at all. I summon as much courage as I can and focus on getting him out and nothing else. I plunge into the room, search frantically for him and, without hesitation, grab Rory by the shoulders and shuffle him out of the room before anyone seems to realize. He emits a small gasp, but doesn't protest.

By the time the alarm sounds and several guards race out of the room after me, I am already around the corner and pressing on the elevator touchpad. Further along the passage, I hear thumps and thuds as my team fends off other guards. We are in the thick of the fight now.

I push him into the elevator and turn him around so I can finally look at his face. His hair is longer than usual and flops down his forehead. I hold my breath.

"Carla," Rory exclaims, slamming into me and wrapping his arms around me. I squeeze him tightly as tears pour down my face. "I knew you would come for me."

That comment breaks my heart a little.

"Do you have him?" Axton blasts in my ear.

"Yes," I say, my voice breaking slightly. I loosen my grip on Rory. "We've got to go," I tell him. "We'll have heaps of time to talk after we get out of here."

Rory nods.

There's so much I want to ask him, but my priority is making our way out alive. It's riskier now that I have Rory with me; he's the treasure I have to protect. I will never let go.

The elevator stops, and we continue back the way I came in. I'm hoping it won't be blocked by guards. We half-jog through the passageways, and are about to reach the exit, when I see a tall figure directly in front of us.

"Stand down," he yells, beginning to run towards us, raising his machine gun.

Rory stiffens and slows down, stricken with panic.

I slow my pace but continue towards the guard, lifting my arms in attack mode.

"No, Carla," Rory yells, clutching in vain at my clothes.

I run forward and swing my fist before the guard can pull the trigger. It contacts the guard's face, emitting a crunching sound. Rory gasps as the guard falls to the ground.

"How did you . . . ?" Rory says, his eyes wide.

"No time to talk," I say, pulling his arm to get us moving again.

We are finally at the exit, and we burst through the doorway. The pod is hovering overhead.

"We're out," I say, my voice barely discernible above the racket of the craft's engines. I know Axton heard me because I can already see him descending from the pod, attached to a long cord. "You're going to have to go up with him," I say to Rory.

He nods, but his chin wobbles with fear. I nearly start to cry because it's so familiar. His chin always quivered when he was upset. Memories flood back to me.

I stare at Rory for a moment. I can't believe he's really here. I get the urge to grab onto him for fear of him vanishing before my eyes.

"What?" he says.

"Nothing," I say.

He narrows his eyes.

"Nothing," I repeat with a laugh. "Just so happy to see you."

Axton reaches the ground and beckons Rory over to him.

I don't want to let Rory go. But I know I have to go back in there to help.

Rory goes over to Axton.

"We're going to strap you in quickly, then you're going to come back up with me," Axton says. "I'll be holding onto you the whole time."

"Wait," Rory says. He runs towards me and gives me a quick, tight hug.

"I'll see you soon," I say, hugging him back.

We let go. "Come back," Rory says.

I will. I promise myself that. I storm back towards the entry for the second time today. I race to the elevator and descend, this time not stopping at the control room level. I reach the bottom and exit. The doors open and there are no guards in sight.

I cautiously walk around the corner and see Merida with a group of fifteen children. I get closer and realize they have a dazed look in their eyes. I shudder. Rory could have ended up like them.

"Keep moving, Carla, we're good here," Merida says.

A guard lies twitching on the floor to my left. I wonder if Merida shot him. I walk around the corner, the sensation of entrapment overwhelming me in the small, enclosed areas. I continue around the corner and come across Eric with another even larger group of children, who appear to be alert. Thank goodness they're not all brainwashed.

Eric spots me and beckons me over. I head to the front of the group where he is standing. The children are whispering excitedly at the prospect of freedom. But between us and the exit is a swarm of guards.

"I've got this," I say to Eric.

I approach the guards. There must be at least a dozen of them.

"Careful," Eric warns me from behind.

Some of the guards start to smirk. They clearly recognize me as the weak, meek Carla. It takes everything I have not to scream at them that I'm going to destroy them all. For everything they've done to me, to my brother and to all of these innocent children. And for what? Why have they been doing all of this?

I run at the guards and they start to laugh. I focus on activating my robotic enhancements more than I ever have. I am mere strides away when one of the guards nudges another and says, "Isn't that the girl?"

The other guard doesn't have time to respond.

I reach them at full speed, punching two of them in the stomach with my two fists, hard. They drop like flies, grimacing and grunting. I do a roundhouse kick and connect with another guard. Before he topples to the floor, another one swings at me. I let his fist pass and it's like a tap on the shoulder by a mosquito. I grab him by the belt and hurl him up into the tunnel roof. He rises, then plummets, and stays down.

Two more guards are a few strides away, backing up. One of them has his gun drawn, aimed at me. I take a step and plant my fist in his stomach. His gun fires off a few rounds as he falls backwards. The bullets hit me in the side, about waist high. In my heightened state, they feel like little goldfish bites. The other guard next to him gets bitten too, but not by bullets. By my other fist.

I take out three other guards, I think. I lose count in the fuzz of battle. But zero is the number that remain standing.

They are all on the ground in a rancid pile of black uniforms. Reminds me of laundry day. I fling several of them to the side to make a path to the exit for the children.

The guards aren't dead, and I guess I'm glad. If I truly had killed them, despite what they've done, I would feel terrible.

Eric is right behind me with the group of children, who are shouting things at me, and to each other, in amazement.

"Thank you," one girl says, her eyes bright.

"Are you the girl we've heard about?" a boy around my age says. "Are you really from the Compound, like us?"

"We'll have plenty of time to talk later," I say. "Right now, let's get out of here."

To my surprise, they let out a cheer.

I don't even have time to react, but Eric says, "Quiet, please." They stop immediately. "We don't want to draw attention to ourselves." Eric turns to me, "I'm glad they missed when they shot."

I feel at my waist, find one of the little holes in the material, and gently squeeze the skin around it. Out pops a bullet. I put it into Eric's hand.

"They didn't," is all that I need to say.

Eric frowns in confusion, then nods.

I want to help Eric take the group out and into the pod, but I know I'll be needed elsewhere.

"I'll see you all soon," I say to them, moving quietly to see if any of our team are at the next exit. There are several guards standing in front of it, but no good guys. I manage to avoid them without being spotted.

"Better hurry, Carla," I hear Axton say through my earpiece. I begin to run to the next exit. If I'm correct, this should be where I will be taking Axton's group of children to escape.

I see the distinct black uniforms of the guards not far away. I hide around the corner behind the wall. The guards have a group of children corralled in the hallway, and I can hear the guards speaking.

"You are to go back to your units and make sure everyone is there. If they're not, work out who's missing," one

of the guards says. "You're not having dinner until everyone is there."

"Get to it," another guard barks. "Now!"

I recognize his voice immediately. I physically feel like throwing up at the sound. For the first time since I've been back at the Compound, panic sets in. It's Silver Belt.

Then I have a new, even more horrific, thought. I don't know what's happened to the other members of my unit. What kind of person am I to totally forget about them? I take a breath, calm myself, and remember why I'm here.

The children begin to scatter to their units, and I realize that now is my chance. I race out of my hiding spot, summon my enhancements and let loose on one of the guards. He falls and I turn on the other guard.

Silver Belt.

He spins around and I see the recognition in his eyes. Could that be fear behind his pupils?

He doesn't say anything, raises his gun, looks at me, then, surprisingly, lowers it.

I can see words forming on his lips. I won't give him the chance. I tense my muscles in preparation for attack, but he beats me to it.

"Carla," he says. "Wait."

"Don't speak to me," I snap, still poised.

"I'm on your side."

What on earth is he talking about?

"You think I want to be in here?" he says.

I need to move on. I need to attack him and move. But has he been trapped in here, the same as I was?

"I've been trying to figure out a way to let the children out for a long time."

I shake my head adamantly, but some part of me hesitates.

"I'm serious," he says. "Please believe me."

I don't believe him. I can't believe him. I try to block his words, but something nags at the back of my mind. Are the guards just prisoners, too?

"I never wanted to be here," he repeats.

I make a decision, and I don't know if it's the right one. My emotion is getting in the way. "All right, stop wasting my time. If you do *one thing* out of line, you're gone." I give him a chance. Even after he threatened to shoot me so many times. Even after the needles. Even after everything else. I'm going to have to watch my back double-time now. But I do take his gun. I grip it tightly and bend the barrel with my bare hands. Titanium fingers have their uses. I throw the broken gun onto the grimy tunnel floor.

I realize that many of the children have stopped a few

steps away to listen to our conversation. "I'm here to help you," I say, loudly enough for them all to hear me. "Follow me and let's get out of here."

"We know who you are, Carla," one of them says.

I give them a small smile, but am kind of disturbed on the inside. It seems that everyone knows more about me than I do. I tell Silver Belt, whose name I still do not know, nor care to know, to lead us to the exit so that I can watch from behind. Watch *him* from behind. I don't speak to the children, and I think they realize I'm not in the mood for a chat. It seems as if they have a million questions to ask. Questions that I doubt I have the answers to, seeing as how I'm always the last person to find out anything. It's only taken me a hundred years to find out who I am. What I am.

We reach the exit, which leads us upstairs to the floor with the elevator on it. The children barely say a word to each other. We enter, and I realize we're going to have to take two trips in the elevator, so I send the guard up with the first batch. I try not to think about the possible consequences.

The rest of the children are left with me. "Sent them up with a guard," I say, hoping Axton will hear me. "Says he's on our side."

"Got them," Axton says. "Send the next ones up."

The elevator comes back down soon enough, so we pile in. As we reach the surface, the children are bubbling with excitement. The pod has landed on the concrete pad now, near where the elevator emerges from the ground. It's making a low whirring sound that I hope anyone below will miss. I'm glad that the Compound is so lightly guarded. Axton's information must have been correct that the main army was deployed to the northern territories.

"Board the pod," I say to the children. "We're taking you to a safe place."

They climb up, and Axton greets them at the front door.

We're going to need to use the back rooms and the downstairs areas to hold them all.

Only when the last of the children board the pod, do I notice Silver Belt standing a little way off. I climb the ramp, and Axton is still waiting near the door.

"Why isn't he boarding?" I say, gesturing to the guard.

"Are you crazy, Carla?" Axton whispers. "He's one of them."

"I know, but . . . " I realize how silly it must sound to want to bring him with us. It's almost ludicrous. But something doesn't seem right about leaving him here.

"What's gotten into you? Has he brainwashed you, too?"

I glare at Axton. That got to me.

"Okay, no. I'm sorry. That was harsh."

"Don't worry about it," I say, moving past him. I decide it's not worth it. I don't know why I should care about Silver Belt anyway. Most likely, he's lying to me. He probably switched sides only when he realized they were going to lose.

I can't stop thinking about his pleading eyes, though. Inside the pod, I see that the rest of the team, are already here.

"Did we get everyone out?" I whisper to Merida.

"We think so. We'll be checking numbers as we leave. But then again, we don't have the correct records for certain to start with."

Axton closes the doors, and I see someone standing next to him. Silver Belt. I guess he's joining us, after all.

"I've checked him for trackers and removed all communication devices. He'd better be telling the truth," Axton says, eyeing the guard.

I head for the back room.

"Looking for somebody?" I hear Theo's question drift down the hallway.

I frown and follow his voice. Sitting in the far corner, next to Theo, is a tiny figure. Rory.

"Rory," I shout, racing towards him and picking him up.

"Is it true that you're a robot?" he asks.

Oh no. I didn't even think of that. How are we going to tell him? Surely, it's better if I'm the one to tell him . . .

I don't know what to say to him.

"It's been a long couple of weeks, and I'll tell you everything very soon. But first I'd like to hear all about where you've been."

He peers up at me with those big, brown eyes. I nearly let a torrent of tears loose at that alone.

"I don't know how long I've been in there. It seems like forever," he says. "I don't remember coming here, but I saw Mom and Dad for the last time before I went to school. I remember going to the school hall, the lights shattered, and it all went dark. Then they grabbed me."

I shudder. I can't believe they did this to him. My brother.

"I don't remember after that," Rory continues. "All I remember is being in the Compound and being yelled at by the guards."

He tells us of his many adventures in the Compound, including pranking a few of the guards, being punished, and telling everyone to push cloth into their ears so they couldn't hear anything in the Monitor Room.

I attempt to talk to Rory more about what happened, but he must have had as little sleep as I in the Compound.

He falls asleep right on my lap in the middle of a sentence. I stroke his hair. Content.

I take to gazing out of the windows for a while, trying to dull the urge to smack the guard who sits in the corner. He's keeping to himself. Probably realizes one wrong word, and we will all rip him apart. The children are keeping their distance.

Axton makes announcements on the loudspeakers as we reassure all of the children that we are the good guys and that they're going to be safe from now on. He doesn't tell them exactly where we're going. We don't want to give the children too much information. And there's a guard on board.

"Where are we going?" Rory asks, nudging me. "Actually, where are we?"

"Prepare for landing," Axton's announcement blasts, saving me from answering.

"We'll talk about everything very soon," I say to Rory.

We land on the same familiar strip, above the dorms.

*     *     *

We lead the children out onto the concrete, and they file into the building. A few of them, especially the dazed ones, begin to wander off, catching glimpses of things in the distance. I hope there's a way to reverse the brain-washing. Luckily, from what I've seen, it doesn't appear that too many of them have been emotionally erased.

"Hey, come back this way," Eric says, as some of the children near the luscious rainforest surrounding the grounds. No wonder they're drawn to it, after all that time in the musky Compound.

Merida and the other soldiers are trying to herd all the children off the pod and into the building. Children are milling around in all directions. Chaos rules.

Suddenly a flash of blue. Sapphire comes running across the concrete yelling, "Carla. You're back."

And she jumps up with a running hug that meets me in mid-air. Good thing I'm a robot, or I would have been knocked off my feet.

I close my eyes and hug her close.

# 30

# AXTON

Despite the spectacle of joy that is Sapphire, I find my attention drawn elsewhere. Instincts are powerful. Guts should be listened to.

I begin to run.

We should never have trusted the guard. Carla is too nice. Humans are humans. Robots are robots. And guards are not to be reckoned with.

I am running at full speed.

The guard with the silver belt has a steel mallet in his hand. He walks awkwardly, the mallet swinging heavily with each step. While the children milled around, he found it in the maintenance shed. He walks slowly and purposefully.

Towards Carla.

He hasn't noticed me running. I am gaining speed. I only need to stay quiet and I can take him. I can make it. I have to. But he is so close to Carla now. I am too far away, and my emotions fail me.

"Carla," I yell a warning.

The guard picks up his pace at the sound of my voice; Carla doesn't hear it. She's too busy hugging Sapphire. Her emotion clouds her senses.

I run faster, but he's only a few steps away from Carla. She doesn't know he's right behind her! There's nothing but empty space between them.

I am not going to reach him in time. He hefts the mallet up high with both of his arms. Any second now, it will come crashing down, onto the back of Carla's skull.

It would kill a human, but I don't know what it will do to a robot.

I'm sure he does.

As he closes in on her, Carla senses something. Perhaps his pounding footsteps or my desperate cries. Still embracing Sapphire, I see Carla release slightly, but she's still facing away from the guard.

I am too late, too slow, too human. He is on her. The mallet begins to fall. Down, down, down. It falls in slow motion. Towards the back of Carla's head, at full speed, with all his power.

Sapphire's eyes grow wide as she sees the weapon crashing towards Carla. She shrieks and reacts. She jumps, and her tiny arm instinctively lifts up to protect her beloved Carla from the deadly blow.

Sapphire's puny little arm up in a brave defence. I can't move, I can't shout. The huge steel mallet slams down. All of the guard's power behind it. Full muscle power. The heavy mallet swings, aimed at Carla's head with deadly force. It smashes into Sapphire's tiny arm.

Clang.

Metal on metal.

The heavy mallet bounces off Sapphire's arm, back up into the air, and spins away into the distance. The guard lands heavily on his feet and his ankle twists unnaturally.

Sapphire falls down out of Carla's embrace. She peers strangely at her arm. She moves it tentatively. It is just fine. She gazes at the guard on the ground in utter fury. She looks at her arm again. Sapphire takes a few running steps towards the guard and plants her swinging foot right into his back. He goes flying. His body arches off the ground and lands crumpled further away.

Sapphire grins in satisfaction.

Carla looks at the huge guard, looks at little Sapphire, and looks at the guard again. She bursts into laughter.

The whole crowd is staring at Sapphire. Everyone is stunned.

No one moves, except Sapphire. She jumps up and down with her arms in the air. "I'm a robot! I'm a robot! I'm just like Carla!"

I arrive, panting. A little late to the party. Carla is kind and she's caring, and she's a robot.

She hovers over the injured guard as if to protect Sapphire from him, or perhaps vice-versa.

I am not a robot. Neither is he. So, I finish him. He will not be coming back.

# 31

# CARLA

Eventually, the commotion dies down, and the new children from the Compound are safe inside. I've been watching Sapphire entertain herself outside, doing cartwheels and occasionally punching dints into the trunks of nearby trees.

Axton beckons Theo and I over to him.

"I'm afraid I still have a special mission for you two," he says. "You're not free yet."

"It's already been a long day." I grit my teeth. "But I'm up for it. As long as we get back soon, because Rory and I have a lot of catching up to do when he's done sleeping."

"It won't take long," Axton says. "We're going in the

pod. I'll be coming with you, of course. We'll talk more about it when we're on board."

"I'm coming too," pouts Sapphire, from several yards away.

Apparently, robot hearing is a thing, too.

"It's too dangerous," I say automatically.

"Uh, actually it's not really," says Axton. "Not for her."

I am not used to this new situation. It has been another interesting day.

*　　*　　*

The four of us board and Axton says, "I've told the others that we're collecting supplies, so we might stop for some food on the way back."

Theo seems as confused as I am, for once. Why would we need to hide things from the other team members? What are we going to be doing?

We resume our regular seats on the pod, and Axton briefs us over the loudspeaker. "We've got to shut the entire Compound down. We have rescued all of the children, but the corporation hasn't been shut down yet. We'll have to go in there and make sure that they're stopped for good. Otherwise they'll continue kidnapping children and making robots, and our work will be for nothing."

I'm confused. Mason was going to be the one to complete the mission. Why is Axton asking *us* to do it now?

"I'm using you two because you're the only ones I totally trust here. Mason is not on our side. He's with the General, and they've been planning together this whole time. Which means he was not intending to take the children back to their families."

He pauses. "I never understood why the other part of the mission failed. It should have been the easy part. Doesn't need a big team. But now I think the General did it on purpose. To keep the robot production lines for herself. They were going to use the children for their own plans. She doesn't care at all about their wellbeing, so we have to step in to make sure it's done right. Enjoy the flight."

*　　*　　*

As we settle into our seats, I turn to Theo. "So . . . care to explain anything? Has anything else slipped your mind?"

"Sapphire is a robot," he says helpfully.

"Yay!" says Sapphire, running around in circles with her arms outstretched.

"Gee, thanks," I say with sarcasm. "About time."

"Why were you surprised? I mean, she stopped

breathing for twenty minutes after we jumped from the pod."

"Yeah, but Axton did CPR on her," I interject.

"And we sliced her wrist open with no problem."

"Because Axton gave her a painkiller! You should've taken one."

Theo laughs. "Wouldn't have done a thing for me."

I look at him.

"It was a placebo," he says. "A sugar pill. Tiger's eye gives you pain tolerance, so long as you can trick the brain . . . "

"Oh."

"The CPR was necessary to bring Sapphire to consciousness, but she could have survived over an hour without breathing."

"Okay."

"And when Axton and Sapphire scared off that man at the cabins . . . did you think he was afraid of Axton?"

I am silent.

"He was scared of Sapphire, because she's young, like most of the others."

"Others?" I am confused now.

"Other children."

"Huh?"

"From the Compound. The other robots."

Sapphire pouts, "I thought I was special."

"You are special, Sapphire," says Theo. "You're the only one apart from Carla who can access your powers. You'll have to teach the others."

Sapphire grins.

"They're all robots?" I ask. "All of the children?"

"Yeah," says Theo. "The Compound uses the mines to train newly converted assets. To teach them to obey without question. And to brainwash them."

"So the guards and the children are all robots?"

"No," snorts Theo like I'm being dumb. "The guards aren't robots. What gave you that idea?"

"None of them?"

"Nope. They're all mean. But human," explains Theo. "The Compound hasn't figured out how to make adults into robots yet. Even teenagers often fail. Cell growth is required for titanium fusing and mitochondrial DNA is—" He's about to go off on a technical rant about biology, so I interrupt before I get a whole lecture.

"But . . . all those people in the pile . . . "

"Oh, those were all failures. They are trying so hard."

"So, there are no adult robots? Only children?"

"They keep trying with adults, but you're the oldest person they've ever converted successfully. That we know of anyway. That's why you're so famous, and why they're always studying you. Also, you've lasted so many more decades than expected. I mean, you've been showing up on our face-rec hits since forever."

I remain silent, which is a mistake.

"Dad's theory was that they study you because they still haven't figured out the tiger's eye themselves. I mean, it's fantastically complicated. It has all these powers and stuff. At first, we thought it was alloyed with the titanium and leeched into the blood. Then we thought it was added to the red blood cells via the bone marrow."

I try to keep up, but I can feel myself zoning out.

"But even that theory doesn't work, because you never age; so all the cell lines are immortal, not only the bone cells. Plus, all the soft tissues are so much stronger, and they heal fast. So, it has to be that there's tiger's eye infused into every cell. Which explains why the Compound needs so much of it."

I think he's showing off, now.

"Maybe it's actually merged into the DNA, with silicone in all four of the bases, so you get perfect replication. And maybe also in the telomeres. Definitely the mitochondria. Maybe the other organelles. I can't wait to start examining cells from all of you under the magneto-scope. Tiger's eye is awesome stuff."

Then, I realize what this means.

"So you want to play with me in your lab?" I say, hurt. "Do you think I'm just a puzzle to solve? That's all I've ever been to you guys?"

"No, it's not like that, Carla," Theo says apologetically. "Far from it."

"Okay," I say. I close my eyes. I find myself beginning to regret starting this conversation.

"Come on, Carla," he says. "You know that's not what this is about anymore. You're amazing. We care about you, and we're here for you. Always."

I feel myself waver.

"Besides," he winks, "I never dreamed I'd be best friends with the deadliest robot of this century."

*　　*　　*

We head to the Compound, and it seems to be far quicker than the previous trip there. This time we fly right past it to another landing pad.

"Prepare for descent," Axton says.

"What is this place?" I say, turning to Theo.

"It's their command center and where they actually convert the children into robots. It's all underground, to minimize detection."

"Makes sense," I say. I wonder how we're going to shut

370

this place down. Axton hefts a large backpack onto his shoulders.

We reach the door, which is strange and angled as if it leads to a basement. It is stark white. So much for blending in with the trees.

"Knock it down, Carla," Axton says.

I hesitate.

"Why do you think I brought you?"

I sigh. "All right, whatever."

But Sapphire beats me to it. She smashes the door with all of her force, perhaps a little too hard. Pieces of door are scattered down the stairwell.

"Okay! Nice job, Sapphire," Axton says, putting his hands out, as if telling her to not damage anything else.

He leads us down the stairs and along several passageways. Nothing had better happen to Axton, because I have no idea where we're going.

I soon realize that this building descends in a cylindrical fashion. We are generally heading in a clockwise direction, with slight changes every now and then. Every so often we reach another staircase that leads to the next level down. A deep empty core forms the center of the stairwell.

There is no one in sight, but we stay silent anyway.

After several flights, Axton stops. "Uh oh," he says.

That's not something I've heard him say before. He's supposed to know exactly what's going on. My heart rate quickens.

I follow Axton's gaze, and spot them. The children. They look adorable. There are five or six of them in miniature soldier outfits. They stand in a triangle formation at the next flight of stairs. Eyeballing us.

"The army was supposed to be up north," says Axton under his breath.

"Look at the uniforms," says Theo quietly. "They're not the main army. This is his personal contingent."

I don't really understand what he means. Army? Personal contingent? They look like nice children, most of them a little older than Sapphire.

We halt. Sapphire waves brightly to them. No response.

"Carla," says Theo nervously. "This is all you now."

I look at Axton, but he provides no clarification. He doesn't seem so brave anymore. Theo gestures to me, urging me to walk ahead. I traverse down the stairs, which follow the contour of the circular building. The children are less than a few yards away now.

I smile at one of the boys as we approach.

He doesn't smile back. Blankness.

I glance back at Theo and Axton, and they are quite far behind. They only followed me part of the way.

When I turn back towards the children, two of them are already in mid-air. Arms out and faces blank. Attacking from both sides. I react and block with my left hand. But I am struck from the other side. Right in the chest. By a girl.

I grunt and am propelled backwards until I slam into the wall. I fall in a heap. Understanding dawns.

These are the scary children. The ones that make up the robot army. An army of children. Theo was right about the guards.

"Carla," implores Axton. "What are you doing? Fight them!"

The two children advance on me with empty eyes, while the other four motionlessly observe. Sapphire jumps in front of me to meet the attack. I nearly yell out to stop her, but then I remember she's a robot, too. She wraps the boy in a bear hug and throws him to the side like an unwanted toy. He stumbles but keeps his balance. He pushes Sapphire out of the way, and continues towards me.

I stand up, this time determined to summon my enhancements. I try to remember what Merida taught me. But there's no time. The two robots are on me. The girl raises her fist, and the boy bends down to grab my ankle. Sapphire tries to help, but it's not enough. He pulls my leg out from under me and twists absurdly fast. I am lifted into the air and hurled towards the stairwell.

Somehow, I contort in mid-air, grab the steel railing and hold on. When I stop, I find myself teetering on the edge, facing the void. It's a long way down. My pulse races. I can't hurt these children. They're just like me. Just like the rest of us robots. They don't even know what they're doing. They are not our enemy, and I won't fight them.

"They can't get hurt, Carla," Theo yells, his words wafting down. "They're robots!"

He's right. They are the enemy. If I don't fight them, this will keep happening to other children. I apologize to them in my mind, before I focus all my pent-up anger. Anger at the guards, the Compound, and the cause of this whole calamity: the Commander. I do not need Merida now.

I regain my balance and drop onto the stairs. I turn to face the two robots. I reach the girl in one long stride. She has her fists ready to attack, but I am incensed. I punch right through her arms and connect with her torso. She staggers backwards and I quickly turn, ready for the boy's attack. As he punches, I grab his wrist and spin him around, then kick him hard in the back. He falls forwards onto the girl, and the two of them drop to the ground.

Now another pair takes their place. They sprint at me,

but I fend them off. I find myself on the back foot. And the first two have re-joined the battle. It's me against four of them, with my back to the void.

Two of them leap at me again. But I'm learning from them. I lash out with a fist on each side and connect. I have repelled them both, but the other two are on me before I can regroup. One jumps onto my back. He seems younger than the others, but his wiry fingers dig cruelly into my eyes and mouth. I can't shake him off. The other three are grabbing my arms and punching me.

I can't see with the boy smothering my face, but I can hear Sapphire's faint voice. I'm still standing, but I am losing. I grab the little boy's hands and pry them from my face. I don't like what I see. The last two of the robot children, the two smallest ones, start to move. Towards Axton and Theo.

The brothers start backing up, but the robots are too fast. Inhumanly fast. The first of them aims a massive kick at Theo, who barely has time to drop his arm to protect his torso. I hear the bone crack from far away. Theo crumples to the ground in agony, clutching his clearly fractured arm.

The two small robot children turn their attention to Axton. He has no chance, and I am too far away. Sapphire can't get to him in time, either.

I can't lose him.

Axton pulls out his gun. He's a soldier at heart; he always has a plan. The gun is aimed at the robot children, but they pay it no heed.

The gun will not protect him. The two robots continue to advance.

I see the fear in Axton's eyes.

My blood boils. Metal shards flood my arteries. Nobody will take Axton from me. Nobody.

I grab the wrists of two robots in front of me and jump with all the might in my titanium legs. I bend forward, and the robot holding onto me from behind smashes hard against a beam in the ceiling. He grunts and his grip loosens. He begins to fall, but so do I. Right before I hit the ground, I slam my arms together, heaving the two robots against each other with a metallic clang.

I am free! But too far away from Axton. He can't prevail against these deadly robot children. My attention is ripped away from Axton as the last child robot launches herself at me. I grab her with both hands, line her up, and fling her with precision beyond human ability, and powered by fury beyond robot ability.

She flies, head first, hurtling like a javelin, spinning like a football. A robotic child projectile. She extends her arms instinctively as she collides into one of the robots near Axton. Momentum sends them both into the other robot. The three robots land in a tangle.

Sapphire runs to stand between them and Axton. The robots turn away from Sapphire and Axton. Towards me...

Axton no longer looks afraid. More importantly, he looks alive. My veins flood with joy, and I droop with relief.

Far too early to celebrate.

Three of the robots are on me before I can summon my enhancements again. Too slow. I am powerless, unable to keep them at bay, my defence inadequate. They pummel me without mercy. There's nothing I can do as three more join the fray. Suddenly it's six against one. They are learning too. My strikes flail.

They tackle me, pin me down, attempting to strangle me, and pull on my limbs to try to dislocate my bones. Six titanium terrors are tearing me apart. Sapphire is trying to pull them off me but she is an amateur against six professionals. Theo and Axton are watching in helpless horror.

There are too many. They are too strong. They have been trained too well by their horrible leader. I try to remember what Merida taught me. But I cannot muster enough anger to summon my powers; there is too much happening to me. I only feel sadness and regret.

Oh, Rory. I should have been there for him. I have failed as a sister again. If only I had kept my promises. If only I could have made my mother proud.

Pain greets me. Air is scarce.

My second life is ending.

# 32

# AXTON

CARLA IS ON THE GROUND. It's as if I'm looking through a tunnel, watching the scene unfold. All I can see is Carla. All I can think about is that I'm going to lose her. And that it's my fault.

The six awful robots are pinning her down, choking her and trying to dismember her joints. Her body writhes in denial.

The struggle is etched plainly on her face. She is so strong, but they are winning. I should have brought backup. I thought it would be a simple mission that only needed a small team. I told them to come here.

Carla will die because of my decision. Not even five

minutes ago, she saved my life. Now, I'm taking hers. I wish I could throw the robot children off her. I want to grab them and rip them apart. I wish I was stronger. But I am hopeless. I am too weak. I am only human.

I should be the one on the ground. I deserve to die. Carla saved me, so I need to save her. I need to repay her. She can't leave us. I need to go. I take a step towards the robots. But I won't be any help. One slap from a metal hand will flatten me. If I die, then it'll be both of us. I hesitate. Please, let me think of something. Before it's too late.

"Theo," I shout in desperation. He gazes at me with a pained expression. He always knows what to do. But not this time. If we divert their attention, it won't help because we'll be dealt with quickly. There are enough of them to keep Carla down and take care of us. What can we do?

My focus turns from Theo back to Carla. This can't be happening. They can't do this to Carla! They can't take her away from me. Nothing in my training has prepared me for this. These robots are too powerful. There is no way out of this.

If Carla fails now, we will all die shortly after. Actually, that's not true. After they dismember Carla, they'll just hold us. Sapphire will be pinned down and reset.

They'll torture me. And Theo. They need to know where the base is, and they'll torture us until we give them the information. Only then will they kill Theo and I. My mother will lose both of her sons. If the robots finish us, at least it'll be quick. If they take us to the guards, it won't be; they'll enjoy themselves too much.

Most devastatingly, the children will be re-captured. All the children will be back in the mines. All that my father worked for will be for nothing.

I hold my gun. It feels good in my hand, but it's a false illusion of power. I've brought a gun to a knife fight. Titanium knives are bulletproof. I need to think of something. I can't lose Carla. Not when I was getting used to her being around. Things are better when she's near. Even when she's being stubborn. Especially when she's being stubborn. My training is wrong. Humans are better with emotion.

I need to stop this. Now. There is no time. Not only for myself. Not only so I don't lose Carla. But so we don't lose the rest of the children. Come on, Axton, you're a soldier. Fight them!

The gun in my hand fires as if it has its own desires. The bullet hits one of the robots. He grunts but doesn't even flinch. He flicks a hand as if a fly were bothering him. He doesn't even glance up.

There's nothing I can do. I'm not strong enough. I'm not smart enough. I turn to Theo, willing him, begging him to think of something.

Anything.

# 33

# CARLA

I won't do it! I won't give up. It was all my fault last time, and I won't let it happen again. I will not relive my past. I am strong. I must be strong. For the children.

I will channel Theo's selflessness. He is so pure. So brave. I am here for the children, because that is my purpose. If I am here on this planet over a hundred years after my birth for a reason, this is it.

But how can I save them when I am trapped? I am held down and my body cannot move. My mind is floating free across a bottomless sea as everything recedes into a distant blur.

I am drifting. My mind is not part of my body. As I

lie here in a swirling world, barely sensing the deadly ministrations of six powerful robots, another moment of enlightenment dawns.

I am Carla.

I am the one they were told about. I am the one everybody knows. Mine is the face of a hundred years.

My bones are titanium. Strong and pure. Full metal power. I am a metal monster.

My heart pumps blood of liquid stone. Every muscle, every fiber, every cell. I am one with the tiger's eye.

I am indestructible. These small robots are feeble compared to my capabilities.

I make my enhancements kick in again. This time without anger. Without emotion. I have control of everything. Of all my enhancements.

I take a breath and activate my muscles, just like I was trained to do. They feel so powerful. As my muscles tense, the grip of the tiny robot hands on my solid limbs ceases to have any effect.

As I ponder my newfound insight into my training, suddenly, I know that I am also destruction. I do not want to know. But I know.

Although I cannot remember the details, somehow I now sense what I could do. What I was made to do. What I have done before. I am inhuman. I am a metal monster.

The desire to crush all six of them one-by-one is almost overwhelming. I know I could send them all on a horrific journey down the void.

Enlightenment is not always pleasant.

Unsettled, I flex my entire body and force them off instead. My limbs belong to me again. Their claws slip from my flesh like chop-sticks off granite. My sinews are rock. All of me is rock. My breath is tiger's eye.

My muscles erupt as I stand. Six tiny little ogres are no trouble. Sapphire steps back as I thrust them away. They scrabble to continue the fight, but they are outmatched. Out-muscled. Out-rocked.

The child robots scatter like pinballs. My eyes look through them to what they are inside. I resist the urge to strike them as they fall.

I could squish them like spiders. Tiny titanium spiders. But I am human. I look at Axton and Theo.

"I am Carla," I say softly, out loud.

Even in defeat, even against the heinous goliath that I am, their faces show no fear, just nothingness. As one, they rise and face me, but have retreated to a safe distance. They move into formation again, and start to advance, cautiously, inching slowly toward me.

"Wait," I say, my voice hoarse. "I don't want to fight you."

For these are not just robots. They are like us. Sapphire and I. Theo, too. They are children with families who love them. I can't bring myself to destroy them.

Something about the emotion in my tone startles them, because they pause. They stare at me. All six of them are watching now. Without emotion. Without fear. Emptiness.

It isn't their fault that they are fighting like this. They were brainwashed of their emotions and trained to attack. I try to imagine a whole army of robot children built in this awful way.

They are calm now, but there is still nothing in their eyes.

"Come on," Axton says. "Let's go."

I refuse. I turn to the children and kneel down to their height.

"I am one of you, you know," I tell them. No response. "I missed my family so much, but then I found my brother. Do you miss your families? Your mom?" There is a flicker of recognition. One of the children tilts her head.

I start talking about my family. About Mom and Dad. And about Rory. How glad I am to have found him. How much I miss them all. That I wish I could go home. How afraid I am that Mom died a horrible death. How much I wish I could go back to her for one last hug.

It takes me quite a while. Axton and Theo watch with bemused expressions. Sapphire is listening avidly. At least she's enjoying my story.

"It's not working, Carla," Theo says softly.

I won't give up. I know they're in there somewhere. All I need to do is trigger their emotional response. Trigger their human instinct.

I continue my story for a long time.

Eventually, I see signs of emotion on each of the children's faces. No longer blank. No longer barren. Confusion. Sadness. They are children once more. Human children.

Just like that, they begin to cry.

"I want my mommy," one of them wails.

They hug and sob.

"Come on," Axton repeats. "No time."

"It's all going to be okay," I say to the children. "Head to the top of the building. There's a pod waiting outside, okay?"

They seem to understand, and the oldest one leads the others. The children are a little disoriented, and some are injured. I feel guilty about that, but they'll heal fast. Because of the tiger's eye, or something like that. In my heart, I know they'll be fine.

Axton smiles at me for the first time today. "Nice work," he says. "Now we have a job to finish."

Back to Soldier Mode.

*　　*　　*

Axton spends a few moments tending to Theo's broken arm. He immobilizes it in a makeshift sling, using cloth from his pack.

"Needs more treatment at the base," he says gruffly.

We continue onwards on our downward spiraling journey. Thankfully, we find no more scary children.

Some of the doors have signs on them, but they're meaningless to me. We come across *P1.0*, *Hope 3.2*, and one that I guess makes some sense: *Maintenance*.

Theo winces, and I follow his gaze as we walk past a door that reads *Heads*. Nothing could make me want to go in any of the rooms that create robots. Imagining them converting real children into such life-like androids makes me feel nauseous.

At last we stop. We are standing at the heart of the building. Right in front of us is a door that leads to the very center of the circular building.

We enter the room.

And there he is.

The leader. The Commander. I shiver. I spent months in that Compound—that prison. Not knowing what I was doing there or if I would ever leave. All because of this man. If you could call him that. I'd say he's far less human than any of us robots.

"If you try to harm us, she will attack you," Axton says. "And that, you don't want."

He waves us in. "I know who she is," he says slowly, almost as if he's bored. "And obviously I know her capabilities. Better than you do."

I want to kill this non-human human. That single thought repeats in a cycle like a train around a track. A train of longing. I try to use the image of him being flattened by a large locomotive to stem the flow of anger within me. It is a hot, angry sea ready to devour this being.

"You don't know anything," exclaims Sapphire.

The Commander turns to give her a condescending smile. "Oh yes? I saw what you did to the door, little one. Surprising."

"I can do lots of things. I'm a robot!"

"Yes, yes, of course." He muses. "I'm not surprised by your capabilities either. What's surprising is that you know about them."

Axton says sternly, "We have solved how to unlock them." A total lie of course. Why is he lying?

The Commander sneers. "So you think you have unlocked the secret of the tiger's eye?" He glowers at Axton. "No? Then how will you build more?" He smiles how a snake would smile if it could.

Theo jumps in. "We know all about the tissue infusion, the titanium, and even the iridium. If we *wanted* to make more, we could figure out the rest in no time."

"Like I said, you don't know it all," the Commander retorts. "I do."

I can feel Axton's gaze on me, willing me not to do anything. He wants me to stay calm. We'll see about that.

I peer deep into the man's sunken eyes. Almost black, and small and squinty. Yet, if you look closely, you can ignore his evil and see him as a person. Like any of us. With his own motives and battles. The problem is, he chose the wrong battle. He chose the wrong side. My breathing quickens as I gaze at his thin, pursed lips. Ugly little things that don't balance his bushy eyebrows. Worms for lips and hairy caterpillars for eyebrows. Maybe I'm letting emotions take over my imagination, but he's not a pleasant man. That is something I can attest to.

I guess I'll never truly understand why he's done this. I don't want to understand. But I ask anyway.

"Why did you do it?" I demand. My hands are shaking, but my voice comes out surprisingly calm.

"Carla . . ." Axton says. I ignore him.

"Tell me why! Why you destroyed thousands of lives, children's lives, and crushed their souls. Why you tore apart families, and left parents to grieve. Why you brain-washed so many children and forced them to tear society apart. Why did you do it?"

He stares at me, unblinking. Clasps his hands in a tight knot. Raises one eyebrow. These things encourage the torrent of hate within me. He does not speak. I want him to speak.

"Tell me!" I shout. I can't do this anymore. I want him gone. No. I want more than that. I want him to pay for all of those children's lives. I want . . .

"Carla." Axton's soft voice carries across the room, easing my pain.

Sapphire is watching me.

"Never mind," I sneer. "I don't want to hear your excuses."

I step back and take a deep breath. We need to get the information out of him, somehow. And we will. We simply have to tap into where his emotions lie. I think about it, and one thing comes to mind.

"Do you have children?" I ask.

The Commander's eyes moisten, as if remembering a time long ago. He slumps, resting his face in his palms.

He doesn't seem so intimidating anymore. Then he straightens up.

"I did," he sighs. "That was a long time ago. I don't believe they are alive." Whatever emotion he felt is gone; he's pushed it down. Back into the depths of his soul. I can tell he's determined to keep it there.

I won't let him.

"What were their names?" I ask.

He pauses, staring at me. "Lavenia . . . and Roscoe." His eyes are no longer glassy. But it's clear he doesn't let himself think about them properly. He superficially remembers their names but doesn't let the emotion get to him.

"And would they be proud of you today?" Axton asks him. The Commander scowls at him, unblinking.

He crosses his arms, then uncrosses them. He breathes deeply. I think I see a hint of feeling behind his eyes, but I can't be sure. I can't believe that he wouldn't care at all about his children. Although he's clearly spent a lot of time trying to forget them.

"I have achieved great things," the Commander announces grandiosely.

"That doesn't answer my question," Axton says calmly, moving his hands to his hips.

The Commander is quiet for a while.

"I did all of this for a reason, and accomplished a lot.

It's amazing, really, what I have achieved. I was handed down the business by my father, and ran with it. I have made it much greater than he ever thought possible."

"There's no point in continuing this," Axton says. "We are here to shut you down."

He ignores Axton. "You're right. I wanted to bring my children back, which is why I kept working on it. But it was never enough. They were never right. They were never perfect."

I flinch at his words. Does that mean that my parents would think I'm too different, now that I'm a robot? I don't feel different.

"It's over," says Axton. "We have taken control of the Compound."

The Commander waves his hand indifferently. "Yes, yes, you have done well with your limited assets. I was far too complacent." He shrugs. "I must be getting old."

"Well," Axton says. "You'd best come with us. Before we deactivate this building."

He waves dismissively. "Hmm, no. Not this time. Do you think I didn't know you were coming?"

Axton has a concerned expression on his face.

"You have the Compound. You and that evil General woman." He seems lost in thought. "Yes, it has been a good site for such a long time. Though, its productivity has been declining. Do you think I sit here all day and do nothing?"

He laughs with contempt.

"Lucky for me, I still have many of my own assets."

Somewhere, he presses a button. A clear glass barrier rockets from the floor, dividing the room in half. He is now separated from the rest of us.

"It was wonderful to see you again, Carla," he says, his words muffled by the glass. "My great-grandfather's proudest achievement, but also our family's greatest disappointment." His voice echoes as he strides through the opposite exit.

*  *  *

We leave quickly, retracing our steps to the flight of stairs. Axton stops every now and then, pulling packages out of his backpack.

"What's that?" I ask.

"Hydro," says Axton. "Concentrated solid form."

"We can't leave him in there," I say.

"After everything he's done?" Theo lifts his sling. "I think we can."

It's a strange feeling, but I can't bear to let this man die because of us. A few minutes ago, I was ready to knock him out of his socks, but now I see that he's only a human. He may have done some evil things, but I don't want anyone to die because of me. Or am I just weak when it comes to the sanctity of human life?

I stop in the middle of the path.

"Carla, we have to go," Axton says. "Come on."

He continues up the flight of stairs, but I am conflicted.

"Carla, please," Theo says. "He won't come with us. We can't convince him. You have to let it go."

I want to argue, but I know we're running out of time. We hurry to the top level of the building, where Axton enters a room marked *Storage*.

After a minute, he comes back out.

"That's the lot," he says. "We'd better get out of here before this place blows up."

I glance back one last time before we race out of the main entrance and into the pod. Axton instructs us to sit in the cockpit with him. The six children sit in the main cabin.

As we begin to soar, a single, circular-shaped pod suddenly flies out of the top of the building.

"Seems like he's got a thing for circles," Theo remarks.

I wonder whether Axton knew the Commander had a secret escape pod. What if he comes back with a bigger, even more ghastly plan than before? How will we stop him then?

Axton seems unfazed. Relaxed, even.

He pulls out a black remote control. Enters a code and taps. Suddenly there is an immense sound, and I look back to see the building erupting into a cloud of dust as it implodes into itself, leaving only a swirling crater.

Axton taps another code.

*Boom!* One more explosion, and the circular pod carrying the Commander disintegrates.

No reaction from Axton. He puts down the remote. Another man is dead. Another day at the office.

"There's one more thing we need to do," Axton says.

Surprisingly, I hear a smile on his lips.

# 34

# AXTON

We arrive once again at Mom's house. The old-fash-ioned house and the rose bushes look intact. It seems as if no time has passed at all.

"They look so real," Carla says, stopping to smell the roses and stroking one of the buds. I always marvel at how real they feel, too. "How do they smell so nice?"

"Artificial fragrance," I say.

We knock on the door. Mom greets us with a huge smile.

"Boys!" she says. "Thanks for calling, Axton. I'm glad you could come. I've just thermo-blasted some pecan pie."

Sapphire steps around us and hugs Mom with a shy smile.

"We'd love to come in," I say. "But we'd like to take Sapphire somewhere first."

"We thought you might like to come with us," Theo says.

"All right," she says, trying to cover the disappointment in her voice. "I'll go put the pie away for a spell."

"We'll definitely have some when we come back," Carla says.

Mom slips on her shoes, and we head to the ship.

"I missed you," Sapphire says to her, as she settles into a seat.

"I missed you, too," Mom says, putting her arm around the little girl.

It will only be about a twenty-minute flight. I'm so excited about where we're going, but I'm not telling any of them. It'll be an excellent surprise. I know Mom will enjoy it, too.

I take my seat in the cockpit. It's almost second nature to fly this thing now. I power it up, press the startup buttons, lift the lever, and we're in the air. I can hear them all laughing in the back, which makes me happy. I check the digital map every now and then, but I know exactly where I'm going. I spent hours searching for it online, so when I finally found the location, it was ingrained in my mind.

I zone out for most of the trip. At the warning beep, I

examine the map, and sure enough the red dot displaying our location is directly above our intended destination.

"Prepare for descent," I say, holding down the button.

"That was quick," Sapphire says.

We have landed in a grassy park near some houses. They're all the same pale shade of green, carefully designed to prevent detection from above. We walk up the street a little, until we reach a certain house.

It has no lawn, only concrete out the front. We make our way to the front door, and I knock loudly. I look back at the others and Sapphire appears scared. She knows it's about her, but I wonder what she's expecting.

The door swings open slightly, and a woman is standing in the doorway with a man protectively hovering over her shoulder. They seem concerned about having visitors. The woman wears the most colorful clothing, which contrasts immensely with her somewhat bland surroundings. And one can't help but notice her gleaming blue eyes, exactly like Sapphire's.

She peers at us, and suddenly spots the small girl in the blue dress. Her smile disappears, and tears well in her eyes. She stares for an eternity. Her lips tremble as she drops to her knees.

A flash of blue as Sapphire throws herself at her mother.

"Mom!" she shouts as they hug.

Her mother is speechless. Endless tears stream down her face. She is shaking with raw emotion. Her father moves towards them. Tentatively, like he doesn't want to believe, doesn't want to change anything at all, doesn't want to risk losing this moment.

"Sapphire . . . " he says, a tremor in his voice, before he is hugging both of them at the same time. Months of lost moments; so much time they could have had making memories. I can see the heartache in their eyes.

Sapphire is home.

*     *     *

Time is at a standstill. They hug for a very long time. We watch without speaking. But not without feeling. Eventually, her father stands up. Her mother won't let her go. She has still lost the power of speech.

"We thought she was dead," says her father.

And he trails off into silence, unable to tear his gaze away.

"Thank you for finding us."

"It's no problem," I say, awkwardly.

A long pause.

We talk for a short while. He wants to know how I

found his little girl. And other things. I don't tell him much.

"Well, we'd better say goodbye for now," I say.

Sapphire looks up at me in surprise. "Okay," she says, her lips trembling. She's still clinging to her mother.

"Goodbye, Sapphire," Carla says. "We will visit you as often as we can."

"Thank you for saving me," she says, and Carla begins to sob. She kneels down and opens her arms wide, welcoming an embrace. Sapphire runs at full speed, accepting the offer.

I only just catch Sapphire whisper in her ear, "Robot buddies."

"Don't make me start crying," I joke. We wave goodbye and turn back with heavy hearts.

A child reunited with her family. The first of many.

We head back towards the pod. We need to return to the dorms. I tell Mom that we're only stopping briefly for pecan pie on the way. She's not happy, but I convince her that we'll visit again very soon.

*     *     *

"Do they know Sapphire's a robot?" Carla asks me as soon as we board the pod, her face full of concern.

"No, I just told them what a good kid she is."

Theo pipes up, "Hope they don't make her angry."

Carla laughs. "'Don't turn off the Animator.'"

"I think she'll be fine." My voice breaks a little.

"Is that a tear?" Carla asks, her mouth agape.

It may well be.

# 35

# CARLA

The team, apart from Mason, is chilling on the comfortable sofas on the top level of the dormitory building. Axton gathered us here. I notice that Theo's arm has a proper cast on it.

"You would have noted Mason's absence." Axton pauses. "He was not on our side. In fact, he was planning selfish and inhumane things behind our back with the General."

Axton is interrupted by an insistent noise. It seems to be coming from Mason's office. The door is unlocked, so he excuses himself and enters. After a moment, he beckons us all inside. "Perhaps this will explain what I mean," he says.

We enter the room, and who do I see on the screen? It's none other than the lady who tried to kill me.

"Hello, General," Axton says. "How are you?"

She seems shocked at first to see us, instead of Mason, but recovers quickly. "Yes, and hello to you, the robot dreamer."

"You wouldn't understand," snaps Axton.

"None of you understand any of this. Too soft-hearted. You are playing with things beyond your comprehension."

"We'll take our chances."

"We can't let the robots live. If we do, they take our entire planet. There will be no need for people anymore. You are letting your emotions blind you to the realities of the world. Every one of us is being put out of business by these robots. They don't have feelings. They are programmed to be emotionless, like a perfect soldier should be."

Theo and I exchange a glance. Aren't I evidence enough that robots do have emotion?

"The company that created these latest robots, including Carla, has produced the most lifelike creatures we have ever seen."

I flinch at the word 'creatures', and I know she sees it.

She counts it as a win. "I started the attack on the robot company because they were becoming too powerful.

They began to produce robots that were very good. Too good. They were small, but strong. And fast, powerful, and very hard to kill. They were perfect. They are perfect. With them, there is no need for us. No need for the human kind. They will take over, and if you can't see that, then you are ignoring the truth."

"Well then," I say. "You must be glad that we've shut it down."

"You've shut the business down," she disagrees. "But you were too sentimental. Now the *monsters* have no purpose." She shudders as she says the word.

"They're humans. Humans with families, memories . . . emotions!"

"It doesn't matter what you think," she says. "What matters is the truth, and that we could have used these robots for great things."

I remain silent. There's no point trying to justify it to her.

Axton speaks up. "Well, Madam General, we simply disagree. You can try to find the children, but you won't succeed. Goodbye." He hangs up the call, and I hope what he said is true.

"Let's head down to the dining hall," Axton says. "I'm starving."

I smile at this, and then something triggers in my

mind. I stop and look at him. "That reminds me," I say. "We have one more thing that we need to do."

Axton looks thoughtful. Then he blurts out, "The cavern."

"Yes." I frown as I think of all those emaciated people in their blankets. "We have to go back."

He surprises me. Instead of objecting, he simply says, "We have supplies in the basement."

"We have lots of children to feed here, too."

"There's enough. We can spare some."

I kiss him on the cheek.

Axton replies without emotion, "There's hydro in the basement, too. We can fit in another trip after we eat."

Sometimes, he's more of a robot than I am.

*     *     *

I walk into the dining hall, a room now filled with hundreds of smiling faces and laughter. Filled with hundreds of robots. All of them like me. Like Sapphire. Like Rory.

Rory is standing to the left of me. I put my hand on his shoulder and he places his hand on top of mine. I vow to be an even better robot sister.

He, too, is gazing intently at the crowd, but perhaps in a different way. I will have to tell him everything about us, our parents, and all that's happened in his second life, but that's for another day.

I notice Axton approach us and give him a smile. He stands on my other side and nudges my arm. He is grinning. It's the first time I've seen him really happy. I am happy, too.

"Look at them," I say, gesturing to all of the children laughing and having fun.

"You know what I see?" asks Axton with a smile.

"What?" I reply.

"The biggest army on the planet."

I gaze at all the children and realize he's right.

"But they don't want to fight," I say. "I thought you were against using them."

"I am," he says. "But the point is, we're safe here." He picks up my hand and wraps it in his. "For a long time."

I squeeze his hand. I am finally home. Sure, it's not the same as my old one—not even close. But I have everyone I could ever need right here.

For the first time in a century, I am home.